WITHDRAWN

GERMAN NARRATIVE PROSE

GERMAN
NARRATIVE PROSE

VOLUME II

edited by

W. E. YUILL

(v. l ed. by E.J. Engel)

DUFOUR
1966

© 1966 OSWALD WOLFF (PUBLISHERS) LIMITED, LONDON

First published 1966
Library of Congress Catalog Card Number: 66–13842

PT
1308
E55
J. 2

PRINTED IN GREAT BRITAIN

CONTENTS

INTRODUCTION

IT is not possible in a collection of less than a dozen stories to give any broad impression of the range and diversity of German literature during the first half of the twentieth century. What can be done perhaps is to indicate, on the one hand, certain themes and preoccupations that seem characteristic of German literary tradition, and to illustrate, on the other hand, a variety of narrative techniques and a diversity of personality among the authors represented. For these purposes the German short story offers a number of advantages. It is a form which has been much cultivated in German literature and which has been regarded by many writers of the first rank, from Kleist and Goethe onwards, as worthy of expressing intense emotional or aesthetic experience as well as philosophical insight into the nature of the world. In this respect it has affinities with the lyric poem. Like the lyric poem, too, it requires, with its economy, its use of symbols, allegorical action or emblematic characters, a technique of considerable sophistication. For the purposes of the present volume, however, the short story has the advantage, over the lyric, of greater reality content : it gives, generally speaking, a more concrete impression of life as it is lived in Germany and experienced by Germans than can commonly be gathered from the lyric. Again, while it allows for the expression of the author's personal view, it tends to be less idiosyncratic than the lyric of the same period.

In point of purely literary merit the stories in this volume would certainly be judged as uneven : no literary critic could seriously place Ludwig Thoma's *Girl from India,* for instance, on the same level as Kafka's *Fasting Showman.* In spite of this disparity in literary quality, however, it is perhaps possible to detect in all these stories a certain ambition to define the nature of experience rather than simply to depict social relationships, to make significant statements about the quality of individual or communal life rather than about its organisation. Even Thoma's story, which is included for its humour and its satirical comment

7

on the stifling atmosphere of lower middle-class life, suggests, in the idealised figure of its heroine, something of this transcendental intention.

This concern with the roots rather than the fruits of experience possibly explains the relatively unpolitical nature of much of the best German writing. Bearing in mind that many distinguished German writers—for example, Heinrich Mann, Bertolt Brecht, Lion Feuchtwanger—conducted the political fight with literary weapons and that many others suffered martyrdom for humane sentiments that were not explicitly political, it would still be true to say that the majority of German poets and thinkers have traditionally tended to concern themselves with existential rather than with social and political problems. For many of them a political song, in words from Goethe's *Faust,* has been a nasty song. It is perhaps characteristic that Wolfgang Borchert, who suffered imprisonment under the Nazi regime, makes of his experience not a social or political protest but an exploration of man's nature and resources, a reflection on the human condition.

The essential inwardness of German literature and its humanism as well as the intense feeling for nature so often manifested in it are inherited from the poetic and philosophical achievements of the Classical and Romantic writers who, at the end of the eighteenth and the beginning of the nineteenth century, made German for the first time the leading literary and philosophical language of Europe. The thinking of men like Goethe, Schiller, Novalis, Friedrich and August Wilhelm Schlegel, E. T. A. Hoffman, Fichte, Schelling and Wilhelm von Humboldt, whether they bear the label "Classic" or "Romantic", is based on certain postulates which are still widely accepted by German thinkers : the fundamental unity of the cosmos, the notion of organic development in nature and man, the prime importance of aesthetic experience, the validity of abstract speculation and, generally, the reality of spiritual factors. To this heritage, preserved as it is by a highly intellectual educational system largely created by Wilhelm von Humboldt, German poets owe their speculative and introspective bent and their concern with the evolution of personality through experience.

Symptomatic of this concern is the prominent part played in the German literary canon by the "Bildungsroman" and its

dramatic equivalents, works which explore the apprenticeship of
the hero to life and his growth through experience. Within such
novels, accounts of childhood as the most clearly formative phase
of life have a deeply significant place. From Goethe's *Wilhelm
Meister*, through Gottfried Keller's *Green Henry*, down to Hans
Carossa's *Boyhood and Youth* and Hermann Hesse's *A Childhood*, writers in German have in fact evoked the atmosphere of
childhood and adolescence and suggested the inner significance
of typical experiences with a subtlety hardly matched in any
other literature. Of the stories reproduced here no less than three
explore the world of adolescence. In view of the prominence of
the theme in German literature this proportion seems justified,
especially as the three authors adopt very different perspectives.

The most subjective and the most delicate of these tales is
Georg Britting's retrospective account of a mildly critical experience in puberty. Through his first erotic encounter and its
matter-of-fact sequel the hero's inner tensions are resolved and
the phantoms conjured up in his overheated imagination by
scraps of conversation overheard from the adult world are exor-
cised. The boy's experience produces the same sort of instan-
taneous change of perspective as Britting describes in his short
story *The Skater*, in which the hero, a boy of thirteen, skating
as he imagines along a hard frozen country lane, suddenly
realises that he is on an ice-covered river and in peril from the
sudden thaw. In *The White Slave Trader* Britting recalls the
turbulence of adolescent feeling, the mixture of guilt, shame,
indignation and incipient lust, but the experience is deprived of
all harshness, mellowed by an idyllic glow of sunshine and green
summer foliage. He describes with warmly humorous understanding the boy's ignominious tumble in the brambles and his
naively sanctimonious resolve to spend the night in corpse-like
repose—only to find next morning "myself nestled voluptuously
in blankets pulled right up to my chin and the sheets and pillows
rumpled, as always". It is with great insight that Britting suggests the adolescent comprehension of the world—blank bewil-
derment and lurid surmise side by side—and the fascination
exerted on the youthful mind by exotic and enigmatic figures
like Herr Berger.

Here, as in Britting's novel, *Life Story of a Fat Man Called
Hamlet*, in his other short stories and, above all, in his lyric,

there is a suggestion of links between man and nature which inspire not only atmospheric settings but also an intermittent pattern of symbols. The hero, offered a seductive fruit, finds himself in the situation of Adam and falls—literally and meta-phorically—and his first erotic entanglement leaves a symbolic stigma on his cheek. In contrast with the "searing welcome" of the bramble patch his new-found serenity is pictured in the half-dreaming image of white lilies, "growing up to either side of my bed, rigid on their long stems, pale and chaste like swans". Whatever these flowers might signify to a Freudian, to Britting they constitute a protective cage within which the boy, having, as it were, undergone his erotic inoculation, sleeps the sleep of one delivered from febrile innocence.

Ludwig Thoma's *Girl from India* also deals with love as seen through the eyes of youth, but here there is less of confession and more of artifice. A double perspective is implied in that the author describes Cora and her suitors through the uncompre-hending eyes of an urchin, well knowing that his readers will appreciate the satire and pathos that are beyond the youthful narrator : a technique that one might perhaps characterise as "narrative irony". Thoma's assumption of the illiterate style of the small boy in this and other episodes of the *Auntie Frieda* col-lection or *Ragamuffin Tales* is not simply whimsical : the youth-ful Ludwig Thoma in these anecdotes and vignettes is not just the eternal *enfant terrible*, a German cousin to Richmal Cromp-ton's William. Thoma, a Bavarian liberal and editor of the boisterously satirical periodical *Simplicissimus*, had ulterior motives : he used the devastating innocence and disrespectful gestures of his young hero to attack Prussianism, the Roman Catholic Church and the suffocating snobbery of German middle-class life. The humour in many of the tales is excruciat-ingly robust and the behaviour of young Ludwig anything but endearing : his revenge on the snobbish and tyrannical adults who surround him usually takes the form of smashing windows or tormenting cherished pets with fire-crackers. *The Girl from India* is, however, set in a gentler key. There is an idyllic quality about life in Weilbach, with its petty social round and sentimen-tal serenades, that is reminiscent of George and Weedon Grossmith's *Diary of a Nobody*. Even Ludwig responds to the benign influence of Cora, and the pathetic figure of Franz

Reiser gives to the story a sentimental tinge that is not common in Thoma's work. The satire on snobbish women is, of course, severe enough, and their henpecked husbands do not escape lightly; there is also a serious implicit criticism of the barriers of class and education in German society, but the picture is brightened, here as elsewhere, by Ludwig's good-hearted if simple-minded mother and by the exotic figure of Cora, who stands for all that women should be in Thoma's opinion—beautiful, frank, sensible, natural and sincere. She is obviously intended as a foil to the vapid and corseted creatures of a world dominated by males: "She hasn't got no corsets on either", is Aunt Theresa's illogical but revealing final condemnation of Cora. Mister Seitz belongs to a type that often forms the butt of Thoma's robust humour; he is effete, conceited—and probably after Cora's money. Weilbach represents a society that is snobbish, petty and spiteful, but it is a society without menace and free from grave psychic deformity. In the end it even appreciates up to a point what Cora stands for, and is hence redeemable. When, in the succeeding episode of the story, she leaves the town to return to India she takes with her the hearts of many and leaves behind some sense of a larger and more gracious life.

An exotic element was bred into the brothers Thomas and Heinrich Mann through their mother, who was of Creole descent. The problematic personality that issues from such a mixture of heredities is well known to readers of *Tonio Kröger*, but it also features prominently in the less celebrated works of Heinrich Mann: it forms the specific theme of the novel, *Between the Races*, and many of the other stories have exotic figures like Cora—Gabriele West in *Eugénie*, Dora Breetpott in *Professor Unrat* and Estela Vermühlen in *The Unknown*. These women and their glamorous sisters from the world of the theatre are not messengers of grace, like Cora, however: they are either pathetic figures or *femmes fatales*. In either case they bring conflict and tragedy into staid communities like that of Lübeck, they release hysterical emotions and repressed desires. Thus the effect of the cabaret singer in *Professor Unrat*—sub-titled *The Fall of a Tyrant* and best known in the famous film version of Marlene Dietrich, *The Blue Angel*. The hero of the story is a schoolmaster, invested with the tyrannical power of the Wilhelmian grammar-school system, who casts respectability to the winds

and finds hysterical satisfaction in degrading himself for the sake
of the "artiste", Rosa Fröliche. In the end he uses her to debauch
his pupils and fellow-citizens. Whereas Thomas Mann—who
described himself as "unpolitical"—is concerned primarily with
the problems of the artistic individual in a bourgeois society, his
brother Heinrich, one of the most "political" of German writers,
explores the dynamics of power within a closely knit community
and describes the distortion of personality by social pressures and
the exercise of authority. Mann is a student of the schoolroom as
a social microcosm, for it is here, in a rigidly hierarchical and
conventional community, that the germs of future political
diseases are implanted. It is in the classroom that Diederich
Hessling, the hero of Mann's satirical novel, *The Patriot* (*Der
Untertan*), acquires the mixture of tyranny and masochistic submission that Mann felt was typical of the respectable middle-
class in Germany. *Abdication*, written at the same time as *Professor Unrat* (1905), might serve as a footnote to this novel and
to *The Patriot*. It is a study in the psychopathology of power which
shows how authority may be seized by the least stable member
of a group. Felix is driven on by the rancorous ambition of the
under-privileged, but he cannot rest content in the possession of
power once he has achieved it. He is compelled to assert his
leadership continuously by ludicrous rituals or gratuitous acts of
self-punishment. In the end he envies the lazy submission of the
oppressed, his tyrannical will is turned against himself and he
experiences a voluptuous longing to be dominated : the hysterical
desire for suffering ends in suicidal mania. To English readers
with a school background less foetid and perhaps more sagaci-
ously supervised the story may seem improbably lurid but it
acquires something of prophetic stature when we recall the bar-
barity and the Götterdämmerung mythology of the Nazi leaders.
The sinister juvenile mentality that Mann describes we may perhaps look upon as a characteristically German mutation of that
depicted by William Golding in *Lord of the Flies*.

In a way that is both more whimsical and more compassionate
Ernst Penzoldt also uncovers the tensions and guilty secrets that
lie behind the ultra-respectable façade of middle-class life. The
literary detective story is not a genre much cultivated in German,
and Penzoldt confesses disarmingly that *The Treasure* is his first
attempt at it. The tone of the story is in fact somewhat self-

conscious, and the construction and unravelling of the plot may not satisfy the more exacting English taste. Short detective stories are perhaps not so successful in any case, as they do not allow scope for the leisurely development of false trails and constantly changing suspicions. Apart from this, Penzoldt tends to vitiate the process of logical deduction and the consequent challenge to the reader's perspicacity by endowing his detective with almost uncanny insight. The ultimate reason for what may seem technical shortcomings is probably the fact that the author is more fascinated by the act of murder and the motives and emotions to which it forms a climax than by the element of the puzzle which is generally paramount in English detective stories. Penzoldt's emphasis on psychology rather than logic, his careful evocation of the dusty grandeur of a decaying household with its outmoded bric-à-brac, his analysis of muffled affection and hatred—all this is more reminiscent of Georges Simenon than of the typical English detective novelist.

In the repeated and detailed descriptions of Agatha's corpse we may perhaps detect a partiality for the morbid which is not uncharacteristic of Penzoldt's work and which may owe something to his upbringing as the son of a distinguished medical professor and to his service as a medical orderly in two world wars. In *The Treasure*, as in many of Penzoldt's other short stories, in his novel *Poor Chatterton* or the account of his war-time experiences, *Admissions*, the morbid element is compounded with whimsical humour and the whole suffused with deep compassion. Penzoldt's emotional constitution is not an unfamiliar one in German literature : one is reminded in particular of the eighteenth-century poet and moralist, Matthias Claudius, who also has the love of the idyllic and the taste for eccentricity that is to be found in Penzoldt. The eccentric Dr. Jokim, although he does not have the specific religious vocation of Chesterton's Father Brown, displays a Christ-like charity that is reminiscent of Claudius. He not only finds the suspect family lovable, but even after he has revealed the viciousness of Agatha's life he can mourn her sincerely and with pity : "There is nothing more pathetic," he comments, "than an unlamented death." His compassion and understanding go infinitely deeper than the cheap indignation of the tradespeople who admired the public Agatha for her cold efficiency and who, as Jokim remarks, "cast the first stone". The last trace of bitterness is removed from the story by the revelation that Agatha was in any case doomed by disease, that her death has spared her the humiliation of her son's disgrace, and that the murder was committed by someone not responsible for her actions. All in all, what we have in the end is not a detective story—*pur sang*, as it were—but a reflection on the workings of Providence.

Carl Zuckmayer shares the Bohemianism of Penzoldt and, in spite of the broad humour and strong sensuality that inform his plays and stories, something of his morbidity also. The powerful appetite for life is balanced by a constant awareness of death. In the drama, *The Headsman of Bergen (Der Schelm von Bergen)*, for instance, the lyrical preoccupation with death is almost Rilkean in its intensity, while the hero of *Carl Michael Bellmann*, a robustly Epicurean poet, reflects on the ever-present shadow of death :

"The end is always at hand—particularly in this world of ours. Even death is born with us. Everything that lives bears in itself its own death. Only, when it comes, it always comes unexpectedly."

But where, in Penzoldt, death is mellowed by compassion, in Zuckmayer it is frequently the harsh issue of a conflict of loyalties —the social conflict of emotional impulse versus convention, or the inner conflict of an individual tempted to break faith with the community to which he belongs. *Love Story*, a tale of *mésalliance*, involves precisely this kind of conflict : the overpowering love of Jost von Fredersdorff and Lili Schallweis comes into collision with the rigid and hypocritical ethos of the Prussian officer caste. But von Fredersdorff's determination to pursue his personal happiness at all costs is not broken by external pressures, it is undermined from within : it is the hoarse farewell of his loyal squadron that makes him aware of the bonds he is breaking and drives him to suicide. This motif of loyalty to a community or way of life is in fact doubly represented in the story : not only is Jost bound to his class, Lili is also tempted to return to her career as a singer and the Bohemian life that it involves—precisely the situation of the heroine of Zuckmayer's drama, *Katharina Knie*. Katharina renounces the prospect of a secure domestic life in order to lead the family circus after the death of

her father. In the circumstances in which *Love Story* was first
published, in 1933, it may perhaps be legitimately interpreted
as a protest against the revival of a Spartan morality that stops
up the flow of natural emotion and sacrifices human happiness
to a false ideal of honour and *esprit de corps*.

Zuckmayer's story is chiefly remarkable for its evocation of
sensual love, the expression of an elemental vigour closely associ-
ated with the moods of nature. The stimulating cold of the
winter night drives the lovers into the intimacy and warm
chiaroscuro of Lili's room, their rapture harmonises with the
freshness of spring. In its construction and characterisation, *Love
Story* shows the skill of the accomplished narrator and dramatist.
If anything, the climax of the story is perhaps too much of a
coup de théatre: the deep emotional ties between von Fredersdorff and his men have not been sufficiently illustrated throughout the action for the sudden suicide to appear inevitably
motivated. There is possibly an excessive nonchalance here in the
working out of a theme which is in itself not highly original.

The situation, the action and even the individual scenes of
Hofmannsthal's *Episode in the Life of the Marshal de Bassompierre*
bear a strong superficial resemblance to those in Zuckmayer's
story. Here, too, we have the impulsive erotic attraction between
virile man and sensuous woman, passion and languor in a fire-lit
room, with death as the climax. The implications and the technique of the two stories are, however, very different. Zuckmayer
describes a whole social context, a society with specific conventions and taboos, he develops a variety of characters with characteristic dialogue, constructs an intrigue. Although it has a
historical setting, Hofmannsthal's tale is not concerned primarily
with society, or even with morality: like his great allegorical
dramas it deals with theological issues, with temptation, sin and
death. In so far as the three principal characters in the story
are identical with their functions in the action they can be regarded as allegorical—the Marshal the personification of intrepid
lust, the woman the embodiment of sensual temptation, the
eternal Eve. The husband, only fleetingly glimpsed, we may
perhaps equate with man's nobler nature, his spirituality, betrayed
and smitten by mortal sickness. As so often in German poetry,
love and death are linked, but in this case it is not a Romantic
"Liebestod"—death is the wages of carnal sin. To explain the

story in such bald terms is, of course, an affront to its subtle symbolism and to the atmosphere of feverish life and impending death that, for all its terseness, it conjures up. The description of the woman offering her body and the legendary apple simultaneously provides a monumental counterpart to the juvenile episode in Britting's story. The cold light of dawn that invades the room when passion is spent is a metaphor that suggests effortlessly the spiritual void which follows on the consummation of lust :

> Then, all of a sudden, the flame sank; a breath of cold air pushed open the shutter like a hand and revealed the livid, hideous grey of dawn. We sat up, knowing that day had come. But the light outside was like no day, and what lay outside was like no street. Things had no outlines. It was a world void and without form, where only shapeless, timeless things could move.

The balance of the story is superb : the firelight casting the shadows of the lovers on the wall is matched by the flickering light of burning straw by which the Marshal glimpses the bodies of the woman and her husband; the corpse-gatherers who pass beneath the lovers' window with their gruesome barrow blunder against the door at the end of the story. Finally, the concluding words of the Marshal, terse as they are, nevertheless cast an aura of mystery round his adventure :

> All my efforts to discover something about the woman after my return were in vain. I even went to the shop with the sign of the Two Angels, but the people who kept it did not know who had kept it before them.

Ever since the Romantic movement, German literature has been particularly strong in stories of the supernatural, and no collection would seem representative without at least one example of the ghost story. The most effective ghost stories suggest more than they explain; they allow us to glimpse only a fragment of some unimaginably vast cosmic pattern and remain, in the final analysis, enigmatic. Bergengruen's *Experience on an Island* is hence not the kind of allegory that we find in Hofmannsthal's story, it is, as it were, open-ended. Like many of the best ghost-

stories, this one gains its effect and its plausibility from an intim-
ately conversational style and from the laconic and congenial
personality of the narrator—in this case an artist with a keen eye
for details of landscape and physiognomy. His precise description of geological formation, of trees and plants and of people
conjures up a world that is vivid and real—and yet alien and
uncanny. Everything speaks of its remoteness : the square houses
of the "shore riders" are like miniature outposts of human
authority in a land which obeys laws that are ancient, and profounder than the laws of nature even. The traveller's ignorance
of the local language is emblematic of the profounder mystification which is to follow; at the same time it sharpens his attention
to atmosphere and detail and puts him into a receptive state of
mind, receptive to communications that are more significant than
human speech. And within this alien world the island is still
more alien. The narrator is drawn to the centre of this remote
universe, the old woman's hovel, where his horrific experience
takes place. Here, he is so far beyond ordinary experience that it
almost seems that *he* is the phantom—the spectre of the dead
son can communicate with the old woman, but the intruder
cannot. In the macabre dialogue between mother and son
Bergengruen suggests the dim outline of some supernatural law
of communication. The narrator, at that time a young man, and
sceptical as young men are, has the impression of being on the
threshold of something undreamed of in his philosophy, of the
ultimate secret of the universe, the secret which would have revealed in one flash of intuition the inner meaning of the painful
chronicle of history. This notion of a "Zauberwort", a magic
formula which will unlock the secret of the universe, is something we frequently find in the writings of German Romantics,
of Tieck, Novalis and Eichendorff. It is perhaps characteristic of
the Romantic heritage that Bergengruen carries his story beyond
the nebulous suspicion of murder committed long ago from
petty jealousy, beyond the unravelling of some mundane mystery, and offers a glimpse into the vast hinterland of the supernatural and—in the serene gaze of the dead woman—a reflection
on the power of love to cross the barrier of death.

The stories of Gertrud von Le Fort, one of Germany's leading
Roman Catholic writers, frequently have a remoteness that is
not simply geographical nor even just the remoteness of past

ages. There is often a dream-like, sibylline atmosphere about her work that gives it almost the force of myth. This is nowhere better epitomised than in the silvery chiaroscuro of *The Judgement of the Sea* : the action and characters hover between history and legend, in a dream world in which the sea, sleep and death become symbolic entities. It is typical that the central figure of the story should be a woman, for Gertrud von Le Fort is repeatedly concerned with the place of woman in God's design and her triple function as virgin, bride and mother. Once more we encounter the dual theme of love and death—this time mythically coupled in the figure of woman. Within herself Anne de Vitré bears the ambivalent power of woman—the lethal power of the witch that is drawn from unregenerate nature, from the cruelly just sea, and the life-giving power of the mother that is a manifestation of divine grace and forgiveness. In the moment of decision, when she is asked to exercise her power as the instrument of retribution, Anne finds herself lifted beyond the natural judgement of the sea, elevated beyond considerations of politics and race, and made aware only of her essential motherhood : the sick child is no longer the prince of a hostile people, he is her dead brother, the murdered Duke, the child which she will never bear in reality. The call of her womanhood is stronger than the call of her race :

> But now she knew. A woman cannot give herself up to being an instrument of death—a woman exists to give life. Anne could feel a yearning rising from the very depths of her being and the remotest sources of her blood, a soft and tender feeling, yet nonetheless strong and powerful and in fact compelling.

Anne's function as a woman is more than a mere natural function, it is a divine ordination. In recognising it and fulfilling it she is defying—even at the cost of her life—the natural law under which her people have lived, the law which prescribes vengeance. Even as she submits to the archaic judgement of the sea, she rejects it, for she has discovered a higher Judgement :

> She felt that she was guilty before the sea, but she felt no remorse. It was as though she had been brought before a different Judge, almighty and holy as the sea, but not only as

just, but, like her heart, merciful as well. Henceforth she could only accept this god become man as her Judge.

Calmly and knowingly, Anne goes to her death at the hand of Budoc, "a creature of the deep, a messenger of the sea", and is united with her lost brother Alain.

Gertrud von Le Fort is perhaps an extreme transcendentalist, seeking to construct myths which express archetypal human functions within a divine plan. Where the literary treatment of experience is concerned, Kasimir Edschmid is at the opposite end or the spectrum : for him the significance of human life is immanent, the subjective and unique quality of every individual experience is paramount. The aim of life for Edschmid, as for many of his fellow-Expressionists, must be to live to the full every passing moment, the aim of art is to express from moment to moment a kaleidoscope of ecstasy, despair or repose. To express, rather than to record—that is the moral of *The Humiliating Room*. The owner of the pictures in the story has passed his life—as did Edschmid himself—in exotic places, pursuing love and danger. His experiences he records—characteristically, not in his own creations but in *trouvailles*, in works of art purchased, given or even filched. Many moods of man and nature are recalled by the gallery—sometimes actually represented, as in the case of the delicate encounter with the girl on the swing, sometimes evoked by association—the sentimental souvenir of a little violinist, the sardonic memento of a Scottish holiday. The scenes, settings and incidents that the pictures suggest are sketched in a typically breathless Expressionistic style. Around the whole narration there hangs the faintest aura of preciosity and snobbery. This is, to all superficial appearances, the "furious life" of a gentleman adventurer—almost a James Bond—a life full of emotion now recollected in tranquillity. Not only recollected, in fact, but worshipped in a kind of secular shrine, a room full of fetishes and confessionals which is emblematic of the owner's soul. For this is a man who has drugged himself with the emotional stimulants represented by his pictures to the point where his emotional constitution is totally undermined : at the climax of his story, whether it be true or invented, he cannot sustain the recollection of its brutality and the loss it implies. The concoction of memories into a kind of emotional stew, this, to the author of the story, is the sin against vitality. One must leave behind nothing but the insubstantial, colourless air. At most, experiences may be briefly registered, as they occur, on a scale that extends from breath-taking motion to serene satisfaction of the aesthetic sense, extremes epitomised in the passage of an express train through a remote country station, and the contemplation of coloured silks on a bright spring day in the ancient streets of Strassburg.

The gloss on the meaning of the story which Edschmid supplies in its closing pages represents a self-conscious reflective element which might be considered to run counter to his philosophy of vitalism : he seems reluctant to allow the episode to speak for itself. In this respect *The Humiliating Room* contrasts with the work of our next author. There are few writers whose work "speaks for itself" like that of Franz Kafka, and this is possibly why his novels and short stories are subject to so many and varied interpretations : the images and emblematic situations of which the works are composed have different associations for each individual reader. Through a style that is clinically detached Kafka creates a world with many of the details of familiar reality, but it is a world of which certain central features are bizarre, perplexing or frightening. His is a method which is not based on an unambiguous and rational translation of concepts and relationships into picturesque terms; the human situation seems to present itself naturally to Kafka as parable or allegory. The tendency to expression in images rather than in abstract terms is a feature of the eidetic mental constitution that Kafka undoubtedly possessed, but it may also be connected with his alienation from philosophical and religious creeds. Lacking faith, like many of his generation, in such traditional systems of thought, Kafka reverted in his attempt to convey the inner truth about life to two primitive sources : the subconscious life of the mind in dreams, and language itself. Corresponding to these sources, we find imagery in Kafka that is more or less intentional. Some of the tales have the gross distortion and the unquestioned absurdity of nightmares : characters and objects swell or vanish with bewildering suddenness, time and space are thrown out of joint, and yet, as a whole, the narrative has an emotional cohesion and may be interpreted in terms of familiar stresses and anxieties. Of this kind is the short story, *A Country*

Doctor. Elsewhere Kafka's technique is the more deliberate one of unlocking insights and truths that have long been imprisoned in simile and metaphor. We may imagine some of his works as springing from trite statements like "Life is a trial", or "The artist is like a circus performer". Kafka proceeds to suppress the first term in such comparisons and to elaborate the second term with a wealth of detail. In the story *The Transformation*, in which the hero is turned into a monstrous and repulsive beetle, Kafka has provided a bizarre literal interpretation of a family situation in which Gregor Samsa might be said to have been "treated like an insect". It is this technique which produces the disconcerting juxtaposition of reality and fantasy in Kafka's work. *A Fasting Showman* belongs to this second category of story, in which a fantastic element is embedded in a context largely realistic. Here, the only feature which is foreign to experience is the fanatical absorption of the hero in his profession and the drastic consequences which follow. Kafka describes with precision the conditions of his hero's life and performance, and yet the story could hardly be mistaken for a straightforward account of a somewhat unusual individual career : Kafka's idiom, for all its apparent objectivity, invites us to look for a hidden meaning. Many interpretations are possible : some commentators have seen the story as satirical, some have regarded it as tragic, some have even seen it as comic, but most agree that it concerns the conflict of idealism and vitality, and that the problematic existence of the artist is involved. The hero is a lone figure seeking to demonstrate an ideal in a society dedicated to materialism and crude vitality. He is, in fact, a voluntary prisoner to his ideal, which, in the nature of things he can serve only by abstention. But even in this would-be idealist there is an element of egoism, of showmanship. He invites the admiration of the public, only to discover, even in the period of his success, that they are incapable of appreciating his motives and the nature of his performance. In his dying moments the showman does not even have the consolation of knowing himself the victim of an idealistic self-sacrifice—his abstention was simply a consequence of his own nature, of his failure to find in the world the nourishment that was to his taste. We do not need the poignant knowledge that Kafka wrote this story practically on his death-bed to feel that it speaks of him, of his complex dilemma as a man and a poet in a

culture which lives more and more by bread alone. But it speaks
not only of its author, it speaks for all those whose moral fastidi-
ousness cause them to languish in a materialistic and sceptical
age. Such "fasting showmen" are bereft of public esteem and
even of a sense of their own merit.

In contrast to the impersonal and parabolic method of Kafka,
Borchert's story, *The Dandelion*, has an impassioned, almost
hysterical directness. Its unceasing monologue expresses the
despair, hatred and ecstasy of a prison life which Borchert knew
at first hand. The story goes much deeper than an account of
the physical and mental privations of a life of confinement. It
goes beyond superficial moral sentiments—questions of guilt,
punishment, justice or indignation—to describe three fundamental experiences. Firstly, the infinite sense of loneliness and
inadequacy, the threatened loss of identity, that comes upon the
individual when he is left face to face with himself. The prisoner
is assailed by claustrophobia, and in a kind of delirium he questions the nature of existence and the reality of God. Release into
the company of others in the exercise yard is only a temporary
relief : no sense of fellowship can flourish under these arid conditions, the only communication that is possible between man
and man is a current of hatred and contempt. A man cannot
love his neighbour, for he has no neighbour, only a Man in
Front, whose face he never sees except in the moment of death.
Deprived of human comradeship, the prisoner's spirit seeks comfort in the tiny vestige of nature that miraculously survives within
the prison walls—the single dandelion. Now the immense resources of human patience and ingenuity come into play to make
possible the acquisition of this precious symbol. In the rapt contemplation of the flower, the prisoner has an experience of mystic
intensity that carries him out of his present condition in a society
of hatred and punishment into a paradise of nature. A spring of
love, almost erotic in its intensity, wells up within him. In his
boundless imagination he is free, and, like the hero of Britting's
story, falls asleep to dream of flowers, to sense that he is a part
of nature, no longer suspended in a void, deserted by God and
reviled by man. It is perhaps fitting that this story should con-
clude our collection, for it epitomises the essential inwardness of
the German poetic genius : within the confines of prison walls,
which have a symbolic force, Borchert concerns himself with

three great existential questions that have repeatedly challenged German philosophers and poets—the nature of the self, the relation of man to man, and the relation of man to nature. To the Germans it seems that the answers to these questions lie within us : as Novalis wrote :

"The mysterious path leads inwards."

Georg Britting

Translated
by
Geoffrey Skelton

THE WHITE SLAVE TRADER

A MOUSTACHE, a brigand's moustache, a buccaneer's moustache hung pale and only slightly greying over his lips. Buccaneer's moustache, I said aloud to myself. Perhaps he would hear and ask me what I meant. But he did not hear or, if he heard, he did not ask, but kept his eyes fixed firmly on the chessboard. There was a rustling in the walnut tree above our heads, it was like drawing a deep breath. A shadow of leaves swayed across the table, the garden was all green light. He seized a knight—*Cavallo* he always called it—with his single arm and moved it. If he could he would never have moved anything else. The knight was his favourite piece, though he never used that name for it, and when I did, because that was its name in my chess-book, I could see in his face that he did not like it. He drew in his eyebrows as he considered his move, shortly and sharply, then gathered up his knight and rapped it down on a new square, and now as before I felt a startled respect as I saw that the hand of the single arm still remaining to him had only three fingers. The little finger and the fourth finger were missing, and that made the hand look strangely narrow. How he had come by this disfigurement—rare in those days before the war—I never knew for certain and I had not the courage to ask.

His name was Herr Berger, and that was all I knew about him. This summer, in the long school holidays, I spent many afternoons with him, playing chess. Sixteen-year-old schoolboys such as I was were strictly forbidden to enter public-houses : only on walks in the country were we allowed by a special dispensation to go into inns to buy refreshments. And so two or three times a week I could go to this village, three-quarters of an hour's walk away, order a cup of coffee or lemonade in a tall glass with a long-handled spoon and a drinking straw, and play chess with Herr Berger. It began quite by chance. He had seen me sitting by myself in front of the board, solving chess problems, which was my great passion, and he came up to my table, introduced himself with a courteous bow and asked whether I would accept him as an opponent. Timidly I agreed and carried the board to his table, and the duel began—the first we fought together, and there were many more to follow. Defying all the rules and instructions of the experts he opened each game with a knight : sending the cavalry out in front, he called it. He began our very first game like that, and with all the confidence of my textbook knowledge I told myself, He'll think better of it when he sees where it leads him. But he won that first game as he was later to win many others, in spite of this completely false opening.

Yet it seemed somehow in character, this reckless cavalry charge in all directions across the board. One after the other his warhorses came up to rear threateningly over me, putting me into difficulties with my bishops and rooks and playing havoc with my defences. I felt admiringly that all these wild equestrian tricks were in line with him, they belonged to this one-armed man with the buccaneer's moustache. Intent on our game, we spoke little on these afternoons. He had a long lean face with jutting cheekbones, eyes a bit slanting, gleaming bald pate and a voice that emerged rough and manly through the strands of his moustache. He was dressed almost invariably in a dark suit, seemed to know a lot and to have seen a lot of the world and had a hardened way of throwing out superior and acid remarks about the things that go on in it. Among other things he was supposed once to have been a fisherman—a Danube fisherman even : that much I had discovered, though I could not really believe it. Not that it isn't a respectable trade, but he seemed too refined for it, too much the gentleman. And even if it were true, who knows what twist of his life, his vivid and colourful life, had brought it about?

He was well known in that rather townified country inn, my Herr Berger : he spent a good deal of money there. Once quite by accident I heard the landlord and his wife talking about him : they were sitting the two of them at the next table and were chatting about him, calling him in an appreciative way a devil of a fellow, and from the bits I heard I gathered that he had not always been simply a fisherman but had also been active—the blood rushed to my head, my hands and knees trembled as I heard it—in the white slave trade. Yes, they used that awful word that sent sweet shudders through me—white slave traffic, and they laughed, and from the scraps of talk that came to my ears I pieced together that he had earned his living with this vicious trade, was maybe still earning it. My feelings were chaotic: in the mind of a sixteen-year-old, greedy for adventure, a white slave trader is as much a hero as a villain, a man both crafty and bold, cunning as a fox, up to all tricks, master of all situations, irresistible, cruel and treacherous, shining in his evil glory.

And I could well believe it of him, of Herr Berger with all his buccaneering looks. I saw him sailing his ship maybe down the Danube, past the whirling currents and the cliffs with their old castles in Germany and Austria, sailing on towards Rumania or somewhere in a festooned ship full of girls, girls in gay dresses, girls singing, girls weeping, girls dancing and drinking wines and spirits with bitter laughter. And sometimes I saw his boatload naked, girls white in their stark nakedness, and I averted my eyes in embarrassment and shame. Hurriedly in my mind I dressed the seething heap again, in rustling silk cloths with red ribbons in their voluptuous black hair—they were all of them black-haired —and they screamed and laughed, bitterly and lecherously.

I did not avoid Herr Berger in spite of these disquieting thoughts. What I knew about him did not really frighten me. It was always possible that I had heard it wrongly, or what had been said about him was untrue. Yes, it was all a pack of lies: what wouldn't people say about other people? But true or not it drew me, the strange evil aura about him beckoned me mysteriously. Slave dealers, traffickers in white bodies, chains and bracelets jangling, and somewhere down there in the Balkans the Danube touching Turkish soil, half moon and harem, the Orient, pashas with their seven horses' tails—it was all mixed up together in my mind, maiden flesh and ransoms, and instead of knight he said *Cavallo*: this was something new and unexperienced. This was truly a man!

Every Friday, the day on which it was forbidden to eat meat —and in those days such things were observed more strictly than today—a fish market was held in our devout little town. It took place in the square near the old bridge, under which the river Danube flowed unseen but spreading coolness around. A fountain dominated this square in which there were a number of coffin-like stones fixed into the ground. On these great stone benches the fishmongers would place their tubs filled with a

gleaming mass of wriggling and slapping and gasping fish:
blackish barbels with blunt heads, greeny-gold sticklebacks with
bristly dorsal fins, flat-sided breams, long-nosed pikes and silly
goggle-eyed carps. Around them housewives and maidservants
with nets and baskets jostled and pushed and wandered from
bench to bench, inspecting what was on offer and sizing it up
with knowing looks, finding one fish too small and another too
bony: they were never satisfied. There were no weighing-
machines, the fish were simply judged by their size, and when
after long bargaining a price was agreed the salesman would
plunge his hands into the water, seize the poor scaly victim and
knock its head against the edge of the tub. In technical language
this was called stunning, and such acts of murder were committed in their hundreds on mornings like this. The merciless
thuds sounded like regular hammer blows, and the fish died as
they had lived, without a sound.

In term time these morning hours would be grudgingly spent in
the classroom, but now I was on holiday, though not many more
days remained to me, only another ten. So once again I had
made my way to the fish market. Mixed up in the jostling among
the heavy curious smells of fish scales, entrails and dampness, I
let myself be pulled along in the current of shoppers, listening
inquisitively to the wordy battles that preceded every purchase.
And it was thus that I came on Herr Berger as he stood there
behind a tub in a collarless shirt, selling fish. He had a place
close to the fountain with its four snarling dragon's mouths spitting out water. I hid myself behind it to watch.

So he still had something to do with fish, this man with the
brigand's moustache, with whom I had yesterday been playing
chess. I did not want him to see me, perhaps he would be embarrassed to know that I was watching him in his business of killing
and selling fish. I leaned up against the fountain and held my
hand over the nearest dragon's mouth, blocking the stream until
the mounting pressure forced my hand away and a great gush
came out. Then the water ran evenly again, and all the time I
kept my eyes fixed firmly on the bald-headed Herr Berger. He
did not appear to have many customers. Standing all alone by
his tub he looked surly and cross, and he slapped the water a few
times, raising a white spray. Then a woman came up to him. I
could see only her back, but I knew her at once by her broad

shoulders, it was our own maid Anna, and she cast a distrustful eye over his wares. With his single hand he scooped up a fish from the flapping mass in the tub, raised it high in the cruel air, and I saw the water dripping from it. Anna shook her head: she didn't fancy the fish, it was anyway half dead—I could clearly hear her high-pitched voice—she had seen the poor creature swimming on its back, no, she was not taking that. And she began to move off to the next stall. Angrily he threw the rejected fish back into the tub, and then I heard this man, the well-mannered and cultured Herr Berger of my acquaintance, in whose mouth I had never known a rude word, I heard my cavalier of the chessboard saying things to the poor woman which made us both, myself and the maid, blush furiously. Were her eyes gummed up, he asked as he pulled on his moustache, that she dared to say it wasn't fresh, a lively leaping fish like that? Well, he had a pretty good idea why, and he laughed coarsely. She probably hadn't slept a wink all night because she hadn't been alone in her bed and had had better things, far better things to do than to slumber in sweet repose. In ugly unambiguous words, gloatingly and exhaustively, he painted the happenings of the night gone by. Anna did not seem at first to know what had struck her, she stood there as if paralysed by the torrent of slops pouring down over her head, and then she fled, as fast as she could, the cruel words of her tormentor echoing after her.

For lunch that day we had barbel, and when Anna carried them in I did not dare look at her. Remembering the vileness of the abuse which she had suffered that very morning, I kept my nose well down to my plate and the fish lying curled and blue on it. But after lunch I slipped furtively into her bedroom to look on the bed with its high pile of feathers and its red and white check cover, in which such exciting things might have occurred last night. For was it not possible that Herr Berger, fisherman and white slave trader, a connoisseur by profession, a hardened expert who could sum women up better than most, was it not possible that he had read the wicked truth in the maid's eyes and had in his fury flung it in her so innocent-looking, so deceitful face? But the bed lay still and silent in its screaming red, and on the wall behind it there was a bright-coloured holy picture.

A few days later I walked again to my chess village. It was

September by now and the end of the holidays loomed with growing menace. I had kept putting the visit off, had even resolved to avoid Herr Berger entirely, but my mind was not at ease and I told myself that it was rude to drop my chess companion without a word. The urge to see him again had been irresistible, and now here I was, on my way to him. There had been a lot of rain in the last few days, I had heard it cascading down through the leaves of the trees outside my bedroom window, and it had washed the summer away, for now that it was fine again and the sun was shining the air had taken on an autumn clarity. Under the chestnut trees lay little prickly globes shaken off by the night wind, the stubble gleamed on the harvested cornfields and giant flowers flaunted their gaudy petals.

I saw Herr Berger immediately I entered the garden of the inn. Seated beside him at the garden table was a young girl in a white blouse, and they were talking animatedly together. This had never happened before, up till now he had always been alone, I felt reluctant to approach him. I was too bashful, I did not want to intrude, not at all, and I looked for a place to sit where I should be out of his sight. But he had already seen me and was beckoning with cheerful insistence, and so there was nothing else I could do, I went over to him, greeting him awkwardly. This was his niece, he said, indicating the girl, who stretched out a small pink hand and smiled at me, and he thought it unlikely that we would play much chess today, the young lady wished to be entertained, and he stroked his brigand's moustache, and I felt very uncomfortable indeed as I looked at the girl who sat there beside me, her bosom rising and falling, I could not take my shy gaze off it. The fishmonger had become the complete gentleman again. He wore a stiff white collar and the empty left sleeve, tucked into his pocket, hung down in dapper folds. He was in high spirits, this one-armed uncle, he talked a lot and the girl laughed at his jokes in silvery tones. Perhaps she wasn't his niece at all—the burning thought shot through my head— perhaps she was destined to be sold, to be traded like a piece of cattle, to be miserably bartered, that young blood and white flesh, and I stirred my coffee and shivered apprehensively, and stirred so vigorously with my spoon that I splashed a brown stain on the white tablecloth and quickly put the sugar bowl over it so that nobody should see.

At this moment the landlord came up to call Herr Berger off to a business talk : the tradesman Moosbacher was there, he was waiting inside in the parlour. I'll leave you alone, Herr Berger said and got to his feet. Be good, he said and laughed for no apparent reason. It may be an hour before we are through, he said, he's a tough fellow, and if things get too boring you can stretch your legs a little. But here at this table—he rapped on its surface—we'll meet again, and before he went off he seemed to give me an encouraging wink.

So I was left sitting with the pretty little girl and could think of nothing to say, and she said nothing either but leaned far back in her chair so that her blouse tightened, and gazed up into the green foliage, and her nearness disturbed me. Suddenly she laughed, then stood up and smoothed the skirt over her hips. Let's take a little walk, she said. We went towards the back of the garden, she going ahead in her bright stockings.

This part of the garden was not kept in order. There were no tables and chairs, the path was overgrown and scarcely visible, there were shrubs and a great profusion of nettles. It was a little green wilderness which I often visited with pleasure. It contained an old rotting swing which I had used many times, it still held even if the posts wobbled ominously when it was in motion. The girl in the white blouse showed no interest in it, but I was not to be put off mounting the wooden seat and heaving myself up, partly I know in the hope of making an impression on her. But I might as well have saved myself the trouble, for she did not even look but went over to the fence between the garden and the fields and looked out across it. I could use my energies as I would to set the swing whistling and singing, she did not even turn her head, and once I thought I heard her sigh.

What is that sigh for, I asked myself, what is going on inside her? Was she the poor deluded victim of that gentlemanly rogue, fallen goodness knows how into his clutches, or was she aware of her fate, did she know what was in store, ready for it, giving herself up of her own free will to a life of sin?

Fiercely I rocked myself to and fro, higher and higher, and the wind whistled round my ears, the rusty iron rings screeched and sang and the lurching posts groaned.

At last the girl turned round. Oh, do come along, she said, a shade grudgingly, and I let the swing run down and then jumped

off, giving the seat a shove so that it started to move again, and
I went across to the sinful creature. There was a little gate in the
fence, fixed with a wooden bolt, we opened it and went out of
the garden, and behind us the rocking swing sang quietly on.

We followed the snaking path across the field, above us the
wide blue sky in which a few white clouds hung unmoving. The
shining hills on the other side of the Danube seemed quite close
and the sunlight gleamed from the stubble fields. The trees were
still fully clad in green, the potatoes were in leaf, though the
leaves now hung limp and faded. We walked along by a turnip
field, which smelled sharp and bitter, and the ditch beside the
path was filled with water just barely flowing. Strands of weed
lay on its surface and from its black bed rose large plants with
sprawling leaves.

My curiosity gave me no rest. Your uncle, I said, trying to
look unconcerned, Herr Berger, is he really your uncle? She
looked at me, surprised and intrigued. Of course, she said and
she plucked a long grass stalk from the wayside, put it in her
mouth and began to nibble at it. What do you mean? In my
exasperation I grabbed the end of the green stalk between her
lips. You can make yourself ill with that, I lectured her. She did
not let go, but held the stalk tight between her white teeth. Rubbish, she said, but then she spat it out. Your uncle then, I started
again, all right, your uncle, I don't care, if that's what he is, and
I laughed carelessly. She did not grasp my meaning or at least
she pretended not to grasp it and simply shrugged her shoulders
in mystification. Your uncle, I went on, eyeing her closely, a
curious business he's engaged in, really a very curious business.
She stopped, her expression was ominous, but now I had the bit
firmly between my teeth and was not to be put off. I know he
deals in fish, I said severely, but there are other things he deals
in, aren't there? Or so people say. She gave no further answer,
simply laughed. Fish, I was almost shouting by now, white fish
—well, there's nothing wrong with that, I suppose, but trading
with white girls ... The words were out, I had said what had
to be said, and I took a deep breath. Yes, she said and seemed
not at all put out by what I seemed to know. Why not? she
went on placidly. It's a job like any other, and as long as he
finds me a good place ...

There she stood, a creature of sin, fresh and crisp, with full red lips and carefree laughter, and I felt hot and cold by turns as I saw the abyss opening up before me, deep and fiery. I looked beyond her towards the town, our good and pious town with its shining turrets, familiar and comforting, to persuade myself that I was not in a dream. It lay there in the shadow of the cathedral, respectable and clean-living, and here I stood beside this depraved maiden, loaded with vice, cast down to the lowest depths, and I felt something like pity for her.

We had reached a clump of brambles, and the thorny branches were full of berries, most of them still green, others already faintly flushed with red, but among them some had ripened before their time and hung there in shining black, luscious and juicy. The girl at my side, taking no further notice of me, began to pick the berries, eating them one after another with slow appreciation. Here is one for you, she said, turning suddenly to me, and the corners of her mouth were stained slightly with black juice. She laughed. Open your mouth and shut your eyes, she said, and she stood so close that her bosom touched me, only very lightly, but a feeling like fire passed through me. I closed my eyes as she bade me and opened my mouth and trembled and tried to hide my trembling. She pushed the berry between my lips, it tasted cool and sharp, and I felt like Adam in the garden of Eden. A sudden violent urge took hold of me and I quickly opened my eyes. That's not allowed, she said. I put my arms about her. And certainly not that, she said angrily and went to pull herself free. Who does she think she is? I asked myself, she is used to other things, things of quite another sort, and I saw the moist sinful lips and the shining teeth behind them and drew her to me and kissed her wildly on the red mouth, twice, three times, again and again, as she struggled vainly against me. She lost her balance and swayed backwards. Watch out, she cried, and now it was she who was pressing against me, not with tender desire but in an attempt to save herself from falling, but all the same I shuddered, sighed ecstatically, and then the fall was past saving. Closely entwined, we sank together into the brambles, which opened with a searing welcome, lashing out at us with their thorns, and then we hit the ground and lay there arm in arm.

We struggled upright and extricated ourselves from the prickly tangle, we felt ourselves and brushed ourselves down and found that nothing very serious had happened. In our fall I had landed underneath, the girl had escaped untouched, but my left sleeve had a large gaping tear which I viewed in alarm, and beneath one eye an angry thorn had inflicted a scratch which burned and bled a little. The girl said not a word, she seemed not to see me at all, but sat down in her bright stockings on a tree stump, took a comb and a mirror from her bag and, as if she were alone, tidied her dishevelled hair, pulled her skirt straight and tied a loosened shoelace. Then she got to her feet and wiped the blood from my face with a small lace-embroidered handkerchief and closed the tear in my sleeve with a safetypin. All this she did in silence, not looking at me, showing no anger, her face untroubled. Then she turned and started back as we had come, walking towards the inn with no particular haste, and I followed her, silent and constrained and ashamed and with a heavy conscience.

I thought, now she will tell him everything. She will tell that one-armed buccaneer of my cowardly assault, and he was not a man to be trifled with, I had seen that at the fish market, and I had done much worse things than our carping maid. For a moment I thought of making a quick escape, dashing straight across the fields to freedom, doubling on my tracks as hares do, never to be seen again, but I fought down the impulse. It's too late now, I told myself obstinately, you must face it whatever happens, and I kept straight to the path, walking behind my accuser in dogged pride, moving with head held high towards an uncertain fate.

Herr Berger was already seated at the table. He was in a beaming humour, his piece of business done seemingly to his liking, and beside him sat a small man with a long black cigar. They looked pleased with themselves, the lean brigand and the fat little man, and both of them were bald. Helen, this is Herr Moosbacher, Herr Berger said to the girl. He's a sly old fox, I'm a baby compared to him. He laughed loudly and Herr Moosbacher laughed loudly too. He's been making rings round me, Herr Berger continued, never in my life have I paid such a wicked price for potatoes. He seemed to find the idea enjoyable, for his eyes sparkled as he raised his glass of pale ale to the victor, drank some of it and then wiped his moustache. And you can start with him on the first of October, he told the girl with pride. He needs a temporary assistant and I said you might do, but he won't pay more than fifty marks. Quite enough too for someone just out of commercial school, said Herr Moosbacher without taking the cigar from his mouth. He held his hand out to Helen. Then it's all agreed, Fräulein Berger, and she took his hand.

Yes, said Herr Berger contentedly, two birds with one stone, nowadays you must have a line on everything, leave nothing undone, fish, potatoes, finding jobs—just as it comes : some of it is bound to stick.

Then he noticed the scratch on my cheek. I suppose you've been having a tussle, he said, and Helen had the sharpest nails? Helen regarded me with round eyes. Nothing of the kind, she said, we have had a splendid time. I was picking blackberries and I nearly fell because I was too greedy, but the young gentleman grabbed me and got caught on a thorn. Her eyes rested placidly on me. But it's nothing very bad : it'll be quite healed up by the time he comes to marry.

I sat there in deep embarrassment, scarcely daring to look up, but now nobody was concerned with me. Herr Berger had gone back to his discussion with Herr Moosbacher about potato prices and Helen was playing thoughtfully with her coffee spoon. Perhaps she was considering the advantages and disadvantages of her new situation, for from time to time, with an absent expression on her face, she would raise her eyes to gaze deliberately at the man who would in future give the orders, at his round bald head and his black cigar and the silver watch-chain stretched across his stomach.

A twirling column of midges moved across from the next table to ours. It reached right up to the leafy roof above us, melted into the branches and extended perhaps up to and beyond the treetops, higher and higher still into the clear blue sky. There was a ceaseless whirring and wheeling around us and a shimmer of silver bodies and glassy wings. Furtively I shifted my chair until the column was between my face and hers, and through that grateful protecting veil I cast timid glances at the girl who had shown me such unaccountable graciousness.

Then I felt it was time for me to go. Helen gave me her hand, calm and unperturbed, Herr Moosbacher kept his cigar in the corner of his mouth as he gave me his, and Herr Berger raised his single arm affably and in his rough voice hoped we would soon meet again at the chessboard: he was looking forward to the intrepid cavalry charge which he had thought out. Then I walked away.

I walked away, but I had not yet recovered my composure and I moved swiftly and had to make an effort to keep myself from running. My one desire was to escape, to put far behind me the scene of my shame and to reach the town that was my home. As its gleaming turrets grew gradually larger I asked myself how I could ever have believed that childish nonsense about Herr Berger being a white slave trader. How beastly, how revolting to have leapt out like a footpad on those red lips, to have molested so insolently that noble girl who had disdained to betray me. I blushed anew to think of it, and yet at the same time remembered with sharp delight the soft feel of her lips on mine. Red as my blushing face the town rose up before me, afire in the glow of the setting sun and scattering its reflected light in the river below.

Arriving at my home, I crept on tiptoe through the darkening hall to the kitchen. Anna, our maid, sat with a bowl on her knees, cleaning and slicing beans, and I put a finger over my lips, commanding silence, and beckoned her to follow me to her room. There I asked her to mend the tear in my sleeve, now at once, so that the damage would not be too soon detected. Later I would tell my mother, but at a time of my own choosing. Today, I felt, it would be enough to have to endure her concerned questioning about the scratch on my face. I took off my jacket and gave it to Anna, who fetched out her work-basket and set to work on the sleeve with tiny cautious stitches after first withdrawing the safety-pin, Helen's safety-pin, and placing it in an ivory box along with other shiny pointed things. I sat on the edge of her bed, the bed about which Herr Berger had spoken so outrageously, and watched her as she sewed. Examining that kind and placid face I wondered how I could even for a second have believed in the wickedness of which she had been accused. She looked up from her work, caught my searching gaze and stopped her needle to ask, why do you look at me like that? Oh, I said, and with the hand hidden behind my back surreptitiously stroked the pillow, oh, I said as if unconcerned, just watching, do finish it please. And she went back to her busy sewing and Joseph, the bright shining Joseph in the holy picture, wielded the plane till the shavings flew.

I went off early to bed that day. Dressed in my long white nightshirt I stood awhile beside my bed, on which the blankets lay pulled enticingly back (Anna's careful work, on this as on all other evenings). The last light of day still lingered in the room and outside the trees made ghostly whispers. I climbed on the bed, but very carefully and deliberately, for I wanted the sheets to stay smooth and unwrinkled, and laid myself down on my back. I pulled my nightshirt down to my ankles, firm and straight, put my arms by my sides and lay stretched out at full length, neither moving nor pulling the blankets over me. It was nice like that, in the pure linen that smelled so good, it was soothing and innocent, and I resolved to stay that way the whole night through, lying quietly on my back, not rumpling the pillows and sheets as I usually did, you could always see it the next morning. The cool evening air blew in through the window and I shivered slightly, but I remained as I was, folding my hands and listening to the rustling outside the window. I closed my eyes and tried to go off to sleep in spite of the unwonted position and the lack of warming blankets.

As I drifted towards sleep I saw in a state of half-dreaming white lilies growing up to either side of my bed, rigid on their long stems, pale and chaste with heads like swans, and within this cage of flowers, comforted, I fell asleep with a deep sigh. When next morning I awoke, I found myself nestled voluptuously in blankets pulled right up to my chin, and sheets and pillows were rumpled, as always.

BIOGRAPHICAL NOTE

Georg Britting was born on 17th February 1891, in Regensburg. He volunteered for the army at the outbreak of war in 1914 and was twice wounded. His subsequent life was outwardly uneventful : in 1920 he settled in Munich and pursued a literary career there until his death on 27th April 1964. Besides his novel, *Lebenslauf eines dicken Mannes, der Hamlet hiess* (1932) and one drama, *Das Storchennest* (1922), Britting produced half a dozen collections of lyrics and nearly fifty short stories. The earliest of the stories reflect the experience of the war, but the most characteristic are probably those which evoke the Bavarian landscape and the scenes of his childhood, stories like *Das Waldhorn*, *Der Eisläufer*, *Der Sturz in die Wolfsschlucht*, *Der Fisch* and, of course, the story reprinted here, *Der Mädchenhändler*. In his lyric, Britting unites the dynamic metaphorical style of Expressionism with his individual perception of landscape and the moods of nature : there is something baroque in the rich imagery and the energetic movement of his verse. This richly poetic style, with its brilliant colours, its evocation of atmosphere and its verbal echoes, is equally characteristic of the Hamlet novel, which, in a series of episodes, portrays a Prince of Denmark who is a lethargic spectator of life, a glutton who defeats his step-father in a bizarre eating contest, laconically successful general who retires to end his days in the sybaritic comfort of a monastery, sardonically observing the ambitious machinations of his mother, who refuses to grow old. In all of his work, Britting shows an awareness of the elemental and potentially destructive forces that lie behind the lush and flourishing countryside of his native Danube valley. The dark undertones beneath a harmony that often verges on the idyllic are reminiscent of Eduard Mörike, and it is significant that Britting edited Mörike's works and wrote an essay on him.

A detailed bibliography of Britting's work will be found in Dietrich Bode, *Georg Britting. Geschichte seines Werkes*, 1962.

Ludwig Thoma

Translated
by
Richard Thonger

THE GIRL FROM INDIA*

ALL of a sudden Cora came to stay, and I didn't know anything about her.

She's Uncle Hans's daughter, he's in Bombay because he never did any work at school and so they kicked him out. But now he's got a lot of money and a tea plantation, and he lies and swings in a hammock, and the slaves have to keep fanning so that the flies don't get on him.

I liked Cora straight away. She's got black eyes and black hair and laughs like anything, but not like Aunt Theresa's Rosa does, Rosa puts her hand up every time so you don't see her awful teeth.

When Cora came she shook hands with me as though she were a boy, and she took hold of my Mother's head and said she was a lovely person, and gave her a kiss.

And she told Annie she was a pretty girl, and if she were a young man she'd be courting her like anything. And she told me I must be working very hard at school and one of these days I'd be a university man with specs on my nose. And then she laughed because my mother gave a sigh. But I told her straight away that I'm not hard-working at all, and I'd like to do the same as Uncle Hans and go out to Bombay and shoot tigers.

She said perhaps she could take me back with her, but I'd have to think it over carefully, as tigers are so dangerous. But I said, I'll sit on an elephant and shoot down on the tiger from up there, and if he gets really savage he can eat my slaves who are running alongside.

She said, that's true enough, and I was a clever boy, and when I'd finished at the Grammar School I must come out.

I said, that would take too long, and you don't need any Grammar School if you want to go to India. They always tell you in the books how a boy runs away from home and makes a

---

* Thoma has phrased this story in ungrammatical German suited to the 14-year-old narrator. I have followed him in comparable English. R.T.

terrific pile in a far-flung continent and comes home rich for
Christmas. And I'd like to do that, as Aunt Theresa's eyes
would pop out and she'd go green with envy when I brought my
Mother back a whole trunkful of furs.

Cora laughed and said I'd have to wait a bit because I had
to do well at school so that our Mother can be happy even if she
doesn't get any furs.

I used to spend all my spare time with Cora. We often
walked to the main square because the band was playing and
everybody was standing about or walking round the fountain.
The gentlemen always looked at us when we came along and
the dispenser from the chemist's looked at us more than anyone.
That's Oskar Seitz, I know his name because Aunt Theresa
talks about him so much as she thinks he might marry Rosa.
He's at the Angel Dispensary and I can't bear him as he gets
so stuck up when you go in to buy barley-sugar. If there are any
girls in the shop you have to wait a terrible time, and once I
banged my money on the counter and said it's disgraceful the
kind of service you get these days. So he said I was a cheeky brat
and he'd box my ears for me. So I said I'd complain to his
superior and I was afraid I'd have to purchase my barley-sugar
somewhere else. So he couldn't bear me after that. I told Cora,
and whenever she saw him she couldn't help laughing. Mister
Seitz used to raise his hat and make his eyes go very big. His
eyes stick out a long way and they're green like a cat's. He'd
always turn round to look at us and walk round so that he'd
pass us again. Once Cora left me alone because she saw a girl
who was a friend of Annie's. Then Mister Seitz came up to me
and got very friendly. He asked how I was and how my Mother
was. I said we're very well thank you. Then he asked if we had
visitors and was it true the young lady came from India. I said
yes, she comes from India. So he said that's very interesting, and
is she staying long, and who are her parents. I said her Papa is
Uncle Hans and he sends big ships back to Europe all full of
tea. He shook hands with me and said why don't I come again,
and he'd give me some barley-sugar. I said, perhaps I
will. On Sunday morning our bell rang and when I went to the
door there was Mister Seitz in a black suit with yellow gloves.
He said he just wanted to pay my Mother a call 'cos he hadn't
seen her for a long time. I took him into the front room

and my Mother was pleased he'd been so thoughtful and she went in, and I went in too. Mister Seitz sat on the sofa with his hat on his knees, and my mother said it was so kind of him to do us the honour, and how was he keeping. He said very well thank you, but do you know, one has to work terribly hard these days, there's so many people come in after dark and want medicine, and it's strange how many diseases there are about just now. My Mother said that's very sad but she hoped it would be better in the summer when there aren't so many colds and chills. He said yes, he hoped so too, and then he held up his hat and gave a terrific yawn so that his eyes watered. Then he said there are a lot of diseases about in summer as well, there's no stopping them. He looked round the room as though he were waiting for someone and then my mother asked how our Dispensing Chemist was, Mister Seitz's superior. He's very well thank you, said Mister Seitz, he's just going off to the country. Mother said of course he needn't worry at all about going off to the country, because Mister Seitz is going to stay and look after the whole business, and she'd heard from Aunt Theresa how very capable Mister Seitz was. Mister Seitz held up his hat and yawned again. Then he asked, how was Miss Annie. Mother looked pleased and laughed and said Annie was very well, God be thanked, she has a wonderful constitution you know. Then Mister Seitz said he was looking forward to the winter when he might have the pleasure of dancing with her, and perhaps she was going to the Harmony Ball again this year. Mother said God willing she'd be going again this year, and taking Annie too, and she was sorry Annie wasn't in, she'd gone out with our Niece. Oh, which Niece would that be? asked Mister Seitz. That's Miss Pfeifer, my mother said. Oh yes, said Mister Seitz, I suppose that is the lady from Abroad? Yes, my mother said, that's the young lady from Hindia. Mister Seitz said oh, he'd heard something about the young lady, and it was very interesting that we had visitors from so far away and being a Dispensing Chemist he found India fascinating as most medicines came from Over There. My mother said it was a shame Cora wasn't in, she could certainly tell Mister Seitz all about it as she was a very well-educated young lady. Then Mister Seitz got up and said he'd have to be going now and God be thanked my Mother was in the best of health and perhaps there might be an opportunity for him to make my Mother's Niece's acquaintance, now that the evenings were warmer and one was sitting out more often. Then he went off, and outside the door he said he hoped I'd be round soon for some barley-sugar.

When Cora came home I told her straight away that Mister Seitz had been round and she laughed, but she didn't say why. I think it's because his eyes are so green and stick out so far.

In the afternoon Aunt Theresa came with her Rosa, and Uncle Joey came too with Auntie Liza. We sat in the summer-house and had coffee. My Mother was very jolly as there was so much company, and Cora took the coffee-pot and began pouring out, and asked Uncle Joey if he liked it dark or milky. And he said, dark was what he liked, and he looked at Cora and laughed. Then Auntie Liza pulled his cup away and said he mustn't drink it yet as the coffee's too hot. My Mother laughed and said did she want Uncle Joey to be better-looking as it makes you good-looking to drink your coffee cold. Then Auntie Liza went rather red and said he was good-looking enough for her and he didn't need to be good-looking for anyone else. Cora didn't know Auntie Liza very well and thought she was joking, and she wagged her finger and said would Auntie be jealous now if Uncle Joey got better-looking? Then Auntie Liza said you don't need to be jealous in Germany as the women in Germany are respectable. Then my Mother put her bonnet straight, she always does that when she's cross. But Cora looked as though she hadn't noticed and poured out some coffee for Auntie Liza, and then she was going to pour some out for Rosa. But Rosa put her hand over her cup very quickly, and said she'd have some later and she'd pour it out herself, thank you.

For quite a while no one said anything, Uncle Joey held his snuff-box in his hand and turned it round and round, and Rosie took a piece of lace out of her velvet bag and crocheted away something terrible, and Aunt Theresa started knitting, and Auntie Liza clasped her hands over her middle and stared about right and left. Cora sat down next to Annie and popped a biscuit in her mouth and then they both laughed quite loud. But Auntie Liza shook her head and looked at Uncle Joey and shook her head again. And Aunt Theresa pulled a needle out of the sock she was knitting and scratched her nose with it and

THE GIRL FROM INDIA

THE GIRL FROM INDIA

looked at Auntie Liza and then they both shook their heads together. And Cora took hold of my Mother's chin and said, "Dear
old Mummy, you're not drinking any coffee at all, and it's real
Indian." And she gave her a kiss. And Auntie Liza shook her
head more than ever, and Aunt Theresa said it was surprising
my mother didn't like the coffee as she was generally so fond of
things from India. Then Uncle Joey picked up his courage and
said it was wonderful coffee and he'd never had coffee like it.
And Auntie Liza rolled her eyes at him and said if his salary
was a bit bigger and if she didn't have to count every penny
they'd be drinking first-class coffee every day, real coffee too.
Cora smiled nicely at Uncle Joey and said if he'd come to
Bombay and see her Papa he could drink the best coffee you
could get. Then Auntie Liza went red in the face again and
said Uncle Joey was properly looked after at home and didn't
need to go travelling. And Aunt Theresa nodded her head
something terrible and picked her teeth with her knitting-needle.
Then she said very slowly, "Stay in your nest, what Mother
cooks is best."

Uncle Joey didn't say anything, and blew his nose. But Cora
didn't take any notice and asked Rosa what she was making.
I'm making an Antimacassar, Rosa said, and didn't look up.
Cora said it must be very boring, crocheting a big thing like
that, and wouldn't it be more sensible to buy one, it wouldn't
cost much. Then Aunt Theresa rolled her eyes at Auntie Liza
and sighed, and then she said the young ladies in Germany had
to spend their time usefully, and not everybody had money to
spend on things. And Cora went a bit red herself and asked if
it was so useful after all if you worked away for six months and
then all you had to show for it was an antimacassar.

Then Aunt Theresa began to squint and I thought, now she's
getting really furious. She said it's much more useful than girls
doing nothing at all, perhaps it's different with the Indians.
Then my Mother spoke up and said you could be a very good girl
and not do any crocheting, and you could do a lot of it and
not be a good girl at all. Then Cora laughed in a very jolly way
and said my Mother was a lovely person and she'd go and fetch
something to work at so that the Aunts would think she was a
good girl. So she got up and Annie went out with her. When
she'd gone mother put her bonnet straighter than ever and said

she couldn't understand how people could behave like that. "Who?" asked Auntie Liza. "You two," said mother. So Aunt Theresa laughed as though it were a terrific joke, and Auntie Liza said very loudly "Ooh, you're a nice one!" And Rosa giggled, showing her dirty teeth, and Auntie Liza said "Yes, you really are!" very loudly, and Aunt Theresa said "Don't take on so, Liza, the Indian girl is a proper treasure."

"What's she done to either of you?" asked my mother. "Has she been rude to you?"

"I should think she better hadn't," said Aunt Theresa and squinted something terrific and stabbed the knitting-needle into her wool as though it were her deadly enemy. And Auntie Liza said "What's her manners like, anyway?"

"She behaves like a real lady," said my mother.

Then Auntie Liza threw down her coffee-spoon on the table and said was it supposed to be good manners for a girl to make eyes like that at old men who never learn sense, and a nice thing, wasn't it, to poison a man's mind against the coffee he gets at home?

And Aunt Theresa said she wouldn't let her Rosa go about too much with this Exotic Person. My Mother looked quite astonished, and said she couldn't think why they were all so cross with Cora, she'd so looked forward to coming to Germany and now the relations were all being nasty to her. Auntie Liza said if you've got eyes in your head you can see the girl's got no manners at all, Cora was here three weeks before she came to call and when she did she laughed quite dreadfully at the stuffed pug in the sitting-room, and then she didn't come any more, but there's one particular man, who'll never learn sense, and now he keeps saying that our stuffed pug Bootsy is disgusting and he doesn't like his coffee any more, but you'll see if I stand there and let my husband get his head turned.

Auntie Theresa knitted so fast that her needles clashed together and said it was disgraceful the way Cora behaved with the young gentlemen. That sort of thing might be all right in Bombay but it wouldn't do in Weilbach, we're still respectable here, and she hasn't got any corsets on either.

Rosie hung her head as though she felt ashamed of her relations, and none of them noticed Mister Seitz from the dispensary come up outside the garden fence. He stood there and kept taking his hat off, but I worked hard pretending not to know him. Then he walked away and kept looking back, and when he'd gone Aunt Theresa was still talking and said absolutely everyone in the whole town had noticed Cora smiling at Mister Seitz the other day. And she thought Mister Seitz would find it difficult to explain that, wouldn't he now.

So I said, perhaps that's why Mister Seitz was standing by the garden fence, perhaps he wants someone to explain it to him.

Then Rosa looked up very quickly and asked "Who was there by the fence?" "Mister Seitz, the one with the green eyes," I said. "That boy's lying," Aunt Theresa shouted. "I'm not," I said, "Mister Seitz was standing there and he kept taking his hat off, but no one took any notice, so he went away." Then Rosa went for me and asked why I hadn't said anything. I said because Auntie was talking and you're not to interrupt your elders, so they looked daggers at me, and Aunt Theresa asked my Mother if she wasn't going to scold, because it was my fault if Mister Seitz had taken offence. "You know, you should have, Ludwig," said my Mother, "you really must tell us next time it happens."

"Next time!" my Aunt screamed, "do you think a person like Mister Seitz is going to put up with this sort of thing?"

"Mister Seitz knows perfectly well I don't mean to be rude to him," said my Mother. "He was here today and we had a very nice talk." "Who came to see you?" asked my Aunt. "Mister Seitz, he came to pay a call." Rosa opened her eyes wide and stared at my Aunt, so I took great care to say that Mister Seitz had promised me some barley-sugar for telling him about Cora.

Then Rosa jumped up and knocked a cup over and threw her crochet-work into her velvet bag and said she wouldn't stay another minute. And Aunt Theresa put her sock away and when she was ready she told my Mother it was a shocking thing for her to be hatching plots, and at her age too.

"Plots? What are you talking about?" said my Mother and looked proper astonished. But Aunt Theresa said for goodness' sake don't look so innocent, you'll see if you get any thanks from this Indian person. Then they both went off. Just then Cora came back with a table-cloth which she used to embroider, but they both walked past her and behaved as if she wasn't there. Cora asked what the matter was. "I don't know," my Mother said. "Do you know, Liza?" And Auntie got up and said "There's things you see and don't talk about, and there's lots of things you could mention, but it's better to hold your tongue."

She flapped her hand at Uncle Joey to come along with her, and he put his snuff-box away and walked off behind Auntie. He did look back while she wasn't looking, but she saw him, and made him walk in front of her.

My Mother sat down in her chair and shook her head.

She didn't know what was the matter with the Aunts. But I know what it is. They get angry because Mister Seitz doesn't pop his eyes out so far when it's just Rosa he's looking at.

*   *   *   *   *

Franz Reiser is a chap I like an awful lot. He's at the Koller Brewery to see how you make beer as his father's got a brewery too. He told me they've got some shooting where his family live and one day I can go over and shoot with him. He lives in the house next door, and we're always talking over the fence. He lets me puff at his cigar and gives a great laugh when I tell him I've made someone cross and says, you don't want to take any nonsense from schoolmasters.

He's strong, he can do the high jump, and he's good at gymnastics. I've watched him having a scrap with the brewery boys for fun, and he chucked the lot of them all over the place. It used to be a few times a week that he'd whistle for me, but now he comes to the fence every day, and I have to go over and talk. And most times he used to leave his collar off and go about in shirt-sleeves, but now he's always got a collar on. And he isn't so cheerful. You know, he used to show me how he could walk on his hands, and do an imitation of Auntie Liza with her one tooth, and once he gave me a fire-cracker to let off somewhere.

But now he doesn't do imitations of Auntie any more and if I say I'd like a fire-cracker he says you shouldn't do that, someone might be frightened when it goes off. I really was surprised at that. And I told him, perhaps this year I'll fail the exam and miss going up to the next form, and he said how sad it was for my Mother and I ought to try to pass somehow. I said I didn't really care as I didn't want to stay at school any more. So he shook his head and said I didn't understand, if I did I'd be swotting away something terrific.

"Why?" I asked.

"Because people don't think anything of you if you're un-educated," he said, "and if you weren't at a Grammar School, and perhaps just working in a brewery, you soon see that you're not worth nearly as much as if you had been, and the girls don't think much of you either."

I said the girls don't learn anything either.

"They don't need to," he said, "if they're pretty and play the piano that's all they need. But a man's no good unless he's had an education."

He looked very sad, and then he asked me how was Miss Cora.

Cora's very well, I said.

Didn't she ever talk about him, he asked.

I said yes she did, but not very much.

So he said did she say nice things about him. I said I couldn't really remember. Once she asked me if it was Mister Reiser who made the beer we were drinking, and it wasn't much good that evening. But I couldn't remember what else she said.

So Franz looked sad again and shook his head and said he didn't think she'd be saying much else about him as perhaps she believes all he can do is make beer. And he was sure she didn't think anything of him, because he didn't go to a Grammar School. And then he said I must keep my ears open for any-thing Cora said about him. And then he went off.

I thought, I'd like to help him because I like him a lot, and I thought about it again at supper-time. We had ham, and salad with hard-boiled eggs on it, and nice beer that was very cold. My Mother said it was lovely and she'd been looking forward to her quart of beer all day, and what good beer it was. So I asked, should you think well of someone if he makes good beer. My Mother said, you ought to think well of anyone who does his job properly. I asked, did she think a Professor knew more about things than a chap who made good beer. You can't compare the two, she said, a person's got to do his duty in the station the good Lord has called him to, that's what counts. I said, if the good Lord has called someone to make beer, why do people think more highly of a Professor because he went to a Grammar

School? So Cora laughed like anything, and said wasn't I a deep young man all of a sudden, and she had a suspicion I wanted to start being a brewer myself.

"Oh dear, oh dear," my mother said, "oh Ludwig, you wasn't thinking of leaving the Grammar School, were you?"

No, I said, but what if I were, why should she go on so? If the good Lord is going to call me to brew beer I've got to do my duty and brew it.

It isn't the good Lord, my mother said, it's just because you're so lazy at school.

I don't want to leave, I said. But now anyone can see that all you think anything of is that old Grammar School.

Then Cora laughed again, and said perhaps it was Mister Reiser's fault that I'd got hold of such ideas, as I was spending so much time in his company. So I got very cross and said no, it wasn't his fault, he keeps saying I've got to work hard at school because you're not supposed to be worth anything unless you do. But I was trying to make him feel better about it.

"How are you doing that?" Cora asked.

"I told him," I said, "I told him the girls only think a Grammar School's something special because they never learn anything themselves."

"What girls are you talking about?" my Mother asked.

"I'm talking about all of them," I said, "because they're all alike. They think that if you wear glasses that means you've got brains."

"What do you know about girls?" my Mother said. "How can you say things like that at your age?"

But Cora stroked her hand and said, "Dear old Mummy, don't be cross with Ludwig. He's just got rather strict views about us girls." Then she winked at Annie and they both laughed like anything.

And when I said good-night Cora was specially nice to me and said she had to tell me a secret. And at the door she whispered right in my ear that I must tell Mister Reiser he ought to buy a pair of specs as if he didn't wear specs the girls wouldn't like him.

But I don't believe she really meant it because afterwards I heard Cora and Annie on the stairs and they were giggling. Next day I went back to the garden fence and Franz was there first.

He asked if I'd done what he wanted me to. I hadn't, but I said yes. Then he pointed at our house with his thumb and asked if anyone had been talking about him. I told him about the trouble I'd been in for sticking up for him and about Cora saying he ought to get a pair of specs. Then he looked very sad again and said she was making fun of him. I said he oughtn't to take on about Cora, I liked her because she was so cheerful, but if she tried making a fool of me I'd soon show her one doesn't take any notice of girls.

Franz shook his head and said it was different for him, and it was terribly sad, and I wouldn't understand yet but it was a great misfortune for him.

I said I'd like to know what all the chaps keep sighing for when they talk about Cora.

"What chaps?" he asked quickly.

"At the chemist's," I said, "Mister Seitz and the other dispenser keep asking me when I go in for something, and they want me to say something nice to her about them, and they look as if they're going to cry any minute."

Franz pointed at our house and asked what she said when I told her.

She laughed, I said.

Did she laugh as if she were pleased, he asked.

I said I didn't know.

So he said, perhaps she was pleased because Mister Seitz went to the university, but he's soapy, and he's got bow legs and he's a stupid idiot, you ought to knock the stuffing out of him, he's so conceited.

I asked what Mister Seitz had done to Franz to make him so cross with him.

Franz said he hadn't done anything, but he couldn't stand the sight of him, and I wasn't to pass any more messages.

And then he went off and kept whacking his stick through the air so that it whistled.

At supper-time Annie asked if I was in a better temper today and didn't feel so grumpy about girls any more. I'm not bothering any more about any girls, I said, if you start bothering about girls all you get for it is trouble and then you feel terribly sad.

My mother put down her fork and looked at me, and then she said it was strange the things I'd been saying these last few days.

And Cora said she was afraid I'd turn into a woman-hater because now I was always so ungracious, and it was strange, she used to imagine I was her gallant young man.

I said girls often get ideas into their heads.

Then they all laughed, but afterwards my Mother said she wouldn't allow me to be rude to Cora.

"He's not being rude," Cora said, "we've just got to see how we can get back into his favour again. He's the only man here with his three women, it's like the Princes in India, their ladies have a difficult time keeping them sweet-tempered."

I was going to say something, but all of a sudden we heard people singing in front of our house. My Mother and Cora and Annie ran to the window and I looked out too. There were four men standing there and singing. I recognised Mister Seitz straight away and Mister Knilling the schoolmaster, and there was a man from the post-office too.

They were singing the sad good-bye song : "Ach wie ist's möglich dann, dass ich dich lassen kann!" First one of them sang it high, then another one sang it low, and then one sang it right high up and made his voice wobble. And that was Mister Seitz.

My Mother kept saying "Oh dear, isn't it lovely!" and she pointed with her finger so that Annie and Cora would notice that the moon was shining at the time, and she nodded her head very sadly while Mister Seitz was singing with his voice all wobbly. And she gave Annie a kiss, and stroked Cora on the cheek, and when they'd finished outside she said once more it was lovely, really lovely, and wasn't it kind of them to do us the honour.

Cora laughed and said she must write to her Papa about our Mother still having people who come and sing serenades outside her window. My mother laughed too and said she thought the honour was intended for our Princess from Hindia. Then we heard them clearing their throats outside, and it started up again. They were singing "Annie of Tharau" and Mister Seitz didn't make his voice wobble so much this time, but Mister Knilling did. And my Mother leaned her head on Annie's shoulder and cried a little.

When it was over Mister Seitz took his hat off and so did the others and they went away. But they stopped at the fountain and sang the Cradle Song, first one sang it low, and then it got

higher and higher, and at the end it was just Mister Seitz singing quite loud and wobbling his voice like anything. And then it
was quiet.

You could hear the fountain splashing and my mother said
we must listen to the murmur of the waters and look at the moon-
shine because it was all so poetical.

Cora asked who the singers were. So I said, one of them was
Mister Seitz, the one with the bald patch and the pop eyes.

So my Mother said she was sorry to see how I kept losing my
manners, and it was sure to be four well-brought-up young
gentlemen and we ought to be grateful to them for giving us
the pleasure. And soon after that we went to bed and my mother
said "Good-night, Annie of Tharau!" to Annie and kissed her
twice.

When I got home from school next day Franz Reiser was
already whistling for me. I went out into our garden, but Franz
said I'd better crawl through to his side of the fence as he wanted
to tell me something. So I crawled through, and we went behind
a woodpile where you couldn't see us.

Franz's eyes were all swollen as if he'd been crying, and he
was in his shirt-sleeves and hadn't got a collar on. He lay down
in the grass and I did too. He kept pulling up tufts of grass and
throwing them away. All of a sudden he asked if I had heard
the singing. I said yes, I had, as it was in front of our house. Then
he asked, had I recognised Mister Seitz. I said yes I had, straight
away. So he said, you couldn't miss him with his bow legs, but
did the others know who it was? I said, what others? He pointed
with his thumb and said "Your Mother and your sister." I said
"Yes, of course they did."

"And did Miss Cora too?" he asked.

"Yes, she did too," I said.

He pulled up a lot of grass and threw it away, and then he
asked if they liked the singing.

"My mother did, she loved it, as it was so poetical with the
fountain splashing," I said.

"It's a dirty thing to do, not letting people sleep," said Franz,
"it's not poetical at all." Then he stopped talking and pulled up
some more grass, and then he asked if Cora had said she liked
it. I said no, she didn't say she liked it, but I think she did all
the same. So Franz pulled a stick out of the woodpile and said

he'd belt Mister Seitz with a stick like that if he ever came singing again.

I laughed then as I was thinking what it would be like if Mister Seitz was singing with his wobbly voice and all of a sudden Franz belted him over the head. But Franz didn't laugh. He turned over with his face in the grass, and suddenly he burst out crying.

I couldn't understand it at all and asked him what was the matter. But he shook his head and sobbed and bashed the ground with the stick. Then he lifted his face out of the grass and wiped his eyes with his sleeves. And I asked him again what it was, but he said I didn't understand. Yes I do, I said, and I'd help him if Mister Seitz had done anything. And I told him I liked him and that I didn't like Mister Seitz. So he said, perhaps I was the only one he could talk to, and he was terribly fond of Cora.

I said I was fond of her too, but why did that make him cry and bash the ground with his stick?

So he said it was quite different, the way he was fond of her, and he wanted her to marry him and be his wife.

I asked why didn't he go over and tell her? And he said he couldn't.

Oh yes you can, I said. He'd have to put on a black jacket and go over. First of all my Mother would be there alone. Then Cora would be told to come in, and he'd have to put his arm round her, and then Annie and me would have to go in, and my mother would cry a little, and then we'd all stand round and each of us would get a kiss.

And Franz shook his head again.

So I said, I know all about it. It was like that when Mister Bindinger wanted to marry our Marie.

But Franz said he couldn't, as he wasn't good enough, and all he'd do later on would be to have a brewery, and he knew Cora didn't like him because he hadn't had an education.

I said I thought Cora would be glad he liked her, as girls like you to like them.

No, he said, Cora wouldn't. He could see perfectly well he wasn't good enough for her, as he hadn't been to the university, and she wouldn't even look at him. So I said, I'll ask her, I could ask her today at supper-time. Then he said loudly, no, you mustn't. He'd tell her himself. I asked if he'd tell her today, and he said it wouldn't be long, perhaps he'd tell her today, if he saw Cora alone he'd go and tell her. He couldn't bear it much longer, he couldn't sleep any more or eat anything or drink anything. Last night when he heard Mister Seitz singing he thought of jumping out of the window. He said he'd never dared to speak to Cora himself, but that disgusting chap from the chemist's had such a nerve that he went straight off and sang like that in front of everybody. But Franz said he wasn't going to be so simple any more, and when he saw her he'd just go straight up and tell her. If she could stand there and listen to that bow-legged idiot singing, she must be able to listen to Franz. And he didn't feel like waiting any longer either.

I asked him why he was fond of her, he hadn't even seen her except from a distance. He said it was always like that, but I wouldn't understand.

We were still talking when suddenly someone called me, and Franz gave a great jump. It was Cora's voice. We looked out from behind the woodpile and saw Cora standing in our garden and calling me. Franz whispered very softly that I wasn't to answer and I was to stay with him or she'd notice he was there too. I said go on, she's alone, go and tell her.

No, he couldn't, he said, he couldn't because he hadn't got a collar on, and I was to keep quite quiet so that she didn't notice.

We lay on our stomachs and just stuck our heads round the edge of the woodpile. Cora looked everywhere and called me again, and then she went to the garden gate and I knew that she'd be walking round the back and would be coming past us. So I told Franz very quickly, and we crawled round to the other side of the woodpile just as Cora came along the fence. She didn't see anything and she was singing to herself and sounded very cheerful.

After she'd gone past Franz got up and I got up too. We could see Cora for quite a long time, as she had a white dress on, and we could hear her singing too. Franz climbed up on the woodpile so that he could see her longer still. I asked him why he didn't go quickly and put a collar on, then he could run after her. He said, today he couldn't. But he'd tell her tomorrow.

But now I don't think he'll ever tell her at all.

BIOGRAPHICAL NOTE

Ludwig Thoma was born on 21st January 1867 in Oberammergau. He studied forestry in Aschaffenburg, but changed to the study of the law and ultimately opened a legal practice in the town of Dachau. In 1897 Thoma became editor of the fiercely satirical magazine, *Simplicissimus*. In this journal and in a small local paper, *Der Miesbacher Anzeiger*, he published his political commentaries, his robustly humorous poems and anecdotes and his biting satires on Prussianism, the clergy, the law and on every aspect of middle-class Philistinism. Thoma is a born raconteur, and his experience as lawyer and journalist provided him with a wealth of material. It is for his Rabelaisian short stories and uproarious comedies that he is best remembered, but, in a sense, collections like *Lausbuben-geschichten* and *Tante Frieda* are minor works: Thoma was capable of much more substantial things. His novels are not merely realistic descriptions of Bavarian peasant life; they show an awareness of the tragic conflicts that are latent in communities where conventions are rigid and emotions all the more elemental for being inarticulate. *Der Wittiber* is a representation of the conflict between father and son in the circumstances of a peasant community that is fit to rank with the stories of Gottfried Keller and Jeremias Gotthelf; *Der Ruepp* is a powerfully tragic tale of deceit and paternal tyranny; *Andreas Vörst* is a bitter denunciation of a scheming clergyman that has validity beyond any immediate propagandistic aim. In all of these novels, too, there is a humour of greater cosmic resonance than the boisterous tomfoolery of the better-known short pieces or the popular comedies, *Die Lokalbahn*, *Erster Klasse*, *Lottchens Geburtstag* or *Moral*.

Thoma died on 26th August 1921. Volume 80 of *Rowohlts Monographien* is devoted to him and provides much illustrative material, as well as a bibliography.

Heinrich Mann

Translated
by
Lawrence Wilson

ABDICATION

THEY all wanted to play football; only Felix insisted on a race.

"Who's the boss here?" he shouted, red-faced and trembling, with such a look that the boy who intercepted it hid himself among a bunch of friends.

"Who's the boss here!" It was the first thing he said to them the moment he entered the school. They eyed each other sheepishly. One big lout surveyed the puny youth and began to laugh. Suddenly Felix had him by the scruff of the neck and was pressing his head down.

"Is that all you can do?" gasped the boy, completely powerless, with his face touching the ground.

"Run a race with me! That will decide between us."

"Yes, a race!" called several of the boys.

"Anyone still against racing?" asked Felix, straightening up and putting one foot forward.

"Couldn't care less," said fat Hans Butt in a sleepy voice.

"Me, too," confirmed others.

There was a stir and some came over to Felix's side. Those who had ranged themselves on his opponent's side felt scared, he gave them such a vindictive look.

"I'll make a note of the lot of you!" he shrilled.

Two went over to him, and then two more. Butt, who was hanging about undecided, was roped in by Felix with a clip on the ear.

Felix won with ease. The wind streaming towards him as he flew along seemed to hold an inspiring melody, and as he came back, his blood pumping with the intoxication of speed, he knew that victory would always be his. When the defeated boy promised to get his own back at football he smiled in his face and shrugged his shoulders.

But next time he subdued someone who opposed an order it was only luck, and he knew it. The fight was almost lost when he managed to break away and give the other boy a kick in the belly so that he collapsed on the ground. Now it seemed inevit-

able that he should be lying there, and yet as Felix looked down
at him he still felt the dizziness of that reeling moment when his
reputation was at stake. Then he took a deep breath and re-
joiced inwardly. But already someone was grumbling : belly kicks
were not fair. No, came the echo, they were cowardly. And once
more he had to confront the mob and assert himself.

With most boys, admittedly, strong words were enough. Felix
knew the two or three with whom he still had to try conclusions;
the others already obeyed him. At times amazement overcame
him—never at school, for there he was always tense with the
task of domination, but at home—amazement that they obeyed.
After all, they were stronger. Every one of them was stronger!
If fat Hans Butt had realised that he possessed muscles! But he
was one of those soft lumps that can be made into anything.
Felix was alone. Restlessly his mind skipped from one to another
of the absent boys, scrutinising them; and his trembling hands
kneaded their faces, his faces, and pushed them away.

In so doing he invented disparaging names for some of them.
On most he had enforced them already, and when the new
form-master asked them their names each had to announce his
own : Clot, Meatball, Pithecos. Yes, there stood Weeke in his
English suiting as the ape-man, and Graupel, whose father was
the mayor, called himself a clot—because Felix had so ordained.
But Felix wore a suit that had been turned and since his father
had lost his life (he could only guess how) on the last of his
adventurous trips he and his mother had been living in three
miserable rooms in this town—where he now gave the orders.

Just as he imposed nicknames on his school-fellows, so he ridi-
culed the teachers until no one could speak of them without
shame. For the writing-master, however, whom even the most
cowardly boy had found the courage to tease, he enforced
respect. Through intimidation and mockery he made it fashion-
able not to prepare for the maths lesson. But when the professor,
to whom someone must have sneaked, warned the class not to let
an untalented boy seduce them to idleness Felix fought his way
to top marks within a week and declared it was child's play. In
fact, he had done violence to his brain and became irritated
almost beyond endurance. To the professor, who tried to win
him over with distinctions, he was courteous and unapproachable. Before the next class he insisted that the iron ruler should

be made red-hot. That was done behind the gymnasium. In trying to convince the sceptics that, in the excitement of his demon-
stration, the professor always suddenly grabbed the ruler with
his whole hand, Felix unthinkingly did the same and gave a
jump. There was laughter, talk of "hoist with his own petard"
and "can't stand it himself".

Felix eyed the circle of boys and frowned darkly. When the
heated ruler was carried in between slats of wood he followed in
silence. They were all in their places and the professor's step
could be heard, when Felix took the ruler from the desk and
shoved it inside his open shirt. There was a sound of hissing in
the class-room. What was the matter with them, why did nobody
stand up, asked the professor. Felix stood up and with white lips
reported all present. Then, sitting again, though overwhelmed at
times with pain he was aware behind his forced and lonely smile
of only one fact: the boys he did not look at were all glancing
furtively at him, horror-struck, submissive, full of surging love,
and he was revelling in ecstasy far above them, despising them
immeasurably.

"Fire is not for you," he said when he came back to school
three days later, "but water is!"

He turned on the water tap.

"Butt! Under the pump!"

Lazily Butt offered his head.

"Weeke! Graupel!"

They came. One after the other they ducked under the stream
of water—with silly, slavish laughs because the one before had
done it, because it might be a joke, because to oppose Felix was
contrary to sense and custom.

When all their heads were dripping water on to the floor and
the furious form-master asked in vain for the ring-leader, Felix
stood up.

"I baptised them all," he declared calmly, and got six hours'
solitary.

He also stood up when someone called "cock-a-doodle-doo"
and no one would own up. He was not the culprit. In the next
lesson he was given a black mark for holding up his grammar so
that the boy behind could read it. In tyrannising over them he
also felt responsible for their sins and their welfare. He could only
endure them as slaves; but when he was not giving the orders

he was jealous of their dignity. The son of a local squire, recently arrived, gave himself airs. Felix found him surrounded by a circle of curious onlookers, declaring that his outstretched arm was the radius. Suddenly he spun round and swept his hand over their faces.

"Why do you let this dogsbody box your ears?" shouted Felix hotly.

"Take care, my good fellow," said the young Count, looking him up and down. Beside himself, Felix flung up his fists.

"Talk like that to your stable-boy, not to me, not to . . ." Words failed him.

"Do you want a thrashing?" asked his enemy. The circle opened up, the boys stepped back.

"What about you?" Felix leapt forward. Suddenly he held back and thrust his hands into his pockets.

"*I* won't thrash you; that's too good for you. But I'll have you thrashed!"

To the others:

"Let him have it! . . . Well? He's insulted you. Don't you care? He's insulted me, too. You know me. Well?"

His words, his eyes brought them into jerky movement. They glanced furtively at one another, sought contact with their elbows: then suddenly, all together, they flung themselves on the boy who had challenged their master. He fell over; their success made them savage. Felix leaned against the wall and looked on.

"That's enough! He's bleeding!"

"Now shake hands on it."

And the astonished newcomer was made a member of the gang and learned to obey with the gang.

Felix trained them. The boy to whom he shouted: "Goodbye to him!" had to vanish at break-neck speed, and to the question: "How is he then?" the compulsory reply was "Middling", whereupon Felix would curl his lip and say: "So it seems." After dark one or other of the boys had to go into the town, relieve himself against a particular house, and return in silence. It might be that by some mystic means Felix would get to hear of offences against his commandments, and the more crass their opposition to reason the more fanatically they were carried out. Punctually at four o'clock, alone in his room, the young Count would bring himself to swing a stick and shout "Hurrah!" thirty times. And

after each hurrah another boy standing in front of the house would
call up "Blockhead!" It was the daily duty of fat Hans Butt to
creep into the class-room during the long break, lie down on the
floor and wait with his eyes shut for Felix to "absolve him from
sin". Felix came up the steps between four henchmen who
stopped at the door and were not allowed to watch the proceedings. Three times, in profound silence, he paced round the
prostrate Butt, then dropped astride on to the patient's stomach.
Then Butt was allowed to get up.

When he felt Butt's fat trembling and yielding beneath him, Felix
was tempted to rest there for a moment. He felt that Butt's sins
really were flowing into his own flesh; the animal apathy of the
other boy tempted him; a bond was formed which he himself
found repulsive.

Butt came from a market-garden and was saturated with the
peaceful odour of earthy vegetables for which Felix longed as for
a poison that promised contemptible raptures. Butt's heavy
breathing enticed him; and in his mad career Felix looked for
some goal or deed which would bring them close together.
Rolled over, Butt lay by the sunny wall. Then Felix had to
pause, captivated by Butt's aroma. He pushed the pliant head to
and fro, never tiring of this, and it hung where he left it hanging. He lifted the flaccid limbs and let them fall, sank into Butt
with a horror that made him weak, as into a soft abyss. A furious
kick marked the moment when he emerged from it again.

His sleep became restless. Sometimes he awoke with tears of
bitter longing and with a rush of shame remembered that he had
touched Butt's body in his dream. With contempt and envy he
thought his way into such a being, a being whose gravity nothing
could shake, no ambition, no sense of responsibility, neither the
stress of self-imposed duties nor of those peculiarities which could
not be confessed. If the conquered could have cast one glance
into what their master kept hidden! If they had known that he
awaited their answer to the ritual call: "How is he then?" in an
ever-repeated agony of suspense. That if that awful "Middling"
had not been forthcoming he would never have been able to
bear it, even in class; would have had to interrupt the teacher
to obtain his tribute. That when he called a boy to him he had
to count the steps and draw superstitious conclusions from the
total. That when he marked someone for rapid disappearance by

a "Goodbye to him!" he hurriedly and anxiously looked at him from both sides, from in front and again from the left, as though to learn his appearance by heart for ever; that he had to do this, and if he did not succeed hours of distress followed.

What an easy life they had, when he came to think of it, the boys who surrendered to him, let him do the willing for them and were now peacefully asleep. Was that sort of humdrum, dull-witted existence desirable for himself? Oh, indeed, it would have been a blessing at times to have someone who gave him orders, took the whole weight off him. Felix got up in the night, stood with a candle in front of the mirror and made his reflection call to him : "Put out your tongue! Put two fingers to your fore-head!"

"No, what rubbish! That's only myself, of course."

With a glance of disgust he turned his back on the reflection.

Then he avenged himself on those whose life was so much easier, tested how far he could go with them.

"Runge, spit in Butt's face!... Now, Butt, spit in Weeke's! And Weeke in Graupel's. And so on."

They obeyed! It was fabulous.

"Whoever hits the other on the nose becomes my henchman!"

He thought : "Don't they notice what they are doing? They are delirious! Why do they force me to despise them so fright-fully? That leaves me completely alone. No one spits at me; that never occurs to them. I should really like that. Oh, I mustn't; but I should like it..." Excitedly, he pulled Butt from the throng and said something in his ear. Butt looked at him aghast. "Hurry up," said Felix, and when Butt still hesitated he raised his hand.

"Do it, or else..."

Then Butt shambled back a step and before the eyes of every-one spat in the middle of Felix's forehead.

Horrified silence. Felix gave a careless laugh.

"Here's something new. I'll do everything that Butt tells me to."

The group looked at Butt and buzzed with relief.

"Well, Butt? Speak up! What shall I do? Can't you think of something? Shall I about-turn?"

Butt couldn't think of anything, and the boys doubled up with laughter.

"Shall I hop on one leg? Haven't you any imagination? Order me to do what I ordered you to do!"

Suspiciously, Butt risked a command :

"Raise your arm! Drop your arm!"

Felix did so, and Butt had no further suggestions.

But in every break between classes Felix came back to the new game. He suggested to Butt the tasks he should give him.

"You can demand anything of me that I demanded of you—anything, get it? What was it you had to do at this time every day?"

"I had to be absolved from sin," said Butt, ready for a repetition.

"No, *I* have to be!"

And Felix went up the steps, lay on the floor and said, with his eyes closed : "Go on, Butt!"

Butt tottered into the room. He paced round Felix : once, twice, three times.

"What comes next, Butt?"

They all held their breath. With a finger stuck in the corner of his mouth, Butt stood gaping down at Felix.

"No, it isn't right," and he turned away.

"Do it, Butt!"

"No, he mustn't do that!" cried the crowd indignantly; and as often as Felix tried the same game the same passive resistance thwarted him. He invented another way of making Butt his master.

"Butt, where does the path lead? Straight on, or round the tree?"

Butt answered doubtfully, Felix did what he prescribed and everyone laughed and applauded.

It was the time of the school excursions.

"Butt, where does the path lead? Over the bridge or through the stream?"

And Butt, plucking up courage :

"Through the stream!"

Felix jumped in without even taking off his shoes.

When the bell rang for class he threw the quick question :

"Butt, where does the path lead?"

"Up the steps," grunted Butt.

"If he had said 'home'," thought Felix, "I should have had to

go. I should have had to do it without question." A temptation
assailed him, fearful and alluring.

"Sometimes the path can also lead through under the desks,"
he explained, and during the next lesson he asked :

"Butt, where does the path lead?"

"Through under the desks," said Butt, and shut his eyes with
terror. When he opened them Felix had gone.

"What is that boy doing under there?" called the professor.

Wild-eyed and scarlet in the face, Felix emerged from under
the last bench. Oh, the cruel violence he had done to himself,
the death-defying abandon with which he had plunged to the
floor! A more splendid sensation it was than when they had
beaten each other on his orders. Full of a terrible sweet pride he
detected in the eyes that scrutinised him the beginnings of
pleasurable malice.

Until then, Felix had had no friends or dealings with anyone
outside school. Now he became inseparable from Butt, brought
him his finished homework, stayed sitting beside him and gazed
at him earnestly.

"Butt, where does the path lead?"

"Into the corner . . . seven times up and down the steps . . . into
the dog-kennel." And with that Butt's invention was exhausted.
But unexpectedly he found something practical.

"To the baker, to fetch apple tarts."

This continued as long as Felix's mother supplied the money.

"Butt, where does the path lead?"

"To the cuckoo."

And Felix ran out of the main gate, slipped through the bushes
with a thumping heart, listened, now red, now pale, in the direction of the wood, and when the cuckoo called he breathed a
heart-felt sigh of relief, as though his life had been saved.

At school Butt boasted of his power over the boy whom everyone obeyed, but he earned only blows from the others. Felix tried
to laugh, then immediately felt ashamed of his hypocrisy and
declared :

"Butt is my friend : what's it got to do with you?"

He was eyed slyly, with disapproval; there were whisperings
about him in corners; pert glances were risked. A guileless child
stepped up to him.

"Is Butt really greater than you?" he asked in a piping voice.

Felix blushed and lowered his head. No one spoke.

All the happiness of which Felix dreamed he expected from the summer holidays, when he would be alone with Butt. He persuaded his mother to pay for the gardener's son to stay at Lake Uklei along with them. The farm-house stood half in the water. They fished from their window. Their ungainly boat rocked over water blackly overshadowed by the wooded shores. Felix shot sticks into the water—torpedoes!—and informed Butt, his captain, of the victory. Carried away, Butt issued proud words of command. But when Felix took from him one of the sticks he had picked out of the water, maintaining it was a shark and he had saved his captain by driving a stick through the shark's mouth and its whole body, Butt failed to understand, declared the whole thing was nonsense, and lay down in the boat.

"Butt, where does the path lead?"

"Into the water, push the boat."

Felix swam and pushed, and began to tire.

"Butt, where does the path lead?"

Butt lay with his hands under his head, blinking, breathing heavily and enjoying himself. Half asleep, he thought of the time when he had jumped to Felix's command, trembled before him and been absolved by him.

"Carry on," he grumbled. A while later, Felix had to admit : "I can't go on. Where does the path lead?"

Butt had a new idea.

"To the ..."

But he broke off, grunting good-naturedly.

"Back into the boat."

"What were you going to say, Butt?"

Felix had to know the answer; he could not rest till he had it. Butt laughed at his agitation. In the night someone shook him. Felix was standing by his bed in his shirt.

"Butt, where does the path lead?"

"For heaven's sake, give over! It leads down to the fishes!"

The next moment he was shouting : "No! Not to the fishes! Back into bed!"

Reluctantly Felix climbed down from the window-sill.

"But you said it."

"It wasn't true. Leave me alone."

"But you *did* say it."

Next morning, his first words after feverish sleep and then insistently, day after day, were:

"Doesn't the path really lead down to the fishes?"

"All right, yes, it does," said Butt sometimes, but then he would call Felix back.

School started again. Felix appeared with pale, hollow cheeks and staring eyes. He had no interest in the doings of the other boys, in the stories Butt told them, in their laughter when he showed himself. From time to time one of them came up to him and without a word gave him a slow shove with his shoulder; after this renunciation of his former lord, the boy would go his way, sour-faced and lowering. With downcast eyes Felix did nothing but creep after Butt, whispering something. Butt shoved him with his shoulder like the others: "Don't ask me," and Felix said in a tortured stammer:

"But you said so."

One morning he was not at school. It was not until the second day that Butt found a slip of paper amongst his books on which Felix had written:

"The path did lead down to the fishes, after all."

BIOGRAPHICAL NOTE

Luiz Heinrich Mann was born in Lübeck on 27th March 1871, the eldest of five children of a prominent merchant. After a brief apprenticeship to the book trade he embarked on a literary career, and had already published a number of novels and a great many short stories before the outbreak of the First World War. Of these, *Im Schlaraffenland* (1900) and the trilogy, *Die Göttinnen* (1902–03), were luridly satirical accounts of decadent life among the wealthy bourgeoisie of Germany and Italy, while *Die Jagd nach Liebe* (1903–04), in much the same vein, has as its heroine the kind of actress and *femme fatale* who features again and again in Mann's work. *Professor Unrat* (1905) is perhaps best known from the film version, *The Blue Angel*: it describes the degradation of a town that hysterically succumbs to a demoralised tyrant of a schoolmaster and the wife whom he takes from the world of the cabaret. *Die kleine Stadt* (1910) tells the tragic but warmly human story of the events that follow from the visit to a small Italian town of a travelling operatic company. In this novel, as in many of his short stories, Mann expresses his affection for Italy, where he spent much of his life before 1914. Mann's second trilogy, opening with the superbly satirical *Der Untertan* (1914-18) and continuing with *Die Armen* (1917) and *Der Kopf* (1925), analyses the causes of Germany's involvement in the war and attributes them to deep-seated social and political neuroses. Mann was a staunch defender of the Weimar Republic and concerned himself more and more with the political and economic problems of Germany, for which he envisaged radical socialist solutions. At the same time, many of his stories and novels, which are set in the underworld and full of exciting and criminal action, reflect the restless and hectic atmosphere of the era between the wars : to this category belong, for example, the novels *Mutter Marie* (1927), *Die grosse Sache* (1931) and *Ein ernstes Leben* (1932). In this period of his writing, only *Eugénie* (1928) harks back to an earlier and more serene age—the aftermath of the Franco-Prussian war.

Exile was the obvious lot of Heinrich Mann as soon as Hitler came to power. But both in France and America he continued to write, and, cut off from contemporary life in his native country, he embarked on a great historical novel based on the life of Henri IV of France : *Die Jugend des Königs Henri Quatre* (1935) and *Die Vollendung des Königs Henri Quatre* (1937) describe the evolution of an ideal ruler and his untimely death. Besides these and other novels and short stories far too numerous to mention individually, Heinrich Mann wrote dramas without conspicuous success, as well as innumerable essays and articles on politics and literature—in both of which fields he showed a strong allegiance to French traditions. Heinrich Mann died in Los Angeles on 12th March 1950. The most complete and up-to-date account of his personality and work is by U. Weisstein : *Heinrich Mann*, Tübingen, 1962. A brief account in English by W. E. Yuill, with select bibliography, will be found in *German Men of Letters*, Series III, London, Wolff, pp. 199-224.

Ernst Penzoldt

Translated
by
Arnold J. Pomerans

ERNST PENZOLDT

THE TREASURE

PETERSEN's cook—for at the time this story happened even simple households still had cooks—yes, Petersen's cook Agatha was dead. She lay prostrate on the bare kitchen tiles, a butcher's knife buried in her heart. It was a commonplace enough kind of knife, with a black wooden handle, the kind Agatha loved and must have used shortly before her sudden death. For on the chopping block, not far from her, lay the freshly plucked and drawn young cockerel whose tiny heart she still clutched in her hand. The blade of the knife, though of Solingen steel, was completely worn down by Agatha's constant sharpenings. With a knowledgeable glance she could always tell just where the blade had to be applied for gutting a fish or dismembering a fowl. Not only was she astute, but so good a housekeeper was she that all the local tradesmen honoured her with the title of Fräulein Agatha. "Do call again soon, madam," the tradesmen would say and shuffle eagerly to open the door for her. Any article she rejected became unsaleable. Her judgement in domestic matters, particularly in the making of cakes and jam, was final. One could see why her employers, the Petersens, were generally regarded with envy.

Fräulein Agatha's death under such unexpected, even gruesome, circumstances, caused general consternation in the town, the more so as, shortly before this brutal and incomprehensible act, the victim had been seen on her errands, glowing with health.

The murder was discovered by the postman when, as usual, he pushed the Petersens' mail through the kitchen window. To do so he had only to climb on the bench where in good weather the indefatigable Agatha Köhler could be seen peeling potatoes, cleaning vegetables or darning stockings. Though she was not at her usual post that day, he never suspected that anything was wrong. The worst he could have imagined was a few tears in Fräulein Agatha's eyes from peeling onions, but never the terrible sight that actually met him—a lifeless body in a pool of blood.

And he had to be the first to see it! For that is precisely what he stated quite innocently, later during the investigation. "The first?" he was asked. Was he quite sure of that? For the first who saw the corpse must have been the murderer himself; from which the unhappy man drew the moral that in the wake of a crime every witness becomes a suspect. He cursed the accident of that fatal discovery and with it his thoughtless self-importance.

Stunned by the murder but certain that no one in the house knew anything about it he had rushed round to the front door. Inside everything was deathly still; he had to knock several times before he heard footsteps and the door was opened to him at last.

It was young Petersen, home from school. So stated the postman during his interrogation, believing it to be the complete truth. But the detective-inspector—the very name reminds one of rattling chains, and of bread and water behind iron bars—the inspector was not satisfied with that alone, he wanted details. In reply to the officer's keen questioning the postman then had to admit that it all happened as follows: in the front door was a little window through which one could see into the corridor as far as the staircase. He had peered in when no one came to open the door, and had grown very uneasy because of the uncanny silence in the house. Indeed, he was expecting to find *all* the inhabitants murdered. However, the sun shone reassuringly through a stained glass window portraying the trumpeter of Säckingen, and then he saw young Petersen come sliding down the banister. At the same time, a girl called his name from above: "Juri," she said—that was what the family called him— and Juri shouted back to her as he opened the door: "Only the postman."

The inspector seemed to place great importance on discovering the exact tone of voice in which the sister had called for Juri. Had it been anxious or admonitory or what? But though most postmen are shrewd judges of character, this one was not particularly schooled in the subtleties of intonation. He did, however, state that the girl's tone had been rather reproachful, possibly because the young gentleman had slid down the banister. A remark that the clerk was expressly instructed to enter in the official record.

Then the officer wanted to know exactly how young Petersen behaved when he was told what had happened in the kitchen.

The good postman became embarrassed for now he was expected to relate at great length and, what is more, in chronological order, events that had occurred in a few confused seconds; to omit no detail, however unimportant, and if necessary to state it all again on oath. He remarked how difficult it was to recall the true course of events even though—or perhaps precisely because—they had all happened so recently. The very questions of the policeman threw him off balance. What he had been expecting when he pushed the letters through the kitchen window, was the familiar Fräulein Agatha, neat as always in a somewhat old-fashioned starched summer apron, pale blue, and beneath it a striped cotton frock. Under her double chin a simple brooch portraying two billing doves. But, oh, how different was the scene that had greeted him through the window! A dead cook spread-eagled on the black and white tiles—tiles whose very regularity produced a series of annoying optical illusions. As on a doubly-exposed film, the image of young Petersen had become mixed up with them, and the postman found himself incapable of recalling the facial expression of the schoolboy or the words they had exchanged. Everything had happened so quickly. Perhaps all he told the boy was that something terrible had occurred in the kitchen, that Fräulein Agatha . . .

"Thereupon we returned to the scene of the crime," he continued, visibly comforted by the reassuring use of official jargon. Further questioning revealed that he had hurried on ahead of the young gentleman, that they had found the kitchen door shut but not locked, that the victim was still lying on the floor just as he had seen her through the window, with her feet towards the door, the heart of the cockerel in her hand like a watch, and her mouth slightly open as if to say: "You, of all people!" And on the chopping block lay the young cockerel, head and neck drooping over the edge, the bluish lids half closed and the parted yellow beak prised open by his little tongue. Perhaps we might mention at this juncture that no one in the house evinced the least desire for the cockerel that Agatha Köhler had so neatly disembowelled. With the agreement of the police it was finally presented to the postman whose finer feelings prevented him from consuming the bird. "I shouldn't have liked it," he said, "because of Fräulein Agatha." So he passed it on to a poor beggar whose hunger outweighed his sensibilities.

"And what did you do upon your return to the scene of the crime?" the inspector now asked. The postman confessed that he was struck by the thought that Fräulein Agatha might not be dead after all, but only unconscious. So he had shaken her once or twice while calling her dear name. Then young Petersen had asked him to fetch a doctor as quickly as possible, to which request, realising its good sense, he had immediately acceded.

From his daily round he knew every doctor in the area. Unfortunately the first one demurred and referred him to one Dr. Jokim, who had only recently settled in the neighbourhood but who was fortunately at home, and—better still—who agreed to come along at once.

The postman noticed at the time—but he was not given a chance to bring this out during the examination—that the doctor seemed to be in no hurry and that, on arrival at the Petersens' house, he lingered outside for quite some time, looking the place over very carefully—rather as a stranger might look at the birthplace of a great man, with amicable reverence, and doffing his hat. Yet there was really nothing to admire about the house, nor did it even look like the scene of a murder. It was built in the unlamented sham style of the late nineteenth century : yellow stone, bluish tiles, and all sorts of unnecessary trappings. Along the coping for instance, there ran a cast-iron balustrade which served no purpose at all since no one could possibly have leant on it. The year the house was constructed, 1885, had been most artfully chiselled on to a plaque in the form of a parchment scroll. The front garden was graced with an oval bed of yellow and violet pansies, made out of tin but deceptively true to nature, and a border consisting of upturned wine bottles. Green agaves stood in terracotta vases on sandstone door pillars, and a tasselled curtain of pressed tin decorated the porticos with their hidden blinds. Above the stairwell, a cherub stood poised on a ball while blowing into a trumpet.

Dr. Jokim had to smile when he saw how much effort had been expended on such utter lack of distinction. Yet he knew that, like so many of their contemporaries, the Petersens were sure to pride themselves on their impressive good taste and great elegance.

This time the door was opened by the pale-faced Herr Petersen himself. He had a very striking, decidedly old-fashioned face, as

Dr. Jokim later remarked. The kind of face you see at concerts, he added.

"I assume you are the doctor, but I'm afraid you are too late," Herr Petersen told him apologetically. "We have already telephoned for the police. We have left everything in the kitchen untouched," he explained, whereupon Dr. Jokim blushed.

Here we must say a few words about Dr. Jokim. To describe his appearance is not an easy matter and moreover unimportant. Who could, in any case, describe his face so accurately that anyone reading the description would, on meeting the character in the street, exclaim at once: "Bless my soul if that isn't Dr. Jokim, from Penzoldt's *The Treasure*." Even I, who know the man better than most, find it hard to say anything definite about the colour of his hair. Nor can I even begin to describe its sheen —a sheen and an aroma that suggested a most unusual blending, if blending is the right word to apply to hair. He was fair, but in saying that I have really said very little. His hair had the slightest, softest wave to it and its colour resembled an old copper jug slightly oxidised and about to be covered with verdigris. Dr. Jokim looked much younger than he really was thanks to his delicate girlish skin which was slightly inclined to freckles. But he seemed in no way feminine. If one agrees with Prohaska, who speaks of the existence of a third sex and supports his claim with much learning but is not entirely convincing, then our Dr. Jokim was not really a hybrid, nor an amalgam of the two sexes with an emphasis towards one or the other. His eyes bore this out, olive brown, honest, capable eyes that did not look, peer, or observe but only surveyed, just as his ears did not listen or hear but simply absorbed. But what he saw and heard, or rather what flowed into him was divided without his active participation, quite naturally, into truth and falsehood, into right and wrong. Thus, much to his own embarrassment, he responded to lies, half-truths, and evasions with varying degrees of involuntary blushing. In that way, he would notice a lie at once, no matter what charming presentation or widening of the eyes accompanied it. He blushed gently from the very depths of his sensitive, delicate skin, and whopping great lies made his ears glow red like signal lamps. Admittedly all he knew was that something was wrong, but as to the truth, well that of course was another matter.

He was unique in having studied medicine and theology simultaneously, thanks mainly to a bicycle that he loved like an old friend. His great success at both these subjects enabled him to take up criminology as a hobby. In this field he soon gained a reputation with a basic treatise entitled "Politics and Crime", a work that tackled the unrewarding task of defining ethics in political life. One of his critics scoffed that according to this wonderful theory more than 75 per cent of all politicians ought to be put into gaol. Dr. Jokim read this opinion with some astonishment but without even the trace of a blush.

After a party, many guests would have difficulty in remembering if Dr. Jokim had really been there, for he seldom spoke, though those who were aware of his presence were careful to mind their p's and q's.

After this unavoidable digression, I shall take the reader back to the Petersens' spotless kitchen and the murdered body of forty-seven year old Agatha Köhler. Stretched out on the ground she lay, skewered by an unknown assassin right through the heart with deadly accuracy. Anyway, that was the finding of Detective-Inspector Schwalbe, who arrived soon after Dr. Jokim. He spoke of a well-aimed thrust delivered with cold deliberation, seeing that the blade, pliant with years of use and sharpening, could so easily have glanced off. It had in fact entered exactly between the third and fourth ribs and, as the police report stated, had led to the immediate death of Agatha Köhler. To Jokim, words were physical creatures, so whenever he heard or read the phrase: "This led to the death of . . .", he had a vision of something or someone actually leading death by the hand, and "dead as mutton" conjured up the image of the moribund animal flat on its back.

The late cook was photographed from all angles at the scene of the crime and then taken to the mortuary.

To all appearances, she more than fully deserved her reputation as a treasure. In the pantry, like ranks of soldiers, stood jars of preserves, each bearing the name of its contents and the year of the pickling in spidery script. Everywhere there reigned the most perfect order; the parquet floor, for instance, was polished to a mirror-like sheen. No wonder then that, in order to preserve it, the inhabitants were ordered to change into their slippers as soon as they entered the house. You could peer into every corner without seeing a single spider's web. In the course of the investigation, it was revealed that Fräulein Agatha would yearly wash and dry the bed feathers of the entire household by herself, and then refill the eiderdowns. This vast undertaking inspired every housewife in the town with glowing admiration and due reverence.

When Dr. Jokim, in his capacity as doctor, had certified the death of the cook, he went upstairs, past the window bearing the trumpeter of Säckingen, to call on the Petersen family. It had been proved beyond the shadow of a doubt that all the Petersens, together with young Petersen's friend, Ole, and the dignified old Frau Consul Petersen—that all of them without exception had been in the house at the exact moment the crime was committed.

After his brief encounter with Dr. Jokim at the front door, Herr Petersen had withdrawn, remarking that everyone was entirely at the doctor's disposal. Dr. Jokim now found the whole family gathered upstairs in a room that was generally referred to as the study. It was dominated by a diplomat's massive desk, resembling a billiard table and bearing heavy bronze ink pots inlaid with semi-precious stones. Quite naturally, there were armchairs and a smoking table, and the bookcase contained the full set of Meyer's Lexicon.

"Oh," exclaimed Dr. Jokim when he saw the family. The word simply escaped him, because he was never given to prevarication. He was as one found him. And he had to admit that despite their utter lack of taste, their hideous furniture, their stand of potted plants, their appalling curtains and their vile wallpaper, the Petersens were exceptionally charming people.

Delighted and yet appalled by his discovery, Dr. Jokim though to himself : "In heaven's name, it couldn't possibly have been any one of these nice people!" Unfortunately all the facts so far elicited confounded this thought. Thus it might have been Herr Petersen, who had a certain artistic bent, and who now struggled nervously to disguise his agitation or the schoolboy who gazed fixedly at the doctor as if he were desperately anxious to read his mind or the old lady, a powder-pale old lady very hard of hearing, in a mauve silk dress partially hidden by a black lace shawl. In her lap lay a matching small parasol with an ivory handle. She had been very beautiful once upon a time and very spoiled, but now she suffered from facial neuralgia, which fact she tried to hide under a studied mask of gaiety. One could see that all her life long she had done nothing that remotely resembled work, and there was something in her that would have been horrified at the very suggestion. She received the attentions of others with a certain grace that was a reward in itself. It was for her that the little cockerel had been intended. There was a rumour that she was the daughter of a Dalmatian prince, hence her nickname, the Duchess. Because of her illness, it was said, and this must be grudgingly admitted, she was rather fond of alcohol and smoked Russian cigarettes with great panache.

"It is time," announced Juri, "for the Duchess to retire to the garden." He said it with finality, as something that must be observed even under the most unusual circumstances, and Dr. Jokim, too, made no objections when the old lady, on the arm of a constable, which she took with obvious condescension, was guided to the ancient cane deckchair in the garden. There beneath the copper beech she allowed herself to be lowered into the cushions that the policeman had duly plumped up for her. Covered by a light vicuña blanket, she rested in regal splendour, toying nonchalantly with the silken tassels of her beloved Parisian parasol, a box of cigarettes within easy reach.

The respect with which she was treated by the family was illustrated by the fact that everyone rose before she left the room. Her daughter-in-law, Frau Petersen, lovingly arranged the lace cape which was slightly awry and delicately straightened the old lady's hair. "Oh, a ladybird," she exclaimed and, holding it in her trembling fingers, she hurried to the window and generously gave freedom to that insect of good fortune. Herr Petersen opened the door for his mother and wished her a pleasant rest.

His wife belonged to the class of person who must continually apologise for being in the world. Though not exactly good looking, she wore a charming expression of loving concern, and after this touching family scene which Dr. Jokim had followed with keen interest, she returned once more to the pretentious settee. Beside her sat the daughter, the very image of her mother. She had a youthful but well-formed face, dominated by features that left little room for the rest. Lacking beauty in the usual sense, she had nevertheless a touching charm. But she did not have her mother's eyes, nor did Juri or his father for that matter —we shall soon learn why.

It was a habit with Dr. Jokim to ask himself whenever he entered a strange room which object in it he would most like to own. But as he cast his eye round this vast study full of furniture and ornaments and trinkets, he found nothing, not a single thing to captivate him. Or was there one object, after all?

"Who might that be?" he asked suddenly. One wall of the room was reserved for family mementoes and photographs. They hung in a variety of frames, some covered with velvet and shells, others decorated with gilded rice grains. There were frames surrounding military decorations, diplomas, children in sailor suits, group photographs taken during family celebrations, and snaps of babies in arms lying on their stomachs with raised heads, popping eyes, and open mouths. The same being confirmed, then as bridegrooms and finally as silvery grandfathers. The whole collection was topped by two crossed swords with the colours of a student society. But Dr. Jokim's acquisitive instincts were now focused on one single picture right in the middle of the wall. It had been taken in the early days of photography when there were still faces, and people who knew how to take them. The person represented must have been a predecessor of these Petersens present today, who sat there awaiting to be examined like patients in a doctor's waiting-room. They too were pale and had the same eyes as the old man in the photograph. Again Dr. Jokim asked "Who might that be?" while those present looked at one another to see which of them was to answer. Then young Petersen eagerly replied. He said the photograph was of his great-grandfather, the astronomer, to whom the town owed its observatory and planetarium, and of whom it was said that he would think nothing of crossing the street in a Turkish dressing-gown and slippers, so as not to keep his precious stars waiting. Or rather he would waft across the street, for he was spare of figure and fleet of foot even in old age.

"What a face," Jokim thought, "what fine eyes! Stargazers' eyes, surely! The hair in a halo round his forehead like a spiral nebula; what splendour, what vision, a really cosmic face, a reflection of the heavens!"

"Thank you, Juri," said Dr. Jokim, but could not help thinking, why, my lad, why did you have to send the postman for a doctor when you could so easily have rung one up? And he blushed when he thought of it. Of course, the shock of the murder might have caused Juri to forget the very existence of the telephone in the nearby corridor. Dr. Jokim would have decided there and then to resign the case, but who, he asked himself, would take it on then? He felt inclined to ask straight out: "Well, which of you was it? Please be kind enough to tell me now. For I'll get at the truth sooner or later."

His floundering embarrassment could not remain unnoticed for long, and, as usual it was infectious. It was later confirmed that the feeling of sympathy he felt for the Petersens was fully returned. Dr. Jokim not only pleased all the Petersens, but also Juri's schoolfriend Ole, a stocky fellow with the face of a sailor who tried vainly to pretend hostility towards the doctor. He was leaning at the window, hands in pockets, as he watched Fräulein Agatha being taken away to the mortuary. He was too sullen to say anything about it or about the morbid spectators in front of the house and their threatening murmurs. But then he did not have to, the Petersens were only too aware of it all. It was more than twenty-five years ago that Agatha had come to their house as a young girl. That very morning she had been seen out shopping with that upright, deliberate, almost soldierly step; now she was being carried out as a corpse.

When the noise of the engine had faded away, the listening faces relaxed. The young man at the window tossed the hair off his forehead like a young colt. Perched on the arm of the sofa —an authentic monstrosity—Juri stirred gently. Everyone breathed a little more freely.

"She has gone," said Dr. Jokim, in an undertone that might have meant: now we may speak freely. He realised how unfair it would be to start from the assumption that the murderer was an outsider. Yet he recoiled from the view that the pleasant father, for instance, or the nearly beautiful Frau Petersen who seemed in such delicate health, could have delivered the fatal thrust. And who in his right mind would credit that young girl with the silver-grey eyes or her brother with so dastardly a crime?

Affection, he thought, while looking at their hands and faces in his embarrassed, inattentive way, surely, affection cannot be a crime. Why then should he struggle to repress it? No, no, a thousand times no, rather must he let himself be guided by it, affirm it and place his complete reliance on it. But whom was he to question first? They all peered at him expectantly, almost eagerly. He turned to Herr Petersen, simply because he had met him first. Again, he asked himself : could one of these delightful people really be a killer? Was it not quite possible for an intruder to have entered the house unnoticed by the family, perhaps through the kitchen window? Was that not why the police, under Inspector Schwalbe, had combed the house from top to bottom? As far as Schwalbe was concerned only the naked facts mattered. He was completely free of prejudice, he had no suspicions, nothing surprised him. His feelings never affected his judgement. In fact, he lacked feelings altogether. It was on his orders that the Petersens had been taken to the study where, until Dr. Jokim arrived, they had remained under the surveillance of a constable. They had been given strict orders not to communicate with one another, and they had not even protested. Some people might perhaps consider their ready compliance suspicious, but from their point of view it was the most sensible thing to do.

In reply to Dr. Jokim's encouraging look, Herr Petersen blurted out that he had spent the whole morning in the house. This, he added, was most unusual, for he was generally in his office by the time the postman called. He was the owner of the optical business founded by his grandfather, the old stargazer with the cosmic face. As a boy, the grandfather had gone with his progenitor from village to village hawking spectacles, a display case hanging from his neck. The business, which had flourished under its present owner's father, was now on the decline. It had been transformed into an optical toyshop, in which little weather-houses with little weather-men and weather-women were now sold. This would have been unthinkable in the old Consul's day.

The obvious question was how Herr Petersen had learnt of the murder. He answered this question even before Dr. Jokim had time to formulate it.

He had, so he confessed, last seen Agatha Köhler at breakfast and he had spoken to her as usual. Fräulein Agatha had been eating with the family ever since the death of his late father. The conversation during breakfast had been about household affairs.

Incidentally, it emerged that Herr Petersen was in the habit of addressing his cook by her first name. Agatha did not of course return this familiarity.

"In other words, she was one of the family," Dr. Jokim suggested. There was no emotion in his voice. He did not even look at the person he was questioning, but stared at the wall with the family pictures in their ornate frames, and at one in particular which to Jokim, at least, was the epitome of bad taste. Man is the product of his environment, he thought, and was surprised that so likeable a family could suffer to live in this room for even a single moment.

Herr Petersen did not reply at once, although the question demanded only a yes or no. "Fräulein Köhler," he said coldly, "was with the family for some thirty years. When my late father engaged her, she was an orphan in Martha's Home." But guessing Dr. Jokim's thoughts, he returned to his original theme. After breakfast he had practised his scales. He played the fiddle a little, and this very evening he had intended to play in a friendly quartet. How sad that nothing would come of it now.

How bizarre, thought Dr. Jokim, that the horrible crime which preyed on his mind, and which had taken place just a few hours earlier, in this very house, might have been committed to the strains of fiddle music from upstairs!

He had heard nothing unusual, Herr Petersen went on, neither screams nor thuds. Then, quite suddenly, the bell had begun to ring very insistently and he had rushed into the passage to see what was going on. Herr Petersen suddenly fell silent, obviously perplexed and visibly agitated.

Although it was not his custom to ask questions, Dr. Jokim now turned to Juri, with words he regretted the moment he had uttered them. For he began in his most formal manner, saying: "Tell me, Juri, wasn't it you ..." At once all those present became startled. "Wasn't it you?" he repeated, "who rushed out to see ..." Relieved, Juri replied: "Yes, it was I who opened the door. As you know, it was the postman," he added. "We were all upstairs at the time," Frau Petersen broke in quite unexpectedly and in an imploring tone. Her daughter nodded as she said it. The friend at the window looked inquiringly across to Dr. Jokim. It was then that Dr. Jokim began to suspect—a word he did not quite like to use—to gain the uncomfortable feeling, then, that, like him, all of them knew that one of them was the murderer, and that they would have to shield him, come what may.

But which of them was it? Alas, the only one who could have answered that question truthfully, the only one who knew, was the criminal himself.

Dr. Jokim was certain of three things, however. Firstly that he had not done it himself; secondly, that this would quite definitely be his last case, and thirdly, that he could not relinquish it now. His self-perception was alarmingly acute; he suddenly realised that he was completely unfit to serve earthly justice, that he was in danger of making common cause with criminals, simply—and he had to admit this to himself—because he liked them.

How he had become involved with detection in the first place was a story in itself. It was because of his peculiar talent, his hypersensitivity to guilt and innocence, that he had inadvertently let the cat out of the bag while serving as a medical expert at Petty Sessions. The accused, a stranger to Jokim, displayed his innocence by behaving in the most clumsy and suspicious manner, and thus antagonising the court. But Dr. Jokim directly spotted the true culprit, who was sitting complacently among the spectators. He could never have told how he realised that this man, who cold-bloodedly watched another being sentenced in his place, was the actual thief. He simply stood up and declared amongst general astonishment: "May it please the court, the real thief is the one over there, in the second row of the spectators' gallery, that sandy-haired youth with the grass-green pullover." Whereupon the youth immediately gave the game away by taking to his heels.

Inspector Schwalbe arrived at the precise moment when Dr. Jokim, now certain of the criminal's identity, decided to stop the interrogation. The inspector had come to find out what progress, if any, Dr. Jokim was making, and incidentally to report that the murder weapon, the kitchen knife, had revealed no fingerprints, not even the cook's. In other words, someone must have wiped the handle clean even while it was still protruding from the corpse. This horrible discovery pointed to astounding coldbloodedness on the part of the criminal.

Dr. Jokim told the inspector somewhat irately that he thought it most ill-advised to blurt out such crucial discoveries in the presence of persons who might possibly be connected with the crime, with which judgement Schwalbe was grudgingly forced to concur. The two of them accordingly repaired to an adjoining room, leaving a constable to keep guard over the Petersens.

Schwalbe now suggested taking the whole lot of them into custody, and Jokim had the greatest difficulty in convincing him that a quick solution of the crime depended on abandoning this drastic measure, at least for the time being. In the end, the inspector contented himself with placing the entire household including Ole under house arrest. Dr. Jokim announced firmly that he would remain with them.

Then he ordered a large supply of ham rolls; the kitchen was, of course, out of bounds, and in any case no one could have entered it without a shudder of horror.

According to Schwalbe, the neighbours were in a threatening and ugly mood. The owner of the poultry shop and supplier of the young cockerel, the last person to speak to Agatha apart from the murderer himself, stated that poor Fräulein Agatha had deserved far better employers, though she herself would brook no criticism of people who were notorious for their arrogance and shameful ignorance of household matters. That very morning she had refused to hear a bad word against them. Moreover, as the witness rightly pointed out, she was the very heart and soul of the house. She alone carried on the tradition of her late master, the Consul, the one who had founded the family fortune and had built the beautiful Petersen home.

It is customary in an investigation to seek for a motive, particularly when suicide is out of the question, as it was in this case. But who could possibly have had a motive for killing a person with the spotless reputation of Agatha Köhler? It certainly was not jealousy. Agatha was an old spinster who had gone quite stale, what fishermen might call a poor catch. In sexual matters she was a neuter. Dr. Jokim had, in his capacity as a physician, delved into the mysteries of sexual transmutation without coming to any conclusive results. He knew that, in the absence of a cock, hens may make comical attempts to crow. Moreover he was not alone in noticing that famous men, especially poets, often resembled old women, particularly in their later years, or that talented women, such as lady writers, painters and sculptors, frequently exhibit male characteristics in old age. Thus do both

sexes blend into each other or rather into a species of hermaphrodite, of which men and women are merely temporary aberra-
tions. Bi-sexual man, Jokim had called his work on this delicate
subject. And he had headed it all with the witty epigram : "Seen
in a scientific light, all humans are hermaphrodite." Moreover
he had quoted Aristophanes' bright remarks on this very subject
and had finally distinguished between benign and malignant
forms of hermaphroditism.

After his discussion with Schwalbe, Jokim dismissed the constable who had been watching the Petersen family. Then, running
the risk that they might plot among themselves, he went round
to interview the neighbours.

This task was facilitated by his excellent gift of creative listening. He scarcely uttered a word, though he would occasionally
make an encouraging gesture, such as a nod or a smile. This gave
him the reputation of a brilliant conversationalist. He did not
ask any questions because he knew that most questions beg the
wrong kind of answer, but kept resolutely, almost enticingly,
silent. Few people can resist this approach, and he came away
with a far profounder picture of the late cook's real character
than a more conventional inquisitor might have obtained.

Agatha Köhler looked like—a cook. One could see from her
face that she made excellent pancakes, apfelstrudels and dump-
lings, that few could rival her soufflés, and that she invariably
made her own noodles, lovingly kneading the dough and then
drawing it out like an edible clothes-line.

To all appearances, Fräulein Agatha had few, if any, enemies.
Her dark hair was pinned up high, for she was a small woman
who also wore exceptionally high heels and held herself very
straight. For some years she had been tinting her hair a chestnut
brown and wore a switch to keep it as full as once it must have
been. Her carp-like little cheeks glistened from the heat of the
oven and her upturned nose was continually poised like someone
who says "I smell gas". Her small mouth was ideal for tasting
and her eyes appeared boiled by the steam to which they were
constantly exposed. Her neck was a little too long, and she
always wrapped it in black velvet. That was probably the reason
why one of Jokim's informants called her an old boiling fowl. It
was said that in her youth she had been a pretty, pert little thing
and that she could have made a number of good matches, but

that she denied herself the happiness of marriage out of loyalty to her employers. Her savings, which must have been considerable, were used exclusively for a nephew, to whom she felt greatly attached. Naturally, she was no longer able to manage the demanding Petersen household by herself, but called in under-servants who, when they left the place—for the work was heavy—were sought after everywhere.

Dr. Jokim's inquiries also revealed that Fräulein Agatha often spoke of the many enviable positions she had refused out of loyalty to the memory of the late Consul, who meant the world to her; for instance, she admired him for ordering his shaving water from afar because the local water was too hard. When she spoke of him her eyes became moist and invariably looked towards heaven. Then she would nod forgivingly, for it appeared that he had also been a bit of a rake.

Among Jokim's willing informants was the Duchess's hairdresser, a vivacious girl by the name of Hildesuse. The same girl, moreover, who had compared Fräulein Agatha to a boiling fowl; in fact, she had had little to say in the late cook's favour. She said quite blatantly : "I'm not going to shed a single tear for her, and that's that." Now, knowing that Hildesuse ministered daily to the grand old lady's needs, Dr. Jokim thought that she might merely be repeating the opinions she had picked up in the Petersen household. Hildesuse obviously enjoyed being part of the Duchess's cosmetic extravaganzas which, she freely admitted, cost the Petersens a great deal of money. "But then, you can't expect to get much for nothing," she added.

About the old stargazer, that misanthrope, whom Fräulein Agatha revered so greatly, Jokim heard all sorts of gossip with keen interest. For instance, that the fabulous old man called anyone younger than himself by his first name, even the highest dignitaries, who did not greatly relish this form of address. To the question of a cynic whether he had not perhaps seen God Almighty after years of scanning the sky, he replied : "Not yet, you young ass, not yet. But rest assured, I shall." One fine morning he was found dead at his telescope, his face bearing, so it is said, so peaceful and ethereal an expression that he might easily have kept his promise.

When Dr. Jokim had learnt enough to get on with, he returned to the Petersens. He was troubled with a visionary nature, thanks to which he occasionally saw the course of events five minutes in advance, without, however, being able to influence them one way or another. Moreover he had to admit that he had come away from his rounds not liking anything he had heard about Agatha Köhler. "The devil take her," he said. He said it aloud, a habit he had acquired through prolonged solitude.

The question of supper for the Petersens caused him some concern, for although Fräulein Agatha was dead and had been removed from the house, everything spoke of her presence, above all in the kitchen, which was still out of bounds and where she continued to live in the countless preserve jars. It seemed inconceivable that Frau Petersen or her daughter should ever enter there again, let alone that very night.

Luckily Dr. Jokim knew a gay young cook—in fact, he was the same whom Dr. Jokim's intervention in court had extricated from what had seemed a pretty hopeless position and who had remained faithful to his saviour ever since. Dr. Jokim had him brought in and the Petersens thanked him wordlessly.

Dr. Jokim knew full well what had happened in his absence —each of the Petersens, except for the criminal, of course, had been suspecting all the others, and hating himself for his suspicions. They might, for instance, have thought that Juri was not in his room at the crucial moment, and that everyone else, too, could easily have crept into the kitchen unnoticed. Any one of them might, moreover, have discovered the crime before the postman, but, believing that the murderer was one of the family, have kept the discovery quiet. It was even possible that the criminal had meanwhile confessed.

In any case, Jokim realised that it was far more fruitful to let matters take their own course than to pursue the embarrassing inquisition. But he made no mention of his decision when he joined the family for dinner; instead he nonchalantly broached the subject of music, and as he warmed to it, so his affection for the criminal family grew more intense, particularly after discussing the art of the fugue with Herr Petersen. For him as a layman, he explained, it was a mystery how some conductors managed to be equally enthusiastic about Mozart and Wagner. It was just like falling in love with a whole family, or with two sisters, or a sister and a brother. Surely two people as individuals were not nearly as attractive as the bonds between them.

Suddenly Dr. Jokim was struck by the irony of his position:
here he was sitting in the company of a suspect and talking
about Bach, Wagner and Mozart.

The old lady meanwhile was being groomed in her own room
by Hildesuse who insisted on seeing to her favourite client's needs
even in the present, rather desperate situation. During supper a
stone was thrown through the window. "Yes, that's how it is,
they are casting the first stone," said Jokim, picked it up and
gazed at it as if he were looking at a stone for the first time in
his life. He weighed it reflectively in his hand, contemplated it
like a jewel, and finally put it into his pocket as a souvenir.
Meanwhile the rumbustious assistant cook, who was also a
capable waiter, was whistling softly to himself and sweeping up
the broken glass.

After dinner Dr. Jokim still had a great deal of work to do.
In particular, he wanted to make a quick inspection of Fräulein
Agatha's room in the attic. The first thing he noticed there was
the complete absence of books (books were the first thing he
looked for in a room). Instead, the wall and chest of drawers
were covered with photographs, including one of the beloved
Herr Consul, his avaricious face set off by a shell frame. Another
showed Agatha herself in her younger days holding hands with
her nephew, for whose future she was working so devotedly.
"Aha," said Jokim and had seen enough. One thing was certain
—there was nothing in that room that he would have liked to
own.

It was quite a different matter with Juri's room, which had
been placed at his disposal for the night. It seemed that Juri had
ejected all the original furnishings, for his room looked more like
a workshop or studio than a bedroom. The walls were covered
with drawings and water colours, not, by the way, from Juri's
hand, but obviously made by Ole, the melancholic and sullen
friend who occupied the spare room. Dr. Jokim particularly
liked the one entitled "Flea Plagued by Human Beings". It
showed a highly magnified flea; tiny men were swarming about
on its machine-like body, tickling and pricking it with swords.
Its face had the same expression of quiet heroism as is usually
worn by itchy human beings. I'd simply love to add that one to
my collection, thought Jokim, greatly impressed. Another drawing was called "Horse with Beard"; it endowed the solemn

beauty of the animal's face with much dignity. Yet another bore the legend "Running Yard", and showed a yardstick scampering through the landscape. There were many more like them. A still-life of an open water-colour box bore the title "If nothing inspires me, I paint the paintbox". Jokim immediately saw the point.

He was sure that Juri would not go to bed without visiting his dear sister, for he realised that they loved each other very much. Tonight Juri would sit on his sister's bed, they would look at each other and each would think: was it you? But surely, you would have told me, for we have perfect faith in each other. . . .

In a detective story, the known events must be recapitulated over and over again. Little knowing what was waiting for her and completely at peace with herself, Fräulein Agatha had returned home from her shopping, and immediately—for she was a creature of almost perpetual motion—had started plucking the young cockerel. She directed the household symphony with consummate ease, much as an experienced musician directs a chamber orchestra from his grand piano.

She had memorised the score throughout the years, indeed, throughout decades. She was delighted by the smooth routine, she was the heart and soul of a well-ordered system, every minute ran its proper course. She was the master of time. In short, she had a near-cosmic nature.

But just when she had plucked the heart from the breast of the dead cockerel, the ordered course of her life was rudely and inconsiderately shattered. Someone had entered the kitchen. We do not know exactly who, and we do not even know what, if anything, was said before the horrible deed was done. A veil is drawn over the next half or three-quarters of an hour—an interminably long period if measured in pain or fear, but very brief if spent in love; nothing at all is known about it. Then the postman looked through the kitchen window and saw Fräulein Agatha wallowing in blood while a black-handled knife protruded from her heart. During all the time it took the postman to go round the house and get someone to answer him, the murderer could easily have been hiding in the kitchen or have escaped from the dining-room. And there were other factors to be taken into account. What had happened when Juri, mistakenly or intentionally, had sent the postman to fetch the doctor, and when the Petersens were left alone in the house for an important half hour?

The murder had been committed in broad daylight, while, if you can believe it, each inhabitant of the house had allegedly been alone on the upper floor. Yet everything pointed to a member of this lovable family, or else to Ole, their friend. The fingerprints on the black handle of the kitchen knife had been so carefully wiped off that even the most sensitive chemical and photomechanical tests known to Inspector Schwalbe had produced nothing but negative results. No one could tell whether the criminal had removed the fingerprints himself or whether someone had done it for him. Nor was it at all certain whether, by the time the postman discovered the murder, the crime or indeed the murderer had already been detected by someone else. In fact, the whole family might have witnessed the crime, and if they stuck by one another, and kept their mouths shut—a difficult task—no power on earth could budge them.

"Lovable people, all the same," Jokim repeated, smiling ruefully, for after all he was not there to like people but to discover the murderer. "Curse all this love I feel for them," he muttered.

But why curse love? Is love not a wonderful, magical feeling, the only true guide there is? Was not the world created out of love, out of tenderness, out of the union of primeval lust with true friendship? It struck Jokim that we are drawn into this process of loving when mere children. He suddenly recaptured that old sinking feeling, as if his body were fashioned of clay. A gentle motion seemed to engulf him, to flow down to his knees, then on between his toes. It was like a gradual immersion in fine sand, and produced a delicious, dreamlike sensation.

But love had now to be torn from his heart and offered as a sacrifice to justice. The criminal must be discovered, lovable though undoubtedly he was.

Jokim saw them all raising their arms for the stroke, all, even the tender young girl. She would have closed her eyes as she delivered the fatal blow, of course. In his mind's eye Jokim could also see the crime reflected in Frau Petersen's gentle, imploring face, and in Juri's shining eyes, those eyes he had inherited from his star-gazing ancestor. In many other ways, too, he bore a great resemblance to the strange old man, for instance in the way his hair stood up on his noble head. Jokim next imagined Herr Petersen's horrified glances as he committed the murder, and Ole's which would, however, be combined with a proud, defiant gesture. Could they all have participated in the crime jointly, like Caesar's assassins? Jokim did not believe it for a minute. Still, it won't be long now, he thought, as he bent over the microscope on Juri's untidy desk, before one and all will come trooping in to me with self-accusations.

And indeed, while he was still examining the wonders of the minute world on which Juri had focused his lens, there came a short but determined knock.

"Here is the first," said Jokim, "please come in." It was Ole: his hair was matted and he looked quite awful.

He had, he began without ado, but opening his sleep-laden eyes, he had to make an important confession. It was he who had murdered the cook. His motives were unimportant; let it suffice that he was very impulsive by nature, and that he had committed the crime all by himself, without any accomplices. Ole held his hands out towards Jokim, as if asking to be hand-cuffed there and then.

"Stuff and nonsense," said Jokim, "it's all stuff and nonsense." Ole's face hardened into obstinacy, "Believe me, it's quite true," he insisted, blushing deeply. "No, it isn't," replied the comical doctor (whose second-sight told him that that was what his friends called him behind his back), "though I appreciate what you are trying to do for your friend. No doubt, at your age I should have done the same, in fact, I did it once, but you are only confusing the issue, for it couldn't have been you. You see, I already know the murderer's identity, or I think I do."

"You know!" the unhappy youth gasped, while the colour drained from his face. "God help us all," he added.

Jokim pushed a chair under him, thrust a cigarette into his mouth and lit it. But Ole demurred and, even now obeying the strict ritual of smokers, motioned the doctor to help himself first.

"I hasten to assure you," Jokim said quickly, "that it wasn't your friend Juri either, although he, as you well know, often swore that he would kill Agatha Köhler one fine day. And he certainly behaved rather suspiciously this morning, I must say."

Ole nodded silently.

"And, let me tell you, he only escaped arrest by a hair-breadth," Jokim added momentously, "for it really was a hair that did it. Do you want to see it?"

Ole turned pale again. "A hair!"

"Don't be afraid, it wasn't the sister either, I sincerely hope. Just forget this whole business. I promise I shall try to do the same. Sacrificing oneself for a friend is a noble deed, but only if it's done in secret. One must never glory in it, that's precisely what is so noble about it."

Ole wanted to object. "I know," the doctor waved him aside, "you meant well—but do go and finish your drawing, for that's where your talents lie . . ."

Alas, the writer is for ever precluded from describing simultaneously events that happened in different places, as for instance the conversation between Dr. Jokim and Ole on the one hand, and that between the Petersen children on the other. He is forced to report them successively although, as we said, they happened at the same time. Nevertheless, Dr. Jokim felt himself present at the second discussion as well, thanks largely to his mind's eye, an organ that unlike the heart and the stomach is not anatomically located. It is best thought of as a mirror, or rather as something combining the properties of ratiocination and vision, and it told him that, while Ole was attempting to save his friend by accusing himself of the murder, Juri and his sister were exchanging confidences, or rather confessions.

"Who is to begin?" they said with one voice. They were young and excited, and they smiled as soon as these identical words were spoken. "I was downstairs in the kitchen," each confided to the other, "before the postman called, and surmising what had happened, I cleaned the handle of the knife . . ."

Naturally they both knew the importance of fingerprints in crime detection, and they had acted upon their knowledge immediately. Now Juri might conceivably have committed the crime, Dr. Jokim thought, but not this delicate young girl. Nevertheless, each had immediately suspected the other, for they had both grown to loathe Fräulein Agatha from the bottom of their hearts. These same young people who yearly recited a poem on the cook's birthday, who gave her flowers and presents, and who suffered her grateful kisses. Of course, each of them was horrified at what the other seemed to have done, but they knew where their loyalties lay and had acted accordingly. The sister had heard Juri creep upstairs and seen him shake all over. That was why she had called out "Juri" when she heard him answer the door to the postman. And it was only because he knew that Fräulein Agatha was dead that Juri had made free to slide non-chalantly down the banister, an action strongly disapproved of from the time of the dearly beloved Herr Consul. What other things hadn't they all been told were forbidden! And oh, how they shuddered in the memory of what they had just done, not a murder, admittedly, but an attempt to protect the murderer. For both of them, the brother with his handkerchief, the sister with her own hair—it had been horrible to bend so low over the corpse—had wiped the black, sticky handle. They would remember it all their lives and dream about it on and off ever afterwards. Bemused and mystified though they were by their own actions and daring, they nevertheless appreciated the cruel humour of their mutual sacrifice. They looked at each other with sharp, knowing glances, and they suddenly fell silent. They were both afraid for each other, and they were both wrong.

Not knowing that, Juri at once set out to find Dr. Jokim. But how convince the good doctor that he, Juri, had murdered the cook? Then he remembered the incriminating handkerchief. With boyish cunning he had securely hidden it, or thought he had (we shall find out how later on). This handkerchief would surely be enough; it and the fact that he had sent the postman to fetch the doctor in order to gain time. Juri said nothing about the hair, of course, never suspecting—no crime is ever perfect— that the comical doctor, whom he liked very much, but of whose detective work he thought mighty little, knew about it already. For guileless Juri had left his sister's hair in the microscope for Dr. Jokim to find—a silky, copper-gleaming hair, which he instantly identified, and which Juri had removed from Agatha's chest. It was in order to get rid of it as quickly as possible that he also had to get rid of the unsuspecting postman.

Just as Juri reached the door to Dr. Jokim's room, it opened. He heard Dr. Jokim's voice say: "Do go and finish your drawing, for that's where your talents lie. And take a few cigarettes with you, you will probably need them." That was certainly true.

Instantly guessing what Ole had been up to, Juri called out: "Don't believe him, doctor, it was I ...". But Ole clapped a hand over his friend's mouth and dragged him away.

It was a warm summer's night, and the two friends carried their mattresses on to the roof terrace and lay watching the stars until they mercifully fell asleep.

When Dr. Jokim woke before them next morning he felt perfectly certain that in his absence much would have happened to help clarify the case. He was sure, for instance, that Juri and Ole had had a long discussion. Those two had no secrets from each other. Had Juri been the criminal, Ole would have been told about it, and vice versa. Brother and sister, too, were unlikely to keep secrets from each other. The same could not, alas, be said of the Petersen seniors, and least of all, of the old Duchess, who seemed beyond good and evil, living as she did in a world of her own. Like a clockwork robot that gets wound up in the early morning and keeps going throughout the day, vaguely human, but cocooned in passivity and dependence, she had no need to think or to do anything; she did not even have to notice events. She could forget every moment as soon as it was gone; for instance, what she had just eaten or what someone had said to her, or what the weather was like yesterday. She even obliterated her aches with opiates. She lived from cigarette to cigarette, from cognac to cognac, from nap to nap, or rather she just existed : she vegetated and felt—in so far as she had any feelings left at all—very happy in her twilight state. She would be the last person to whom anyone would reveal the identity of the criminal. One would have had to shout it into her ear, in any event. Perhaps she did not even realise that Fräulein Agatha was dead, or else she had forgotten it already.

Occasionally the Duchess's clockwork existence was disturbed by a childish tantrum, as when her supplies ran out. On one such occasion she actually threw a precious vase, a hideous thing, through the big window with the Trumpeter of Säckingen and looked terribly proud of what she had done. The stained glass proved very difficult and costly to repair, but this did not deter the tearful Agatha, who immediately gave orders for its restoration—out of reverence for the dear late Consul, she explained.

By now the reader must feel fairly sure that the murder was not committed by Juri, his sister or, for that matter, by Ole. The friends had been lying awake for a very long time, their last cigarette travelling to and fro like a pipe of peace, when they were startled by an eerie call. It was the Duchess calling for Agatha in her deep voice; Agathaaah she called again and again, wailing on the last syllable. Her Agathaaahs reverberated through the night until Dr. Jokim came to her aid. She looked a terrifying figure with her tousled white hair and ravaged unpowdered face. "Who are you?" she asked Dr. Jokim sharply, "I do not know you. Kindly introduce yourself." Fortunately Herr Petersen came along just then. "A friend of the family, Mama," he said. "So," she answered, "I cannot get to sleep." Dr. Jokim brought his little bag and conjured up sleep for the irate Duchess. "I like you, doctor," were her last words as he left the room.

In the early morning Inspector Schwalbe roared up on his powerful motorcycle to boast about what he chose to call an important new clue. "How is your murderous family this morning?" he asked. "You are much too soft, my friend, much too soft. A real detective can't afford to like people."

"As far as I am concerned," Jokim answered coolly, "I have always detested that Roman general in the Latin text book who was so impartial that he had his own son executed."

"That's my man," Schwalbe answered. He had spent the whole night on the telephone trying to locate Agatha's nephew, a bank clerk in a nearby town. He had disappeared without a trace, had simply melted into thin air, so to speak. Dr. Jokim listened to this important bit of news in complete silence. You fool, he thought to himself, but nevertheless left poor Schwalbe to roar away again on the wrong trail.

Soon after breakfast, Hildesuse came in to perform her daily chore of dressing and beautifying the Duchess. She had a black eye and scratches on her face—the righteous indignation of the neighbours had been visited upon one who had been imprudent enough to make invidious comparisons between the Petersens and Agatha. She had given as good as she got, she declared with satisfaction. As Dr. Jokim listened to her, a faint smile of gentle interest played on his lips. Hildesuse became annoyed. "Don't act the Chinaman with me," she shouted at him. But all the good doctor did, with a minimum of effort, entailing a barely visible shake of the head, and with expressionless eyes, was to indicate that, in actual fact, he had nothing to say to her, nothing to say to her at all.

Hildesuse stormed off to shout abuse of the doctor into the

Duchess's left ear. That lady, unfortunately, failed to grasp what Hildesuse was talking about and of whom. A minute or two later, Frau Petersen came into Jokim's room. For the first time in her life she was acting with a purpose. Visibly moved by this fact, her head inclined a little to one side, but without looking at the doctor, perhaps entranced by the new thrill of deliberately lying, she declared she had something to confess. It was she who had murdered Fräulein Agatha, and, what was more, all by herself and without any accomplices. Jokim readily entered into the game. But this time he did not remain silent.

"Why," he replied with apparent interest, "is that really so? Fancy you being the culprit, dear lady, I should never have guessed. But what were your motives, if I may ask? Why murder her when she was already dead? Come, I shall not mince my words with you, you overgrown schoolgirl. I could, of course, take you at your word and have you arrested here and now. Then your husband will probably insist that you are trying to shield him, the real murderer. In this deceptively simple case it is as difficult to convince each member of your family of his innocence as it is to prove that he committed the crime."

"I hated Agatha Köhler," Frau Petersen began again, without paying the slightest attention to Jokim's biting irony. "Yes, I hated her, cruel though you might think me for finding so little love for one who slaved away for us all from dawn to dusk, who fulfilled our least wishes before they were ever expressed . . ."

"Stop," the doctor broke in very crossly. "Let me tell you something. Stop me if I'm wrong. Actually, there is no good reason why your husband, for whom, by the way, I have a very deep affection, and your children and that charming sullen friend equally dear to me, should not hear what I have to say as well. But then, you and I, dear lady, are the only ones to know who committed the crime. This terrible crime, for God knows that's what it was—I only wish we could wash our hands of it. It is sometimes better not to know. Yes, perhaps we should keep it quiet for the time being."

"How right you are," murmured Frau Petersen softly, her eyes brimming over with tears. "I really did think it was a lady-bird at first. I am a little short-sighted, you know, and would wear spectacles except that I look like a governess in them. But it only took me a moment to realise that what I saw on the

Duchess's hair was no insect—it was a drop of blood. My God, now I have let it slip out! Still, no court in the world can make me admit it—it's only your word against mine. And I had carefully planned to take the blame myself, to do something worthwhile with my life for once!" With a childlike gaze she implored the doctor to keep her secret.

"People like you and me should not think," replied Jokim. "When we begin to think we do everything wrong. But it is time for us to repair to the study."

On the way, they met the Duchess on the arm of Hildesuse, who had just performed her masterpiece on the old lady's face. The Duchess, by the way, needed no support for she was still sound on her feet, but felt that it looked better that way. In fact, she looked magnificent, almost like a queen-mother, particularly now as she stepped down the broad, majestic red stair-carpet with its unbelievably tasteless design and unsafe brackets.

The Duchess, who was again carrying her old-fashioned little parasol, stabbed it with great accuracy at a certain repetitive pattern in the hideous floral wallpaper. She was followed by Herr Petersen bearing cushions, the ubiquitous new cook with blankets, and Juri with a box of Russian cigarettes and a book elegantly bound in pliant red Moroccan leather, its title embossed in gold. For years the Duchess had been opening this self-same book, reading two or three lines through her lorgnette, then getting bored and leaving it open on the vicuña blanket while the wind rustled in the pages. Today as every day, the old lady was on the way to her favourite spot in the garden.

When Dr. Jokim bowed to her, she thanked him wordlessly by inclining her forehead just the slightest bit, closing her eyes for an instant and at the same time smiling with her nose, the sides of which wrinkled in the process. Quite suddenly she froze, pointed the parasol at him and said in her masculine voice: "I don't think I know you, introduce yourself." Then she used her parasol to push her ear forward for better hearing, but had already forgotten what it was she was listening for. Smiling bemusedly she walked on, while Hildesuse indicated with up-turned eyes that the old lady was a perfect darling if a bit queer at times.

Only when the old lady, smoking with great satisfaction and playing with the silken tassels of her parasol, was safely deposited in the back garden there to slumber regally under the copper beech, did the rest of the family gather in Herr Petersen's room. Jokim, who noticed that the photograph of the stargazer was askew, carefully placed it back in position and began to speak with some embarrassment.

"A most unforgettable and unusual picture," he said, looking at it intensely, and then continued. As a newcomer to the area he had not until yesterday heard of the Petersen family, but even he had not been left in ignorance of Fräulein Agatha's remarkable achievements. It was of this treasure of a cook that he now began to speak, of this poor creature, who so reminded him of someone he had known and feared in his own early childhood— a resemblance that had helped him considerably in getting to the bottom of this terrible case.

Agatha Köhler had been an orphan, a buxom young thing, when the late Consul had hired her as his maid. Now the old gentleman, though a great dear, was perhaps a little too fond of young girls, and just a trifle vain and possessive.

"I was told yesterday," Jokim said, "that soon after Agatha Köhler joined his household she had to retire for a time, ostensibly so as to make provision for a nephew—the same nephew whom she spoiled ever afterwards as only a mother can, and for whom she scraped together every penny she could. In due course, she sent him to a good school, for he was a clever boy, with very strange eyes, by the way, stargazers' eyes, some would have called them."

At this point, Juri glared at the doctor, as if to say: How dare you! Only the Petersens have stargazers' eyes; what utter impertinence to suggest we share them with that miserable fellow!

"Agatha's nephew later devoted his life to banking. Inspector Schwalbe, a very capable officer, is just about to track him down, and I should be very much surprised if that doesn't entail a trip abroad. Perhaps the good inspector will even discover that the nephew quite recently called on his devoted aunt. For my part, I am certain that he did so. If I know Schwalbe, he will pin something or other on him, but he will never catch him, for the nephew is a very shrewd and imaginative person. And, believe me, imagination is a very dangerous legacy—for instance, when it comes to hiding an incriminating handkerchief from the police. Only an imaginative person would think of wrapping it round a

roll of black paper and fitting it carefully into the tube of a telescope, and then admire the stars unhindered by its presence."

Juri turned from red to white, but Jokim continued evenly:
"But all that is irrelevant. Agatha Köhler was attached to the
Consul by other ties as well. She ministered to him body and
soul and quickly cooked herself into his heart. She was truly a
treasure. One would have to search far and wide to find someone
who did the housework so thoroughly and who became such a
fanatic exponent of this laudable art. But no one is indispensable,
you will say. Could she not be given notice? Of course, the
question was considered. Am I not right? But it never came to
that. She herself occasionally referred to, though never really
threatened with, her possible departure. Her lust for power was
insatiable. How many schemes did the luckless Petersens not
think up to rid themselves of her quiet tyranny, which unfortunately did not restrict itself to domestic matters, but even extended to the choice of acquaintances! She guarded the door
and the telephone, only delivering messages when it suited her,
and telling all visitors whom the late Consul might have disliked
that nobody was at home. In particular, she kept a watchful eye
on the children's playmates. Thus she would hotly defend poor
Ole against reproaches no one had raised against him, at the
same time making it clear that she considered his influence on
the children as being of the worst kind. She called Frau Petersen
a weak mother, and whenever that good lady tried to make
herself useful in the house, Agatha's condescending smile would
remove any joy from the enterprise. She would follow Frau
Petersen, duster in hand, and if her employer had the temerity
to lay the table she would quickly rearrange the plates or change
the whole dinner service. Nor did she approve of Herr Petersen's
musical interests. She would use the occasion of certain anniver-
saries to pillory innocent enjoyments as lacking in respect, not
with words but simply through her behaviour. For instance, she
might ask for permission to pay silent tribute to the memory of a
deceased member of the family by going to the cemetery, and
would Herr Petersen please carry on with whatever he was
doing; she had no wish to disturb him in any way. She fully
understood his position and, in other circumstances, had a deep
love of music herself.

"To preserve the delicate polish of the furniture she used all manner of loose covers and antimacassars, turning the house into a kind of mausoleum.

"She hated to be left out of anything, including, for instance, the children's friendship with Ole. There was something unhealthy in all such relationships, as she let slip out during meals, citing horrible examples from other families. She would often compare Juri and Ole to her nephew, whose perfect behaviour and outstanding school reports were perpetual sources of joy to her. All such comparisons were always to the detriment of the two friends. Another of Agatha's endearing qualities was that she insisted on giving the Duchess her daily ration of brandy, thus bringing the old lady into her power. She also made a point of keeping silent about some of the children's misdeeds, only to terrorise them with her knowledge later.

"It was said that although she was ignorant of business matters she had lent Herr Petersen a considerable sum of money, thus jeopardising her beloved nephew's future. No doubt, she had been repaid in full, but it was galling to know that the Consul's inheritance was safer in his cook's hands than in those of his son.

"Although she usually stood on ceremony, she would occasionally participate in the Petersens' musical evenings, especially when relatives were present with whom she was on good terms, and who treated her more as a friend of the family than as a cook. Although normally quite devoid of humour, she would on these occasions jocularly refer to herself as an old house-dragon. Uncles and aunts would always protest at this and dig good old Agatha smilingly in the ribs. No wonder, therefore, that Agatha never guessed how hated she really was. She was dazzled by her own capabilities and by the unshakeable belief that everything she did was for the best. So she ruled over the Petersens obdurately, just as the dearly beloved Consul would have wanted her to. And the best guarantee of her supremacy was her employers' utter dependence on her—and of this she made perfectly sure.

"Here I must mention the late Consul's widow, the Duchess, and her charming art of allowing others to spoil her. Her origins were veiled in darkness. The late Consul had met her on a pleasure cruise, and I should be very surprised if her parents had not been circus performers! No doubt, she had a spotless reputation, though, seeing that her father might have been a knife-thrower and she his target, this was only to be expected. I can still imagine her in a tiny tutu clutching her little parasol and perching charmingly on a tight-rope. She was very beautiful and one of nature's noblewomen. She was no more educated than her cook, but people tended not to notice, chiefly because of her deafness and her foreign accent. I might suppose she came from Montenegro, where so many women look like queens. And then, she had great charm, where as Agatha Köhler had none at all."

At this moment there was a knock at the door, and the new cook entered.

"I beg your pardon," he said, "but the old lady has left the garden and cannot be found in the house. I'm afraid she might have wandered out into the street . . ."

The news caused some consternation, but Jokim pacified the family. The cook would look for her; meanwhile her great dignity would help to protect her against the wrath of the incensed populace.

In fact, the Duchess was promenading quite gaily through the streets of the neighbourhood, and no one molested her in the slightest. If the truth be told, her unconcerned appearance contributed largely to pacifying the ugly mood of the tradesmen.

"Fräulein Köhler," Jokim was saying at this point, "saw to it that no family birthday or anniversary was ever forgotten. And at table she would glance towards the ceiling as if to commune with the late gentleman. Everything in the house and garden had to remain as he would have liked it, the flower bed with its yellow and violet pansies in the front, every piece of furniture in its usual place, the choice of dishes, and the morning ritual of distributing the post. She balanced the household accounts down to the last penny—I've looked at them myself, and I've found that she tended to round off all the prices, no doubt in the interests of tidiness. Thus if an egg cost nine pfennig she would write down ten in the book, just to make it a nice round sum. And incidentally, it went a long way towards meeting the cost of the nephew's education, for, needless to say, she never took anything for herself.

"Still, the fact remains that she looked after the Petersen children very well, even though, to my mind, they were dressed in the worst possible taste—if we are to judge by the family photographs. She knew the weaknesses of the entire Petersen family—even the exotic origins of the Duchess and the moral laxity of the late Consul. Even the fact that the present head of the Petersen family had married for money in obedience to his father's wishes. (But being possessed of an independent spirit Herr Petersen has revenged himself upon his autocratic father by falling in love with his wife—at least that's how I see it.) And now Agatha Köhler is dead. There is nothing more pathetic than the death of a person for whom no one grieves, after whose demise everyone breathes more freely. Please don't think that I am trying to condone her murder, even though, as Hildesuse says, she was no great loss. (Agatha, by the way, would have said the same of Hildesuse.) But then, which of us can honestly claim he is perfect?

"For the rest, I shall be mercifully brief. Can we rest content in the knowledge that by her death Fräulein Agatha was spared great pain, for surely the embezzlements of her nephew—or let us call a spade a spade : of her son—and his headlong flight into perpetual exile would have cut her to the quick? Or that she, who had never known a day's illness, bore within her the seeds of a slow and painful death, for this the post-mortem has revealed? Or finally that the murder was committed by a person who was of unsound mind? No, none of these things can be our excuse. We cannot approve of what has happened. Never.

"Perhaps it would be best to send the Duchess to a mental home, where she can be given the treatment she needs. In any case, this house will never be the same for you. I cannot imagine that you, Herr Petersen, will want to continue living here, let alone make music in this house . . ."

"The Duchess," announced the ubiquitous cook.

She floated into the room, cradling her beloved parasol like a doll, holding a cigarette affectedly between thumb and index finger, and wearing an expression normally found only in children and occasionally in very old people—a look of complete innocence. The sides of her nose were wrinkled in a smile. When she saw Dr. Jokim she said in a pronounced Slavonic accent : "And who might you be? I don't think we have been introduced."

Dr. Jokim took his leave, promising to return under happier circumstances. They had formed a lasting friendship. As he stepped into the street accompanied by the temporary cook, Juri ran out and implored him to accept a token of his affection. It was Ole's drawing of the flea plagued by human beings. "You must have read my thoughts," said Dr. Jokim.

BIOGRAPHICAL NOTE

Ernst Penzoldt was born on 14th June 1892 in Erlangen, the son of an eminent physician. He studied art at Weimar and Kassel, and later became a sculptor in Munich. His first literary success was the novel *Der arme Chatterton* (1928), a romantic account of the tragic life and death of the eighteenth-century Bristol poet. Its success was eclipsed by *Die Powenzbande* (1930), sub-titled "Zoology of a family". This novel, which remains Penzoldt's most popular work, is an entertaining and intermittently satirical account of the highly ingenious and not over-scrupulous money-making enterprises of a family of outsiders. Amidst the economic squalls of the 1920s the family of Baltus Powenz—their motto is "Furchtlos, Fröhlich, Fruchtbar"— labour in devious ways to attain to a monument to respectability— a family dwelling. Penzoldt served as a medical orderly in both world wars, and his experiences in the second are movingly described in *Zugänge* (1947). One of his best-known short stories, *Korporal Mombour* (1941), epitomises, in the fate which sends a young German volunteer in the Napoleonic wars to live with the family of the Frenchman he has killed, the perverse brutality of war. This story was turned into a successful film with the title *Es kommt ein Tag* (1950). Penzoldt also wrote plays (*Die portugalesische Schlacht*, 1931; *So war Herr Brummell*, 1933), but these have little distinction, apart from witty bits of dialogue and a certain flair for the construction of ingenious situations. More characteristic of his talent, which is essentially narrative, are the novels *Die Leute aus der Mohrenapotheke* (1938) and *Squirrel* (1954). Penzoldt died on 27th January 1955. His work is suffused with a warm humanity and a whimsical humour that are reminiscent of Matthias Claudius and Jean Paul. He has an eye for atmosphere and a predilection for the eccentric personality that are at times almost Dickensian. Above all, Penzoldt was an artist and a Bohemian who delighted in indulging an impish sense of humour and took a sardonic pleasure in lampooning the more solemn aspects of middle-class life. An account of his life and work—*Leben und Werk von Ernst Penzoldt*—was published by Ulla Lentz-Penzoldt in 1962.

Carl Zuckmayer

Translated
by
Sheila Rooke

LOVE STORY

Do you know what she came to mean to the Captain by
loving him?

—Lessing

JOST FREDERSDORFF, captain of cavalry, who, as a young lieutenant, had fought with the Brandenburg cuirassiers at Rossbach
and Leuthen, and, on the very day after the victory at Torgau,
had been decorated for bravery in the face of the enemy and
then promoted, spent New Year's Eve of 1767 in the apartment
of his regimental comrade, Count von Prittwitz.

It was on this evening that he first made the acquaintance of
Lili Schallweis.

Lili Schallweis was no longer in her first youth, but she was
one of those women whose face and figure scarcely change at all
from their mid-twenties to their forties. She had a natural tendency to plumpness, but in spite of this her body had remained
taut and lissom. There was something suggestive of the supple
flexibility of a pedigree filly—not merely about her knees and
ankles, but even in the curve that ran from her hips to her
shoulders and neck. On occasions, when she was tired or out of
sorts, her lower lids were suffused with bluish shadows, and tiny,
fleeting lines hovered round her nostrils and brow. Yet at other
times, especially if the hour was late and the conversation
animated, her face, framed in the soft cascade of her pale blonde
hair, would display the freshness and the robust complexion of a
healthy country child. Her hands, too, with their slender fingers
and beautiful shape, were nevertheless strong and firm rather
than delicate. Little was known of her life, except that she had
originally come from South Germany with a troupe of strolling
players and had lived for some while as the mistress of a high-
ranking officer in Berlin. Later, she had come to Brandenburg with
another officer who had been posted on account of a duel. He,
however, had subsequently married, and since that time she had
lived quite openly from the gifts of her frequently changing lovers.

Now she was the acknowledged mistress of Count Prittwitz.

Count Prittwitz, who was entertaining several bachelor friends this evening—amongst whom Lili Schallweis, as the only woman present, naturally formed the focal point—was what women, then as now, would call "an interesting man". His dark, lean face, that even at the age of fourteen had probably seemed somewhat weary and remote, revealed that mixture of gentleness and selfish harshness that always seems to indicate dark, dangerously repressed undercurrents and passionate, restless feelings, even when nothing of the sort is hidden there. Amongst his comrades he was regarded as a fine fellow, dashing, witty and broadminded. Yet it would never have occurred to any of them to rely on him in a difficult situation, nor to expect any special favour or self-sacrifice from him. This, of course, was what gave him his charm and attraction : one could not be completely sure of him, and yet had no positive reason to distrust him. Sometimes, quite out of the blue, he could assume a child-like sincerity in his enjoyment, contentment and pleasure, an impetuous, heady gaiety that was irresistibly infectious. In particular, he flaunted his success with women with such boisterous self-congratulation, with such undisguised delight in his conquests and in his self-esteem, that people found him scintillating and congenial and no one grudged him the good fortune that was all too easily won. Although still relatively young, he held the rank of major and, in view of his family connections, was considered to be on the threshold of a great career.

Lili Schallweis was assuming to some extent the role of hostess this evening; looking after the guests and also the wine, for the servants had been let off from eleven o'clock so that they could participate in the troops' midnight celebrations. A good deal had been drunk and the talking and laughter grew noisy as the hands of the clock gradually approached twelve, and here and there from the streets of the little town, the hiss of fireworks and the whoops of premature New Year celebrations could be heard.

Although all the guests, apart from Fredersdorff, who rarely visited Prittwitz, had known Lili Schallweis for a long time —one or two of them indeed knew her rather well—the fact of her presence nevertheless gave the evening a special, faintly exciting quality. No one attempted to be too familiar with her, nor did the conversation take on a purely masculine tone, but by no means did the reticence in speech and manners prevail, which is customary in the company of a real lady. It was precisely this mixture of levity and slight reserve, adherence to outward formality despite general good-humoured understanding, that led to a more and more relaxed atmosphere and imperceptibly filled the air with excitement and tingling expectancy. Prittwitz drank manfully to his guests and seemed a little too indifferent when they flirted with Lili. When, however, she went into the kitchen to fetch more drinks, he would hastily lean forward, and, supported by the other connoisseurs, would extol the way she walked, her figure, her skin and other charms.

Young Jost Fredersdorff was a rather monosyllabic onlooker. He was not by nature a very talkative person, although in keeping with his age, he was lively and enjoyed sociable occasions. This evening, however, the atmosphere oppressed him somewhat. Whenever he looked at Lili Schallweis, intentionally or otherwise, not, it is true, in an intimate or challenging manner, but coolly, enquiringly and thoughtfully. Even when he did not look in her direction, he seemed to feel the cool gaze of those eyes on his forehead or eyelids. This disconcerted him so much that he found it difficult to follow the conversation. His face took on an unnaturally aloof, wooden and chilly expression, and at intervals, he was jokingly asked if he was hoping for an audience with the King or a seat in the Supreme Military Court in the New Year. Once when Lili Schallweis crossed the room to trim one of the wall lamps he could not restrain himself from following her with his eyes. Prittwitz suddenly interrupted the others' conversation; leaned back in his chair, and laughingly pointed to him : "Jost's burning his fingers," he remarked in tones of exaggerated amusement. The others grinned. Fredersdorff neither lost his composure nor blushed. "Why not?" he said, after a short pause, inclining his head politely to Lili, who had turned towards them again and was approaching the table. She stopped in front of Jost and looked at him as if her thoughts were elsewhere.

At this moment the chimes which preceded the striking of the hour rang out from the garrison church. "Attention!" cried Prittwitz and hastily filled their glasses. They all rose and even Lili stood still where she was. From the barracks a bugle call blared out with clear, resplendent tones and at the first stroke of midnight the bells began to boom, shots thundered into the air, and the trombones sounded the traditional hymn of praise after a battle. "Long live the King!" cried Prittwitz in a loud, rather rasping voice; all the gentlemen drew their swords and brought the points of the blades together high in the air, which flashed with the naked metal and the gleam of the candles. Lili had stepped back and was looking out of the window until the silence in the room, and the clinking and jangling of weapons as they were replaced in their sheaths, died away. Then, when the glasses were tinkling amidst noisy, laughing cheers and everyone was embracing and exchanging brotherly kisses in accordance with a Masonic custom which at that time was usual amongst the Prussian officers, she went over to Prittwitz and laid her hand on his shoulder. He took her head in his hands and kissed her on the lips. Then he pressed her to him and caressed her arms and throat, her head almost disappearing into his lapels. The others came up and asked if they might clink glasses with her. She turned and her face was serious, pale and clouded. "Now Lili will give you a sisterly kiss," laughed Prittwitz and pushed her towards the man standing nearest her. He placed his hands on her hips and kissed her respectfully on both cheeks, just as if she had been a niece or a cousin of good breeding. But after he had already released her, he seemed to have regrets and quickly bent over her again and kissed her on the mouth. "Bravo!" cried Prittwitz. "Courage, gentlemen!" And now each one kissed her wherever it pleased him and Lili smiled silently. Fredersdorff also kissed her on the mouth, and noticed that she kept her lips firmly closed.

Prittwitz had drawn back the curtains and was opening the window. Outside, the regimental band was drawn up and was playing a tune to each officer outside his apartment. The gentlemen stepped over to the window and acknowledged them, appearing to call down a few words to their drum-major; and assailed by the cold night air, they moved in time to the rousing march. Jost had remained in the room next to Lili, still holding his glass in his right hand and watching the others. Suddenly he felt her grasp his left hand in both hers and press it to her breast. He looked at her. She had closed her eyes and her lips uttered silently a word which he did not catch. This only lasted the space of a heart-beat and then she moved sharply away from him while he went over to the window.

He stopped beside Prittwitz and by chance his eye followed the other's gaze which lingered on the oblique glass pane of the window. Its shining blackness reflected the entire room clearly, and with every detail of light and shade. Fredersdorff stared at the window-pane and it seemed to him that he could still see reflected in it himself and close to him, Lili Schallweis, her hand, her mouth and her closed eyes. In fact he saw only the shimmer of her dress, for she was just leaving the room by the hall-door at the back. Then Prittwitz turned to Fredersdorff and looked him full in the face. The latter returned his gaze calmly and evenly. Prittwitz looked the same as ever, except that in the velvety brown iris of his eye and in the large, dark pupils a triangular, sharp, dead-white light was to be seen. The two of them stayed thus for a moment, whilst the other gentlemen returned to the table and then Prittwitz struck Fredersdorff lightly on his sleeve with the flat of his hand. "Come on," he said and closed the window, pulling the curtains to. From below there still came the beating of drums and the marching of the retreating bandsmen. They went over to the table and sat down. Lili appeared in the door. In her hand she held a large ladle and an aroma of hot red wine and rum wafted into the room. "Here comes the seven-year old!" she cried, and the officers applauded enthusiastically. The "seven-year old" was the name they gave to a particularly potent punch which had helped to shorten the winters they had spent in their quarters during the seven war years, while they waited for Friedrich's tardy paymaster and for the beginning of the spring battles. "You must come now, Count," called Lili to Prittwitz, "I dare not set it alight myself." The punch had to be brought burning on to the table; outside, a sugarloaf, previously saturated in rum, had had arrack poured over it and now hung poised in a pair of tongs over the steaming brew; it was set alight and then the bowl wreathed in blue flames, was raised aloft and carried into the darkened room.

"No," said Prittwitz, "I've had too much to drink. You do it, Jost." The latter shook his head. "I'm not familiar with the art of making punch," he said. "That's news to me," replied Prittwitz, "or else you've forgotten a good deal since Bohemia!" The two of them sat stiffly and looked at each other. "The beautiful alcohol is evaporating all this time," said one of the others, disapprovingly. "There you are, then!" said Prittwitz, without

making a move. "Come on now, captain," called Lili to him
from the door, "the rum won't wait any longer!" Fredersdorff
stood up. "Bravo," shouted a voice, "Jost doesn't lack spirit!"
and was the only one to laugh at his feeble pun. "Make a good
job of it, Jost," Prittwitz called after him as he went towards the
door, and the others bellowed simultaneously "Don't make it too
weak! Make a good blaze! And have plenty of fuel! Don't spare
the powder!" "Put out the light," ordered Prittwitz and the
youngest lieutenant leapt to his feet and extinguished all the
candles in the room. For a moment an almost solemn stillness
reigned. From somewhere outside came the sound of distant
music and the screeching voice of a woman. Then the door
opened, and the bowl of punch with its strong, heavy aroma was
borne aloft by invisible arms, the flames darting and leaping. In
the flickering, uncertain glow, which now spread round the table,
one could see Lili Schallweis' white dress gleaming and next to
her the dark outline of Fredersdorff's tall figure.

"What about the song, then?" said Prittwitz in a bored voice.

A deep bass started up and the others joined in. The song,
which might well have seemed gay and vigorous at some war-
time carousel, now hobbled through the room like a veteran on
crutches.

"Fire has to burn,
And love burns too—"

During the song Lili had gone out, and returned now with a
spill and lit the lamps again. Fredersdorff dipped the ladle in the
gradually dying flames of the punch and filled the thick, tall
punch glasses. "Have you had a taste?" asked Prittwitz. Jost did
not reply; possibly he had not heard the question. He was just
handing a full glass to Lili as she approached the table. Prittwitz
raised his glass and took a sip. "Damnation!" he bellowed suddenly and banged the glass down on the table, so hard that the
hot liquid in the bowl of the glass spattered over the bodice of
Lili's white dress and even stained her throat and arm. She gave
a slight scream and started back. The others jumped up. Everyone exclaimed simultaneously. Jost stood pale and silent before
Prittwitz, who also stood up now. "What do you think you're
doing?" he said in an undertone. "Damnation!" cried Prittwitz
a second time. "It's bitter. Poison!" he bawled, completely beside

himself. "You're out of your mind," said Jost and shrugged his shoulders. Then he turned to Lili Schallweis who was dabbing herself with a cloth. "You must put oil on it," he said. Lili left without a word. There was a red glow on the white satin of her dress. The others stood around in embarrassment.

"Good night," said Fredersdorff after a pause, and bowed to Prittwitz. He did not reply. The others made clumsy attempts to make them both see reason, although none of them really knew what the trouble was all about. Jost turned on his heel and went out. Inside, the Count, who was staring glassily into the air, was besieged with requests to call Jost back. Eventually he seemed to come to a decision and hurried along the corridor after Jost. Everyone expected a prompt, gentlemanly reconciliation and so stayed behind laughing and drinking. Jost had flung his cloak round his shoulders and donned his hat. He was about to leave the apartment and already had his hand on the door-knob. Then Lili appeared from an adjacent door, also clad in cloak and hat. "Take me home," she said to Jost. "Please—," she added. Before he could reply, Prittwitz came out and stopped in front of them. "Do you have money on you?" he said to Jost. "It'll cost you something." Jost moved half a step towards him. "Go to hell!" he said loudly. And then, opening the door for Lili, he left with her without glancing back.

It was a clear winter's night. The moon had already faded and the stars were flickering brightly. The streets were swept free of snow. Only at the corners of the houses and by the lamp-posts were some frozen, dirty-grey mounds to be seen. Lights were still burning in many windows, but now that the first hour of the New Year was past, it had grown quiet again in the town. Occasionally they encountered a few masked revellers returning home after a party. Now and then there was the steady, echoing tread of a patrol on guard duty.

Fredersdorff did not know where Lili Schallweis lived. She had taken his arm and he left it to her to direct them. Their hands touched as they walked. Neither of them wore gloves, but they did not notice the cold. After a while Lili thrust her fingers between his, which he closed firmly over her knuckles. The palms of their hands were pressed close together and they could feel the pulsing of their blood at every step. They walked on for a long time without speaking. Soon they were in the suburbs, where the houses stood detached, amidst tiny vegetable gardens. The cobbled surface gave way to a narrow and uneven road. Eventually there were no more houses to be seen; a broken-down fence ran a little further into the country and then there were only flat fields, covered with a thin layer of snow, which glimmered softly in the starlight. The tracks of a carriage stretched straight ahead, leading towards the dark outlines of a pinewood. In the silence their boots crunched and rang on the ground, and when they trod in a rut, the brittle, splintering ice snapped. From the town they heard the church clock striking; it sounded faint and silvery. Lili stopped for a moment and listened.

"Do you live much further out?" asked Jost suddenly.

"No," she replied, laughing. "I live somewhere quite different. Over there, where we've come from!"

"I thought so," he said. "But it's glorious to walk like this."

"Yes—it's glorious."

"Aren't you tired?" he then asked, as she was still standing motionless.

"Please just let's go as far as the wood!" she said, "It's not much further."

They walked on. They had not loosened their handclasp. The wood towered gloomily above them. More and more sky disappeared behind the back of hunched tree-tops, which gradually thinned out. Now they could see a pale streak where the coach road penetrated the trees. To the right of it stood a sign-post, which resembled a cross. They went up to it and stopped.

"I thought it was a crucifix," said Lili.

"No," Jost said, with a smile, for he knew every landmark in the district. "We don't have any here."

"Where I come from, you see them everywhere," she replied, "statues of the Virgin as well."

"You won't find any here," he repeated. Then he looked at her. She was still gazing at the sign-post. He put his free arm round her and pressed her to him. She looked up at him and bent her head back. He kissed her. Her skin was cold, even her lips were frigid in the icy air. He held his mouth a long time on hers until her lips thawed and clung firmly to his. Their faces pressed against each other and they did not move. Through the fur and the heavy coat each was aware of the other's body and pounding heart.

"Come on," she said after a long time had elapsed, "Let's go home."

This time he took her arm and slid his own beneath it.

They strode out smartly, sometimes stumbling over bumpy furrows in the frozen sand, but always managing to end up in step. Above the rooftops of the town, which sloped down to meet the gently undulating fields, rose the mighty flashing figure of Orion, the huntsman of the winter sky. With feet apart, he straddled the rim of the world, his loins, with their blazing girdle, sloping sideways; the short sword flamed earthwards, while his starry fists stretched the bow, aiming far out into the northern dome of the night.

They had to pass Prittwitz' house, where the lights were still burning. They went past almost without noticing. A few streets further on, in the other direction, Lili stopped outside a door and rummaged for her key. "Here it is," she said. Jost helped her to open up and then followed her upstairs. Down below, beside the front door, was a grocer's shop and an aroma of burnt coffee, cinnamon, cloves, nutmeg and other strong spices pervaded the stairway. Both floors served as storage rooms, apart from the two front rooms of the top storey, which Lili had rented. At night or on holidays, she was quite alone in the house. She had no lady's maid or maid servant living with her, but a housemaid came every morning and left when her work was done. As it was very dark on the staircase, Lili had half-turned to him as she mounted and led him by the hand. Once upstairs she opened the door of the landing in the gloom and they stepped into a little hall, dimly lit by a smoky, glittering oil lamp. Lili turned the wick up, so that a kitchen, with open doorway, was now visible on the left hand side. Straight ahead lay her room, and she let Jost in, still clad in his hat and cloak. The living-room lay in darkness and all that could be seen were the outlines of a large, tiled stove, still radiating heat. Without pausing or speaking, she led him through into her bedroom and removed his cloak in the gloom. Then she left him and he heard her hanging up both their cloaks somewhere. The darkness in the room must have been intensified by very heavy curtains, because he could not see a hand in front of him. Lili then went out and returned at once with a burning candle beneath a narrow, cut-glass shade. She placed the light on a small table near the bed, then came up to him and stroked his hair. He wanted to kiss her, but she drew away from him and left the room once more. He surveyed the room: a wide bed stood against the back wall. It was of dark polished wood with the head and foot carved in the shape of a boat. The floor was covered by a thick velvety carpet in plain, deep red. The stove had been built in between the two rooms, so that it was lit in the living-room, but also heated the bedroom. Between the bed and the window a section of the room was curtained off, and consequently, when the curtains were drawn, no light penetrated from outside. In the corner stood a kind of card table with a smooth, patterned surface and two upholstered wing chairs. Jost drew in the air through his nostrils and was aware of the extremely delicate, indisputably feminine scent of the room. It seemed to come from the silk bedcover and from a cupboard with its door ajar. Jost went to the door. From the adjoining room came a smell of withering flowers and a slight scent of wood-smoke. Lili seemed to be in the kitchen. He could hear her moving about. He unbuckled his sword and stood it in the corner. Then he sat down on one of the wing chairs and waited. The next moment, Lili came in, bringing a bottle of Tokay, which she had opened, and two glasses. She put the wine and the glasses in front of him on the little table, and sat down opposite him. Not a word had passed between them since they had entered the house. Jost raised his glass to her and started to say something. But, with a smile, she quickly put a finger to her lips. Then they clinked glasses and she drank a little. They sat there for a while, looking at each other. It was so still that they could hear their own breathing. After a time, a grandfather clock struck in the adjoining room. Lili's lips moved silently, counting the strokes. The clock struck three. She rose, went to the cupboard, rummaged a little, drew out a red silk dressing-gown, closed the cupboard door and then disappeared behind the curtains, taking the candle with her. The room lay in semi-darkness and the light flickered with a yellowish glow through a crack in the curtains. Jost heard her undressing and the rustle of her falling clothes conjured up a strange feeling of unreality, which profoundly excited him and at the same time gently calmed the quiet thumping of his heart. When she returned, barefooted, clasping the red dressing-gown across her breast, she left the light behind the curtain so that the room remained almost in darkness. Without looking at him, she went to the bed and drew back the cover. Then she let the dressing-gown slip to the ground and lay down. "Come here," she said softly, almost in a whisper. Then, with a quick movement, she pressed her head into the pillow and remained thus, so that he could only see her hair and her bare arm. Quietly he undressed in the dark, and approached her bed. She held open the bed clothes a little without looking up. He lay down beside her and felt the warmth of her body. Very gently she stroked his arm and drew him nearer to her. His heart pounded and breathing heavily he kissed her closed eyelids, as she raised her face a little. She wound her arms round his neck and they both lay motionless, clinging to each other and breathing quietly. Although his pulse was racing, he felt a luxurious, childlike fatigue—a tingling, bitter-sweet languor throughout his whole body such as he had never known before. It was as if he were floating in a dream and as if his body would lie there weightlessly for ever, gradually losing itself in the steady rhythm of their breathing. He lay there with his eyes open, and watched the pale reflection of the hidden candle on the ceiling, as it grew fainter and fainter. After a while he noticed that she was asleep. A little later his own eyes closed and he glided into a sleep which, even while he was still awake, had flooded him with calm and release.

Their sleep seemed unfathomable and boundless. From time to time they awoke, but without the usual wrench of waking, and only to drift off again, secure in the knowledge of their closeness and seclusion. It was the sort of sleep that children imagine of animals in their lairs or the sleep of seeds benenath the snow—only sweeter, more blessed, and more rapturous. They hardly even changed their positions. They lay motionless, cast in the enchanted form in which this cradle of sleep had first moulded them.

Jost, who, like many soldiers, had cultivated an inner alarm mechanism, which woke him at the hour that was required by his duty, opened his eyes as the grandfather clock in the next room announced simultaneously with the chimes of the garrison church, that morning had come. He felt himself clear-headed, fresh, charged with a current of vigorous strength. In his finger tips he could feel a pricking and tingling sensation as when a shower of sparks fly from a wand. He lay with his head nestling in her armpit and with every breath that she took, his lips touched her breast. It was dark in the room; the candle had long since burnt out; only a narrow strip of opal dawn light penetrated the slit in the curtains. Suddenly desire and a wild tenderness made him tremble and almost overcame him. But he remained motionless and listened to her gentle breathing, as he held his own breath. Then she raised her shoulders and propped herself up on her free arm. "You're awake," she said and he felt her looking at him in the darkness. He groped for her hair and covered her face with kisses. Then he sat up. "What is it?" she whispered. He told her that, in accordance with his orders, he had to return to barracks to be at the head of his squadron for the New Year's Day service. "And after that?" she asked him. Then he had to pay his commander a New Year's visit and afterwards dine with the other officers in the casino. But then? she wanted to know. Then he would be free until the morning of the third, because the second fell on a Sunday. "Come back then!" she said. He kissed her and got up. While he dressed hastily in the dark, she had also risen and had brought in a fresh candle. She stood now before him in her red dressing-gown, which was open in front, displaying the loose folds of her night-gown. She handed him the light and the keys of her apartment and the front door. Then she placed her hands on his shoulders. "You will come back?" she asked once more. "Of course!" he said. "When?" "As soon as I'm free. Round about four." "That's late," she replied. "But I'm looking forward to it." Whilst he buckled on his equipment she fetched his cloak from the corner behind the cupboard and placed it round his shoulders. Then she went round and fastened the cloak in front. She bent her head back and he kissed her on the lips. Then, as he hurried away, he heard her return to bed.

Count Prittwitz did not appear in the mess the next afternoon. He made the excuse that he was indisposed. Since he was not the only one in this state the day after New Year's Eve, everyone laughed and made jokes about it. All this scarcely penetrated Jost's consciousness; he lived in a twilit world in which he moved, ate, drank, spoke and answered mechanically, until at last, after an eternity of meaningless being and doing, which he at once forgot, he found himself alone and completely composed again. His one thought was to return to her as quickly as possible. But in his apartment, as he changed his clothes, it occurred to him that he should take her something, and in haste and confusion he hunted through all his things. Everything edible that he found he crammed into a leather wallet—a few apples from a friend's orchard, nuts, and some Christmas fare, a bottle of Danzig brandy and a jar of preserved fruit. On the stairs it occurred to him that he also possessed something valuable, a tiny cross set with precious stones, on a golden chain, which he had been given as a present in the third year of the war. But in the very same moment he decided not to take it with him, for he was afraid she might misunderstand such a costly present. And when, after some slight hesitation, he had unlocked the door of her apartment, and was standing alone in the tiny entrance hall, he left the wallet with the presents in the kitchen before entering, for he suddenly felt ridiculous with his apples and nuts. He knocked first on the living-room door and as he heard nothing, opened it. During the night and early morning, this room had lain in darkness, so that now, with its bright furniture, it struck him as strange and hostile. He hesitated for a moment, as if filled with foreboding. Then he went to the bedroom door and knocked again. From inside he heard her voice and the spell was broken. "Come in!" she called. He opened the door quickly. Daylight flooded the room, which already seemed as familiar to him as if he had spent his whole life there. The curtains between the bed and the window were drawn back revealing a kind of dressing-room, the main wall of which was covered by a huge mirror. She was standing in this room, quite naked, her hair pinned up. On the floor at her feet, was a shallow wooden tub in which she had presumably stood to wash herself. The red dressing-gown lay across a chair, her clothes from the night before were strewn carelessly around the dressing-table. She was standing with her back to him and had glanced over her shoulder. Now she turned round to face him and he saw this movement reflected in the large mirror. At the same time, however, his glance took in every detail of the room so sharply and precisely, that he was never able to forget it. She had probably been in bed all this time, because nothing had been tidied up. But the maid must have been here, for the bottle and glasses had disappeared from the card-table and in their place stood a coffee-tray with a half-empty cup and some biscuits. Her cloak still hung where she had placed it yesterday evening with his own. Jost closed the door slowly behind him, then he took off his cloak and hung it in the same place. He put his sword there too, and then walked calmly up to her. She stretched out her hands to him, but he clasped her body in his arms. In so doing, he could see himself and all his movements, but was so overwhelmed by his feelings for her, that he acted almost unconsciously. He stroked her hips and with his mouth, felt the soft resilience of her breast, the down in her armpits, the polished sleekness of her shoulders. The perfume of her skin overwhelmed him, and his whole body became tense with the urgency of his desire. He seized her roughly, almost violently, and she relaxed in his grasp with a tender, eager willingness. As he picked her up she touched his face with moist, parted lips. He carried her to the bed, drew the curtains so that it was nearly dark, and came to her.

This happened at twilight on the first day of the New Year. Outside it had become warmer; low, billowing clouds swept over the town. Darkness fell swiftly and in the night it began to snow. The fluttering, swirling snow veiled the houses with such a muffled, breathless silence that the hourly chimes of the church clock were scarcely audible. All living things seemed to be banished behind the double-windows of the rooms, which were thickly encrusted with snow. And everything inside, breathing, throbbing, flaring up, reaching a climax and dying away, seemed as if sunk to the bed of the sea, enfolded in the black waters of the deep, eternally removed and severed from time and place. The next day too, dawned sluggishly and late, the sky would not brighten, the clamour of the church bells was drowned in the snow clouds and was conveyed as a far-off, indistinct rumble. Then night fell again, it had stopped snowing, the starry sky sparkled with the cold fire of frost, and ferns of ice splayed over the windows, ran riot, and crystallised; while solitary sleigh-bells tinkled thinly and then died away. Hardly sleeping at all, yet in an oblivion deeper and more powerful than intoxication and more nebulous than a dream—hardly closing their eyes, but sometimes groping through unheeded hours in the midst of semi-consciousness—almost continuously embracing, caressing, delighting each other in silence, only occasionally exchanging in shy, quiet, private whispers, words of the deepest intimacy—they passed through the eternity of this encounter—a night, a day and then another night—as if after this, no return to forgotten times were possible—as if, its end was also the end of their own mortal lives. Sometimes their eyes discerned the onset of twilight, without their knowing whether it heralded the dusk or the dawn. Although feet shuffled in the next room, and knuckles rapped cautiously on the locked door; fresh wood crackled in the living-room stove and a tray with gently rattling cups was placed outside; nothing, not a living sound actually penetrated their threshold. When they parted from one another for a brief interval, it was as if they were sleepwalking and had never wakened; their separation was noticeable only by a new desire and a new passion, which drove them into each other's arms again. When he left her early on the second day, he went silently and without any farewell, for it was only a shadow of himself which glided into a lost world; his whole being remained intact in her room.

His boots creaked strangely on the bare wooden steps and he was almost startled by his spurs clinking on the stone flags of the downstairs hall. He put out the light and placed it in the corner behind the door, then stepped out and locked up again from outside.

The stars had already grown dim and a long, reddish streak hung over the rooftops. The sky above it was bluish-grey, like fish-scales, gleaming with the reflection of frozen snow. The footprints of a man in riding-boots, who must have gone to the front door and then walked up and down many times, ran in a zigzag line across the street, the bumpy cobbles of which were completely shrouded in snow. Jost did not notice them and strode right over them, making fresh, dark prints with every step in the glittering surface of the virgin, sharply crunching snow. His face smarted from the biting cold; it felt like a wild, searing caress against his skin. His breath billowed from his mouth in white steam, like the clouds of smoke which issue from the nostrils of horses. The peace, the ever stronger morning light and the solitude at this hour of the day filled him with a miraculously serene composure, a flow of confidence, an entirely new sensation of breadth, freedom, unrestricted buoyancy and strength which spread into every fibre of his body. He quickened his pace, the blood surging in his ears. In his breast he seemed to hear the booming and resounding music of a mighty army advancing. He pictured himself several years younger, riding into the glittering turmoil of a battle-morning—with that radiant sharpness and clarity of vision, which has almost overstepped the bounds of human thought and emotion. Even in the bare barrack yard, at the customary trumpet-call for reveille, in the pungent, steamy atmosphere of the stable and on the springy back of his gently trotting horse, this readiness, this strong, silent alertness, this free irrevocable alignment of all his powers, remained with him for better or worse.

He met Prittwitz at the barrack gate, as he returned from duty. They greeted each other briefly. But in the next few days when he went to his small apartment on the crown property near the barracks, which he visited now only for short periods in order to change his clothes, he heard frequently from his batman that Count Prittwitz had been there and had asked after him. And so, about a week after the New Year, he decided to go and see the Count himself and render him an account and an explanation. When he entered, Major von Prittwitz was sitting on a narrow silk-covered stool at his spinet; his left hand tinkled restlessly at little runs and arpeggios, while, with his right, he waved Jost to an armchair. Then he rang for the servant and ordered him to bring an Italian wine, glasses and biscuits. He poured the wine himself and clapped Jost on the shoulder with his free hand as he did so. "It's nice of you to come," he said, "several times I've wanted to visit you—but it seems you don't live in your apartment any more!" "I heard that you had called," replied Jost without stiffness, but none the less in a deliberately reserved tone of voice "and it's for that reason that I'm here." Prittwitz raised his glass slowly. "Your health," he said. "And yours!" answered Jost. They drank. Suddenly Prittwitz laughed in his face quite easily, in a happy, boyish,

uninhibited manner. "You old scoundrel!" he cried and laughingly bent towards him. "Aren't we really ridiculous? Should
we poison the wine just for this?" "No," said Jost and smiled.
"Not even the hot punch!" Prittzwitz stood up and stretched
out his hand to him. "I was crazy," he said, "and you've made
us even. Are we quits?" "Quits!" said Jost and pressed his
hand. "Well, thank God for that," exclaimed Prittwitz softly,
"now perhaps we can have some sensible talk." And he winked
at him, as he placed his hands fondly on his shoulders. "Are
you happy, my boy?" "Yes, I'm happy!" replied Jost seriously.
"I don't bear you any grudge," said Prittwitz and he poured
more wine, and played a trill on the keys. "It wouldn't have
lasted much longer with me," he said. "And after all, she's
destined to bring us all happiness. Each according to his rank!"
He laughed and stopped playing trills. "Change the guard!"
he called and saluted in the manner of one soldier relieving
another. Jost stood up and said quietly, "Please don't talk like
that. I consider her as my wife." "What do you mean?" said
Prittwitz and stared at him. "She is my wife," repeated Jost,
meeting his gaze firmly. It seemed as if Prittwitz would burst
out laughing, but he remained silent and his face twitched.
"Tell me," he asked after a while, "have you never had an
affair with a woman before?" "Yes, of course," said Jost. "But
I have never been loved before." "Does she love you?" asked
Prittwitz. "Yes," replied Jost, simply. "Well, congratulations,"
said Prittwitz cynically and with resentment. "Thank you,"
said Jost. For a time they were silent, then Jost held out his
hand to him. "Goodbye," he said. "What a minute," said Prittwitz, without taking his hand. He paced up and down the
room. Then he stopped in front of him. "Are you really living
with her?" he asked. "Yes," said Jost. "I only come to the barracks when I'm on duty." "Are you aware that people are
already talking?" said Prittwitz. "They can, for all I care," replied Jost. "But I must go now." "Very well," said Prittwitz,
grasping his hand and holding it fast for a moment. "Don't do
anything foolish, Jost," he said. "Get it out of your system, but
then be yourself again!" "I am myself," said Jost with a smile,
"more than I ever was. And I'm glad that there's nothing to
come between us any more." "I'm glad too," said Prittwitz and
let go of his hand. He would not meet his gaze any longer, and

after Jost had gone, he stood motionless for a time, the tip of
his tongue playing in the corner of his mouth.

Towards the end of the winter, when the melted snow gurgled
in the gutters and the mild wind carried with it a tang of puddles
and acrid birch bark, the famous Viennese Opera Company
Coronelli-Schlumberger came to the town and gave a guest
performance in the large hall of the hotel "The Elector", which
was normally used for balls and festivities. Since the orchestra
had to sit in the auditorium at the foot of the hastily constructed
stage, the chairs for the audience were arranged in ever-
widening semi-circles which took advantage of all available
space. The whole room was surrounded by a type of opera box.
These were built on to a raised dais and separated from each
other by small, low partitions and had been largely reserved by
officers of the cuirassiers. The musicians tuned their instruments,
and these chirping, trilling, plucking, scraping and fluting sounds,
as well as the flickering of footlights through a slit in the swaying
of the lowered curtain and the murmur of numerous semi-
audible voices, generated waves of unusual excitement in the
room. In the meantime the gentlemen in dress uniform, many
accompanied by their ladies and others in smaller groups with
their comrades took their seats in the boxes and each observed
the others through lorgnettes and opera glasses. Soon everyone's
attention, which had been first directed at the commanding
officer, who was seated in the centre with his wife and three
daughters, was directed to a small box at one side in which stood
two single chairs. Captain Fredersdorff had appeared in it and
accompanying him, in a magnificent fur-trimmed silk gown, was
Lili Schallweis. He waited until she had sat down, placed round
her shoulders the shawl which he had been carrying on his arm,
then stepped up to the railing and acknowledged first the commander and then the other ladies and gentlemen politely and
without a trace of embarrassment. Before they could make up
their minds how to react in such a situation and before the hostile glances of the ladies and girls, who had heard a great deal
about the life and notoriety of this woman, could penetrate each
detail of her appearance, the lights dimmed, the short, sharp
swell of voices gave way to complete silence and the orchestra
began to play the overture. Jost's chair stood somewhat further

back than hers and after the curtain was raised, he could see her
hair gleaming softly in the reflection of the stage-lights and her
pale, motionless profile turned towards the stage, completely
absorbed in the music. Her hand lay next to his on the arm of her
chair, but he did not touch it. From her hand, from her body,
he sensed a profound remoteness; it seemed to him as if the very
sounds which reached his own ears separated her from him in an
uncanny and inexplicable way. An opera by Gluck was being
performed, and when the great vocal quartet began, he saw her
lips move silently and a dark, self-absorbed gleam come into her
eyes and without understanding why, he was filled with a sudden burning, searing pain. Then, almost as if by chance, her
hand touched his and groped for his and she pressed his fingers
in a passionate, yet tender clasp. Without turning she acknowledged him with a scarcely perceptible movement of her lips, her
bent neck and her averted gaze. And at last, as if some key, some
concentration, some outlet had been necessary, the enchantment,
the thrill, the subtle strength and the elusive realisation of this
intangible element, this fantasy made substance, filled his whole
being. When the lights came on again, they sat next to each
other in silence for a while without raising their eyes. Later,
during the interval, when the audience rose in order to greet one
another from their boxes and in the corridors outside the hall,
Jost noticed—and he had already anticipated and calmly
reckoned with this—that people avoided his greeting, glancing
from behind fans, over shoulders and between fingers, weighing
up the woman at his side and finding her wanting. He seemed
indifferent and unaffected and they talked quietly to each other,
bending over their opera programme. Prittwitz, who had to pass
very close to them, felt their gaze riveted on him and he greeted
them briefly and formally. Then, outside, after he had kissed the
hands of the wife and daughters of the commander, the latter
drew him by the arm to one side. While the ladies vainly tried
to catch a few words they whispered together, Prittwitz with an
eager, anxious but somewhat impatient expression; the commander seriously, indecisively and without any visible emotion.
A few other gentlemen approached and were drawn into the discussion, which had now become more heated and betrayed its
theme by occasional ejaculations. But the colonel warned them
off with a shake of the head and returned to the ladies, while

the younger officers collected round Prittwitz, who had this evening invited several regimental friends and the members of the Opera Company to a small reception at his apartment after the performance. Even there, although people did not arrive till nearly midnight, the conversation revolved mainly around Fredersdorff's inexplicable behaviour and Lili Schallweis. It was a topic that concerned the guests, particularly the women artistes, so that it was easy to make conversation with them; for it transpired that Lili Schallweis had been a singer in this very Opera Company, and had left it only a few years ago. Herr Schlumberger, their manager, who, Prittwitz assured the other gentlemen, was completely in the picture and would disappear immediately after the meal, insisted repeatedly that neither before nor since had he had in his troupe, such a worthy and good-hearted woman as Lili Schallweis. Clearly this was only intended to annoy Madame Coronelli; who as leading lady of the company, spoke with patronising indulgence and devastating sympathy of her former colleague, claiming that she had always wished her every good fortune. Little Fräulein Zuckerstätter, a tough, scatterbrained person, whose Viennese accent and contrived spontaneity affected the Prussian gentlemen like an exotic drug, expressed herself particularly forcefully, however. She could have no respect for women who flaunted themselves, she cried, and the more so when an artiste was involved, although, she added, there were artistes and artistes. People agreed with her politely, although basically they themselves did not recognise such a clear distinction; and after supper when Herr Schlumberger had left, accompanied by the tired, sleepy tenor and the bass-buffo, still thirsty and resisting energetically,—the assembled company refrained from any further clarification and from too sharp a definition of terms. Finally Madame Coronelli was taken home by a very young lieutenant, the other ladies were driven back to their lodgings under male protection and little Fräulein Zuckerstätter had forgotten the key of the inn where she was staying and had to spend the night at Prittwitz' apartment. When, next day, he missed his valuable snuff-box and a gold watch, his impulse was to hush the matter up, but his batman, and particularly his charlady felt themselves under suspicion and so fetched the police before he could prevent them. That very afternoon his belongings had been returned to him and little Fräulein Zuckerstätter was relegated to a police-cell.

Towards evening as Jost was hurrying along the accustomed road to Lili's house, duty over and orders received, he bumped into a strange, shabby-looking man wearing a soft hat and a cloak just outside the door. As soon as he caught sight of Jost he stepped off the pavement, turned to face him, doffed his hat, and with a hasty bow muttered "Schlumberger!" Jost took no notice and hurried quickly past. Not until he reached the hall, between the empty packing cases and the piled up sacks of groceries, did it occur to him to connect this figure with Lili. He stopped and reflected for a moment, then went on his way. But something made him stop again on the first landing. He listened and held his breath, then was aware of his heart gradually beginning to pound with anxiety. Musical notes wafted down to him, at first softly, far away, then suddenly all at once swelling to a climax; dying down again almost as if groping tentatively for the clear line of a melody, then delicately elaborating on this with sustained and trilled notes. It was the first time he heard her sing. He had never thought of her as a singer. Slowly he mounted the stairs until he stood outside the door of her apartment. He waited indecisively, weighing the key in his hand. The voice broke off suddenly, then started up again in a mighty, triumphant crescendo. He considered whether he should go in or not. Then he heard the faint sound of the chimes striking the hour. It occurred to him that she would be expecting him at this time, must be expecting him, and that he was not crossing the threshold of a secret, jealously guarded private life, but that she, because she was expecting him and waiting for his arrival, was singing, singing for him—and this image buoyed him up so much, that he almost laughed at his hesitation and at his gloomy fears. He turned the key and went in. The melody broke off as he opened the drawing-room door; her voice tailed off into a gentle, restrained laugh, which seemed to him just as unfamiliar as the music. She was standing amid suitcases, one of which was open and half unpacked. A slight smell of silk, calico, lavender and a touch of mothballs filled the air. On chairs and couches, even on the floor and across the wide open suitcase lid lay costumes, scarves and theatrical wardrobe pieces of all kinds. Right across the table lay a page's costume adorned with lace and with knee breeches of yellow silk. She had a tiny, flowered bodice in her hand and was holding it up to the light and examining it. As he entered and approached her, she let it fall to the ground. "Here," she said, stretching out a hand to him and pointing with the other to various costumes lying all around : "Lucinda! Rosamunde! Coelestin!" Then she caught his glance, fell silent and looked him full in the face. He walked up to her and embraced her. "What is all this?" he asked softly. "It's my old company," she said, "I travelled with them for years. The manager was here. He lost one of his members, who used to sing my parts today. He asked me if I would like to take over, would like to join them." Jost fixed his gaze on her hands. His face registered nothing. "Do you want to?" he asked, his voice steady. "I don't know if I'm still able to," she said. "I was very ill when I gave up. I had hardly any voice left." Jost involuntarily took a step back, then plunged his hands into his pockets. "And if it were possible," he then said, "would you want to go away?" As she did not reply he repeated his question after a time—"Would you want to leave me?" She stood motionless, her head slightly bent; the lamplight cast shadows over her eyes, then she raised her head and the tiny lines at the corners of her mouth stood out sharply. "I think it would be best," she said slowly. "Why?" he asked. "Because it won't work," she replied. "Why not?" he repeated, his voice unchanged. "Because it won't work," she said again. "Why not?" he asked for the third time. "We shouldn't have gone yesterday evening," she said painfully. She turned slightly. He came up behind her, took her head in his hands, and turned her face towards him. It was bathed in silent tears. "I won't leave you," he said firmly. "Never." She turned rapidly, clutched at him, buried her face in his neck and smothered it in the lapels of his coat. He could feel her teeth tearing the material of his shirt. He bent his mouth towards her head and murmured into her dishevelled hair. His words were lost, drowned by their breathing, the surging of their blood and the pounding of their hearts. Their hands met, touched, pressed and tortured each other. Then he felt her mouth seeking his, was aware of her face looming large, with closed eyes before him, her knees weakening and of her body drawing him to the ground.

In the next few days, the commander of the Brandenburg Cuirassiers, an elderly experienced warrior, who came of a middle-class military family, decided, after conversation with some of his officers, who had informed him of their wives' complaints and their personal displeasure, to have a private talk with the young captain to indicate the unsuitability of his companion at the opera and reprimand him in a friendly manner for the dubious change in his way of life. However, before the orderly could reach him with the command, Captain Jost von Fredersdorff sent word to the commander and presented him with an application for permission to marry the singer Lili Schallweis.

On the second day after Easter, Jost called for her in a carriage, which he drove himself and took her out into the bright, sun-drenched countryside. Larks, like stones thrown at the sky, were already hovering and warbling in the silky air of this April day; flocks of starlings twittered and whistled on the edges of the barn gables and from the distant marsh meadows came the cheeping call of young peewits. Here and there the canal was veiled by young birches and willows. On her breast Lili wore a bunch of freshly picked violets that a boy had sold them on the main road. Jost made no mention of their destination, but it was easy to see that he had some purpose in making this special and unusual excursion. He said little, but seemed rather pleasurably excited and sometimes a gleam of calm expectation was discernible in his eyes. The further they went from the town and the villages bordering on it into the flat countryside, and the worse the road became, and the more monotonously the unending view extended across the wet meadows, fields with their feathery crop of young seedlings and distant woods, the happier and more high-spirited he became. He laughed a great deal, would let her take the reins of the horse as it lashed out in pleasure at its own strength and at being in the fresh air, at the same time teaching her the rudiments of driving; and would suddenly, with great emotion, point out to her places of note and interest in the district, which could not be distinguished from similar landmarks in other districts—the sails of a windmill on the horizon, a church tower far away beyond the hills, an old stork's nest on the mossy roof of a farmhouse, and finally the façade of a bright, castle-like building which shone out from between the elm trees. He tugged at the reins and brought the carriage to a halt. Lili fell silent and looked at him. She sensed that something held him back which she could not coax from him by questions. She moved closer to him and waited. "That's my family home," he said at last, pointing with the handle of his whip to the manor house, beside which could now be seen the domestic buildings and the stables. "And it's here that we're going to live," he added after a while. She still said nothing, but pressed herself against him. "When my parents died," he said in a tone of calm explanation, "I had already entered the Army. I had no brothers and so a cousin of mine who had grown up with us, took over the estate. But I can lay claim, as an heir, to half of it. I am now going to take advantage of this. It will be ours." "Will your cousin give it back to you?" she asked. "He'll have to!" laughed Jost. "And apart from that, we've been friends since we were children. I want to give him a surprise." He released the brake and was about to drive up. She placed her hand on his arm. "Wouldn't you rather go to see him alone?" she asked, "I can get out here and go for a walk." And as his face clouded she added weakly, with a smile, "and survey our estate!" "We'll do that together later!" said Jost and seemed reassured. "But now you must come with me!" he said in a voice that was almost commanding, and all at once he drove the horse into a trot. They turned into the bare avenue which led up to the stone steps of the simple old manor house. "This is the Wendlitz estate," he said, "it has a few thousand acres of arable land, meadows, woods and pasture." "It's beautiful," she said softly. A groom in his shirt-sleeves ran towards them from the stable and held the horse's bridle. Jost looked at him closely, but he did not seem to recognise him—he was only a youngster. "Are your master and mistress at home?" Jost asked. "Yes, indeed, sir," replied the servant, "shall I unharness the carriage?" At that moment the main door above the curve of the stairway opened, and a man in riding-boots stepped out, wearing an open, military-looking jacket with a high collar, which he was buttoning up with his left hand. Lili stared hypnotised at the slim, almost lean figure framed in the doorway, who shaded his eyes with his hand, as he examined the new arrivals in astonishment. There stood Jost's double, except that he was somewhat older, harder, more reserved and less animated—as perhaps he might have been portrayed on a graveyard monument, if he had died a heroic death on the battlefield—and he seemed to exude such unfriendliness, and unapproachable reserve that her blood ran cold. "Fritz!" called Jost and cracked his whip. The other may have recognised him immediately, but his face did not change its expression. He stood still a moment or two longer, then surveyed the two of them with a composed glance, like a man who is accustomed to weigh up events and their effect in a flash. Then he came down the steps with an unhurried but buoyant tread. Jost had jumped from the carriage and helped her out. Now he turned with outstretched hand to the master of the house, who clasped it and shook it in a friendly fashion. "I'm glad to see you here on a visit, Jost," he said, "it's a long time since I've seen you." Then with a cool, questioning look he turned to the lady. "This is my cousin, Fritz," said Jost warmly and steered him somewhat nearer to her. "Fritz von Fredersdorff. And this is my fiancée." The master of the house bowed low over her hand, then stepped back and, with a movement of his arm invited her to lead the way up the steps. Turning, he called to the servant, "Unharness the horse and feed it, Kilian!" He turned to Jost, who was ahead of him—"Can you stay for an hour?" "It all depends," he replied and half-turned with a grin, "perhaps longer." One of the older servants appeared in the doorway and bowed low to Jost with expressions of pleasure. Jost held out his hand. "Well, how are things with you, Martin?" he asked. "Very well, sir!" the servant murmured and was about to back away. The master of the house detained him with a look. "Show our visitors into the reception-room!" he commanded, as they entered a dimly-lit hall adorned with antlers and ancient weapons. From somewhere to the left— apparently from one of the corridors which led to the reception-room—a woman's voice and the laughter of children could be heard distinctly. Jost turned in this direction. "Your wife?" he asked. "My wife is unfortunately not at home," replied his cousin without any change in his voice. "She's gone to the country with the children and won't be back before evening." Jost stopped and looked at him. He returned his gaze evenly and then, turning to Lili he said, "Please excuse me for a moment," and disappeared quickly to the left. The servant opened a door on the right. They entered a room whose severe furnishing combined with the presence of a desk gave it an office-like air. Jost stopped at the door, opened it a crack, then closed it again.

"Damnation!" he said and stamped his foot. His face was pale, though his eyes flamed. Lili glanced quickly at him, then tore her eyes away from him. She went to the window and looked out on to a bare garden in early spring, adorned with the branches of fir-trees. The blood welled up into her temples and at the same time an involuntary and unexpected spirit of defiance, rage and angry indignation arose in her. She was deeply shocked, for she was aware that this budding hatred was not directed at these strangers but against him, the man who was her lover. She sensed how much he was suffering as he stood there with clenched hands in the doorway and a blind, cruel hostility which she was powerless to resist, stirred in her. She pressed her hands to her forehead and silently intoned all the tender names and words, all the good, intimate things that they shared, like a litany on his behalf. But in doing so she could not really recall him, just as one is not always able when saying a prayer, to be aware of the one to whom it is addressed. Behind her she heard a voice, that was so sharp, strange and cold, that at first she could not distinguish it from that of the cousin. "Since your wife prefers," he said to the latter, who had entered unheard, "not to meet my fiancée, I do not wish to detain you any longer." "I've had some refreshment prepared for you," replied the other, "can't I persuade you?" He turned unmistakably in her direction, but she would not face him. "No thank you," said Jost rather drily, "we'll do without. I would like to request only a short tête-à-tête with you." "As you wish," said the other after a short interval. "May I ask you to take a seat in the drawing-room for the time being?" "I should prefer to wait outside," said Lili and indicated with an indeterminate movement of her arm the garden which lay beyond the window. "You'll be cold," said the master of the house, politely. "No," she replied, "I'll take a walk." He bowed slightly, opened the door for her and beckoned to the servant outside. She inclined her head and went out. The cousin shut the door and turned to Jost. He was standing at the desk, one hand resting on its writing top. They looked at each other without saying a word. Then the master of the house said: "You must understand, Jost. I know Lili Schallweis by sight. It's quite out of the question for my wife to be introduced to your—," he hesitated, "to your friend." "You are referring to my future wife," replied Jost coolly, "and to the future mistress of the Wendlitz estate. Or at least of half the Wendlitz estate," he added. His cousin nodded, as if he was now hearing something he had expected. Then he said, "Won't you sit down?" "No," replied Jost. "Let's be brief. I am going to get my discharge. I have handed in an application to get married and it has been refused." "Are you surprised?" asked his cousin. "No," answered Jost, "but I am prepared to take the consequences." "Jost," said the other, without showing any particular emotion or emphasis in his voice—more as if he were repeating a formula which he knew to be worthless, "if your career is a matter of indifference to you, you might at least think of the family name." "The family name," said Jost softly and earnestly, "will never be obliterated from the war record of my regiment. My career, too," he added with a smile, "can be read in the same journal. But my life is only just beginning." They remained silent. Then Jost said, "Half of this estate belongs to me as my inheritance. I wish to claim it. We must come to an agreement about the division of it." The master of the house did not reply, but looked in the direction of the window for a long time. Then he went over to the desk, took a small key from it, stepped over to the wall and opened a concealed cupboard. He took a large, heavily sealed document from a wallet and spread it out on the table. Both men bent over it. The cousin tapped his finger several times at a particular paragraph. "It says here," he said, "that if I have managed the estate for longer than ten years I have the right to exchange your share for a certain sum in cash. The amount would be assessed according to an official estimate of its value. I have managed the estate for more than eleven years." "Do you have the money?" asked Jost. "No," replied the other, "it wouldn't be easy. But if you force me, I'll raise it." "I don't want the money," said Jost, "I want my share. I want to live here." "With that woman?" asked his cousin. "With my wife!" replied Jost, emphasising every word. They were silent. The master of the house put away the document again and locked the wall safe. Then he said, "You must give me a month. That's customary." "Certainly," said Jost, "I haven't handed in my petition for discharge yet." "Thank you," replied his cousin simply. "Goodbye, then," said Jost and held out his hand. "I hope that in a month's time we'll be able to agree on how to

partition the estate!" "Goodbye," said the master of the house
and shook his hand. "I'll keep you informed." Jost left the room.
The shrill laughter of children reached his ears. Lili was standing
behind the house in the orchard; the blossom was not yet out.
She was playing with two little girls with flaxen hair and she
was imitating the dull, plaintive croak of the first spawning
toads, which could be heard from a reedy pond nearby. It
sounded so convincing, that one would think she had been imitating toads all her life. She was puffing out her cheeks and
pressing her deeply curved eyelids tightly together, so that she
looked exactly like a frog. The children tried to do the same,
but they were unsuccessful. They merely pulled ugly faces and
made noises appropriate to other animals, or simply yelled.
Suddenly the sharp, commanding voice of a woman came from
the window. The children stiffened and stood stock still. Then
with a sudden movement they rushed into the house.

Jost went up to her and cautiously took her arm. She did not
look at him; her eyes were following the children. They walked
a few paces. Then, as he stroked her hand, Jost said: "It'll be
all right." She made no reply, but the corners of her mouth
twitched. When they were sitting in the carriage and he was
turning the horse prior to trotting out of the courtyard and
down the avenue, she moved her face close to him and whispered: "I'm sorry!" He bent down sharply and kissed her bare
hand, which lay on the rug. He drove the vehicle indiscriminately across sandy, bumpy lanes, through diminutive copses, past
cattle pens, sometimes only able to follow hoof-tracks and wheel-
ruts. Again and again from different angles and distances they
caught sight of the manor house. Finally, in a hollow, he halted
and bound the reins to the trunk of a willow tree. He climbed
up the grassy slope ahead of her, followed a narrow footpath
through a beechwood in bud for a few minutes and then stopped
at the entrance to a clearing. Under a solitary, gnarled oak-tree
a stunted, untidy box-hedge had been planted. He bent down
and parted the leaves with his hands revealing a flat, grey
stone. "A dog's grave," he said and smiled, his thoughts elsewhere. The sun glanced down across the edge of the wood and
the pale expanse of winter pasture, through the middle of which
ran a narrow ditch of water. They sat down on the dead leaves
which crackled drily at the foot of the oak-tree, and leaned

against its sunlit trunk. The pulsating coolness of the ground and the increasing warmth of the sundrenched air mingled with one another, creating a mild, aromatic haze which they inhaled and absorbed through their skin. Like some heavenly ether it bathed their brows and lips and pervaded their bodies. The deep, overwhelming lethargy of spring which cannot be dispelled by sleep, seeped through their veins in this flood of hazy light. Their hands and knees touched, their eyes consumed each other like fire. "I could die," said Jost after a long, uninterrupted silence and his voice, distorted by mist and desire sounded somewhat hoarse, "I could die of happiness." His eyes left hers and gazed far away into the distant light on the horizon. Diffidently Lili raised her right hand and, unnoticed by him, she made an unobtrusive sign of the cross on her forehead, mouth and breast. "Is it true," she asked after a while in a quiet voice, almost like that of a frightened child, "that your King doesn't believe in God?" "Our King," replied Jost, and his face narrowed with pride, "our King doesn't need any God." "But we need Him," she said softly. "We're lost without Him." "Yes," said Jost, "but He has shown us three wide roads which always lead into the open." "What are they?" she asked. "Courage," said Jost and then fell silent for a time and looked at her. Then he continued, "love," "And what else?" she asked quickly. "Death," he replied and stood up and stretched his legs. She leapt up from the ground and embraced him with all her strength. He kissed her for a long time. Then he said, "Come on." They walked back to the carriage. They set out at a sharp trot, and as they turned into the wide main road, which led back to the town, he looked round once more and whistled between his teeth. "He won't be able to find the money!" he said with a short laugh and whipped up the horse.

Jost's application for discharge from the army had been lodged for several weeks now with the commander of his regiment. The latter, however, could not bring himself to pass it on to the personnel section in Potsdam and tried repeatedly, but unsuccessfully, to persuade the young officer to change his mind. Early in May the commander received Count von Prittwitz for a long discussion behind closed doors. Shortly after, Jost was sent on a military mission which necessitated his departure from the town for a few days. He was required to lead the guard of honour for a prince who was passing that way, and who had to change horses in the town; he would then be accompanied by a squadron of cuirassiers as far as Berlin. Jost had secretly been surprised at this mission, since two officer escorts from a Potsdam regiment had already been appointed for the procession. The day after he had ridden away, there was a knock on Lili Schallweis' door. She never left her room because, for some time now, passers-by were wont to stare at her and shout many coarse things after her, whenever she ventured out by herself into the street. As she was alone, she opened the door herself. Prittwitz was standing outside, shrouded in his long cloak. She look at him without a word and did not invite him in. "I beg you," said Prittwitz, "to allow me a short conversation. I must talk to you." "I wasn't aware," she rejoined, "that we had anything to discuss." "It concerns von Fredersdorff," said Prittwitz. "It's about Jost!" he added urgently, as her expression showed no sign of allowing him in. She hesitated for another moment, then she stepped back. "Please come in," she said, opening the drawing-room door. Once inside, she stopped near the window and did not invite him to remove his cloak nor to sit down. He went towards her and looked at her a long time. "You must go away!" he said then, quite suddenly. Not a muscle moved in her face. "What do you mean by that?" she asked, slowly. "I mean,"—and he stepped a little closer to her and laid a hand gently on her arm—"that Jost must not be ruined." She was silent and drew her arm away. After a time she said, "Have you been ordered to come here?" "I beg you to understand," said Prittwitz emphatically. "I haven't come here on orders. But I have come on a matter of general concern. Jost is an officer. He's one of the best." She nodded and gazed at the floor. "You think that I ought to leave him?" she said in an incredulous voice. "I think that you must!" replied Prittwitz in a decisive tone. "Otherwise you will be responsible for what occurs." "I am responsible for his life," she said as if to herself. "Yes," cried Prittwitz, "and it really is a matter of life and death!" She looked at him. "I can't," she whispered. Prittwitz stepped up to her and laid his arm on her shoulder. She remained passive and stood motionless. "Be brave, Lili," he said and his voice took on a warmer tone, "you know yourself that it won't work!" "I know nothing of the sort," she said. "I love him." "If you really love him," said Prittwitz, "then you must understand what I'm saying. You can only make a choice between a quick cut which will heal and a slow bleeding to death." She leant against him slightly and he felt her knees trembling. "Do you really think that we can't live together?" she asked. "Do I have to answer that?" he asked quietly. "I can't do it—" she said and moved away from him, sinking into a chair. "You don't have to make any decisions," he said hastily. "It will be sufficient if you don't resist." She looked at him questioningly with dull eyes ringed with bluish shadows. "I will take the responsibility for everything," he continued, "I'll explain everything to him. I won't leave him alone. He has friends!" She did not move. "Everything is prepared," he said. "The police are serving you with an expulsion order. Don't be afraid," and he stepped quickly up to her and passed a hand over her hair. "It's only a formality. It relieves you of the choice and removes all the bitterness from your action. When he returns, you will have disappeared because of powers beyond your control." She still made no reply. "It will make him sweat blood," he said, "but then he'll be saved. Even you won't die of it," he added. "One dies and goes on living," she said, her voice barely audible. Prittwitz paced the length of the room twice, then he stopped by the table and said in a voice that was dry and almost official, "Everything will take place unobserved. Tomorrow at the same time a carriage with its blinds drawn will drive up to the house. It will be accompanied by two mounted policemen. They will wait at the nearest crossroads and no one will notice them. I myself will be here to collect you." "Where shall I be taken?" she inquired in the same indifferent tone. "That's up to you," he replied. "Preferably to Berlin for the time being." Then, after a pause he went on : "If you are without means, you can be cared for for a while." She rose lifting her hand. "Not that!" she said in a hard voice, "please, not that!" "I'm sorry," he said, "I didn't want to insult you." "I know," she said softly. He went up to her and stretched out his hand. "I can rely on you, then?" he asked. She made no reply, ignored his outstretched hand and turned away. He noticed her head drooping lower and lower. Without another word he bowed and departed.

Jost had been given leave of absence by the commander of the guard of honour in Potsdam. Tormented by a feeling of deep unrest, he had hastened on a day ahead of the squadron, which was returning home under the leadership of a lieutenant, and towards evening, followed at a short distance by his groom, he rode into the town. When he reached the square he stopped in front of the garrison church as if a thought had struck him; then he forced his horse, which could smell the stable and was making in the direction of the barracks, to face the other way, and urged it at a quicker pace into the street where Lili Schallweis lived. He drove his footsore horse faster and faster and bending over its neck, he peered into the rapidly deepening twilight. From quite a long way off he noticed the carriage outside her front door, and when he saw two figures emerge into the street, he brought his horse to a trot, in spite of the cobbles. The mounted policemen waiting behind the corner of the street saw him fly past and attached themselves to his groom who was following at a slacker pace. Jost flung himself breathlessly to the ground as he drew level with the carriage, whose door had just been opened by Prittwitz. He left his horse where it stood; the groom dismounted and held its reins. Lili, wrapped in a travelling cloak, had placed her foot on the running board. She remained thus, rooted to the spot and when she caught sight of him all the blood drained from her face. In three strides he was at her side. With a faint cry she collapsed. He caught her and held her in his arms. Prittwitz' fist closed round the door handle as if he would crush it to fragments. Jost stared at him, his lips white with hatred and rage. Lili raised herself in his arms, released herself, and stood between them. Quickly he stood in front of her, coming right up to Prittwitz. "What do you want here?" he asked in menacing tones. Faces appeared at windows; several lads came out of a gate-entrance, craning their necks. Prittwitz, madly obsessed with the idea that he must carry out his intention, and end this scene as soon as possible, straightened himself and said softly, but acidly, "Captain von Fredersdorff, I command you to obey my orders and return immediately to barracks!" Jost did not move. "I wish to know what is going on here," he said coldly. Prittwitz replied hastily, "These are the orders of the chief of police. There will be no opposition." He made as if to come a step nearer to her and force her into the carriage. Then Jost raised his clenched fist and punched him in the chest so violently that he staggered to one side. The two policemen had dismounted and came forward, indecisively. Prittwitz, propped up against the back wheel of the carriage, waved them away. Jost placed his arm round her waist and led her quickly to the door of the house. There, he turned round once more. "I am ready for satisfaction," he said loudly, "but I will protect my wife from any attempt at violence." Then carrying, rather than supporting her, he went back into her apartment. Prittwitz stood there a moment or two longer as if turned to stone, then he gave a subdued command to the policemen and the coachman. He climbed into the carriage which moved off swaying and creaking. Behind him, slowly, came the gendarmes and the soldier with two horses.

On the very same evening Jost received a summons via an orderly officer to relinquish his sword, as he had been suspended from his duties until his application for discharge had been granted. This was being delivered by a messenger on horseback. However, the next day the third squadron, on its way back from Berlin, refused to obey Count Prittwitz, who had been given temporary authority over them, because they were convinced that their captain had been unjustly treated.

They had not left the apartment since he had brought her there from the very running board of the carriage; they lived as in a dream in a new passion which made every earlier occasion seem nebulous and fleeting. In her heart, too, any doubts were burnt to ashes by the furnace of faith which such a love engenders. Sometimes in the night she would quiver deep down with a quiet, nagging fear, but this was quickly stifled by the pounding of her blood and the stormy passion of his embrace. They looked forward to the day when he would finally be released, as if it were a secret festival which would be succeeded by that of their marriage only as a final, visible seal. He had received a letter from Prittwitz in which the latter refused to demand satisfaction, since Jost had not come into conflict with him personally, but rather with military orders, for which he would have to take the consequences alone and in a different manner. In the letter he also begged Jost to understand that he had acted as he had done from great affection and to preserve a memory of his comradeship. They also discovered that all horses and arms had been removed from his squadron until the matter could be dealt with. The commander had been personally summoned to Potsdam in the last few days to explain and answer for recent events. This he did in such a way that any suggestion of dishonourable or unpardonable conduct on the captain's part was removed and he made a recommendation to the King for mercy and understanding for Jost's action. None of this affected the latter any more. Like murmurs of a far-off world, whose atmosphere he had long since left behind him, and whose role and destiny were no longer comprehensible, it hardly penetrated his ears. On one occasion a clerk called on him and tried to persuade him to see a lawyer in connection with some important matter or other. But after a brief exchange of words, Jost sent him on his way alone. The next day the lawyer called himself and had a long conversation with him in the living-room. When Lili, who had been waiting in the adjacent room, entered the living-room after the lawyer's departure, a large sum of money, made up in bundles and small bags, lay on the table next to a duplicate copy of a sealed document. She looked questioningly at him. "He found the money after all," said Jost in a voice almost of indifference. She sensed that this was no feigned indifference and her last fears disappeared from her heart. "Now we'll be able to travel far away!" he said with a gentle smile. "Here, you take it; I can't be bothered with it!" And since she lifted a hand in protest, he heaped it all together and put it in the drawer of her tiny, polished bureau. Lili left the house for the first time that day. Towards evening she went out on some errands and as she was passing a flower stall, she bought from the gardener's wife an armful of fresh roses hardly out of bud, the first of the year. While she was away an officer of his regiment came to the house and delivered to him a highly official communication in which, in recognition of his services in the war, the King had allowed him to take his leave from the army with full honours. The commander of his regiment also returned his sword. On her return, Lili found him standing by the table, his sword and belt and his pistol in his hands, his face happy and serene. They were awake a long time that night. The window stood wide open, the scent of the roses, which bloomed like a thick hedge in the centre of the room, mingled with the intoxicating atmosphere of the moonlit hours. They did not speak; they were immersed in the floods of their own happiness for which no words were relevant. When at last they closed their eyes, the northern early summer dawn was already rising rapidly in the east.

With the triumphant warbling of the birds and the first flashing shaft of sunlight they were awakened by an unusual sound which gradually came nearer and nearer and which reaching their house from the town centre like the thunder of a distant battle. Suddenly Jost jumped up, threw on his uniform, put on his sword belt and went into the living-room and up to the open window. Then they came, turning the corner and marching down the empty street, step by step and foot by foot with heavy tread, the clatter of iron, the jingle of spurs—the cuirassiers of his old squadron, without horses or arms, with the drummer beating loud and muffled sounds at their head and in their midst, borne aloft, the battered Torgau ensign. In front of the window they stood in *front* formation, the drum fell silent, and the many faces, the bearded and scarred ones and the smooth, young and eager ones, looked up at him in silent, manly devotion. And as he stood there, looking down at them, unable to say a word, utter a sound or make a movement, they called up to him, at first with throaty, embarrassed shouts, then more freely and in a wild, surging roar, the names of their battles and skirmishes, and the bad and proud years which they had experienced with him. Then the drum boomed again and as they retreated, their old cavalry song rang out to the rhythm of their marching feet. Lili did not come into the room. She sat motionless on the edge of the bed, spellbound as if she were half in a dream. From the other room she heard his voice which had a changed, strangely elated timbre. "That was the farewell!" he said. His words sounded like a cry of triumph. She still did not move, afraid of spoiling the atmosphere of this, his own special hour by a single wrong word or sound.

"That kind of thing cannot perish"—she heard him again—"that kind of thing cannot perish!" She felt that he was speaking to her.

"You're right," she said loudly and hardly recognised her own voice—"it can't perish!"

"Thank you!" he cried from the other room, "thank you!"

She wanted to jump up, but her knees were paralysed by a sudden icy chill. Simultaneously with the last echoes of the drum beat came the hollow sound of a shot.

The shock made her fall; she groped along the floor with her hands till she reached the door. Then slowly, she straightened herself and entered. He was leaning back, sitting upright in a tall, narrow armchair close by the window, the smoking pistol still near his heart. She looked at his face. It was beautiful and still and so filled with everything in life that matters to a man, that she knelt down and could find no tears.

BIOGRAPHICAL NOTE

Carl Zuckmayer was born on 27th November 1896 at Nackenheim in Rheinhessen. Like so many of his contemporaries he went straight from school to the army in 1914 and served throughout the war with distinction. After a brief period of study in Heidelberg he entered on a career as a dramatist and producer. His first drama, *Kreuzweg* (1920) was an unsuccessful exercise in the Expressionist style, but five years later Zuckmayer scored a resounding success with *Der fröhliche Weinberg*, a play which was free from such literary pretension and which allowed full scope for a natural, robust *joie de vivre*. He continued to work this vein in two further popular plays, *Schinderhannes* (1927), which takes as its hero a Rhineland Robin Hood figure, and *Katharina Knie* (1928), the story of a tight-rope walker who renounces the prospect of a secure domestic life in order to take over the direction of the family circus after the death of her father. This kind of conflict, to which Zuckmayer frequently reverts, is one that he no doubt experienced himself in his youth when literary and dramatic interests drew him away from the rural life in which he had been brought up. About the same time as he wrote *Katharina Knie*, Zuckmayer began to publish novels and short stories which show a strong narrative talent, scurrilous humour and a sympathetic understanding of simple people. In the early part of his career Zuckmayer advocates the natural and uninhibited way of life followed by simple peasants and is an enemy of convention—particularly sexual convention—and unhealthy intellectuality. This is the theme of the more thoughtful and more successful of his two novels, *Die Magdalena von Bozen* (1936), which contrasts a rarified, and ultimately effete intellectual atmosphere with the elemental strength and untrammelled emotional fulfilment of the peasant life. The other novel, *Herr über Leben und Tod* (1938), is a rather jejune and sentimental account of a difficult marriage.

Zuckmayer's reputation is principally founded on his dramas. His early successes were confirmed by *Der Hauptmann von Köpenick* (1931), which uses for satirical ends the true story of a confidence trick perpetrated on the authorities by an out-of-work ex-convict masquerading as a Prussian officer. *Der Schelm von Bergen* (1934) and *Carl Michael Bellmann* (1938) enjoyed less success, but Zuckmayer's fame reached a climax after the Second World War with *Des Teufels General* (1946), again a work based in part on authentic figures and incidents : a bluff and heroic air force general, Harras, is trapped between allegiance to his service and the dubiously patriotic activities of the resistance movement against Hitler. The same problem of divided loyalties is the theme of the more imaginatively conceived drama of the French resistance, *Der Gesang im Feuerofen* (1950), and *Das kalte Licht* (1955), which is in essence a dramatisation of the Klaus Fuchs espionage case. Zuckmayer spent the war years farming in America and eventually took American citizenship. Since the end of the war he has lived in Switzerland. His autobiography in English, *Second Wind*, London, Harrap; New York, Doubleday, Doran, was published in 1940.

The two main studies in German of Zuckmayer's work are by Ingeborg Engelsing-Malek : *"Amor Fati" in Zuckmayers Dramen*, Konstanz, Rosgarten Verlag, 1960, and W. Adling : *Die Entwicklung des Dramatikers Carl Zuckmayers*, Leipzig, 1956. In English, there is a useful general chapter in H. Garten : *Modern German Drama*, London, Methuen, 1959, and a well-written brief account, with bibliography, by Sheila Rooke in *German Men of Letters*, Series III, London, Wolff, 1964, pp. 209–33.

Hugo von Hofmannsthal

Translated
by
Mary Hottinger and
Tanis and James Stern

HUGO VON HOFMANNSTHAL

AN EPISODE IN THE LIFE
OF THE MARSHAL DE BASSOMPIERRE

AT one time in my life I had, in the course of my service, to cross the little bridge (the Pont Neuf not yet being built) fairly regularly several times a week at the same hour, and as I did so, some labourers and others of the common people came to recognise and salute me. But the most insistent and regular greeting came from the very pretty shopkeeper whose shop bore the sign of the Two Angels. Every time I passed during those five or six months, she would drop me a low curtsey and watch me out of sight. Attracted by her behaviour, I returned her look and acknowledged her salutation with care. Once, towards the end of the winter, I was riding from Fontainebleau to Paris, and as I mounted the little bridge, she came to the door of her shop and said, as I rode by, "Your servant, Sir." I returned her greeting and, looking back from time to time, saw that she had leaned yet farther out to keep me in sight as long as she possibly could. I had my man and a postillion behind me, whom I had meant to send back to Fontainebleau that evening with letters for certain ladies. On my order, my man now dismounted and approached the young woman, telling her in my name that I had remarked her eagerness to see and greet me, and that if she desired to make my closer acquaintance, I would wait upon her at any place she appointed.

She replied to my man that he could have brought her no more welcome message; she would herself come to any place I would name.

As we rode on, I asked my man if he knew where I could meet the woman. He replied that he could take her to a certain procuress's, but this man of mine, William of Courtrai, being a most careful and conscientious creature, he at once added that there was plague here and there in the city, and as it had already carried off not only men and women of the mean and dirty sort, but a doctor and a canon too, he would advise me to have my own mattresses and bed-clothes taken with me. I fell in with his proposal, and he promised to prepare me a good bed. Before we dismounted, I added that he should take to the place a proper wash-basin, a small bottle of sweet-smelling essence, and some cakes and apples; he should also see that the room was thoroughly warmed, for it was so cold that my feet were frozen stiff in the stirrups, and the sky was heavy with snow-clouds.

That evening, going to the appointed place, I found a very beautiful young woman, some twenty years of age, sitting on the bed, while the procuress, her head and bent old back muffled up in a black shawl, seemed to be urging something upon her. The door stood ajar; in the fireplace, big, fresh logs were blazing noisily. The women did not hear my approach, and I remained standing a moment in the doorway. The young woman was gazing steadily into the fire with wide open eyes, a single movement of her head seemed to have put miles between her and the old crone; in the movement, a few locks of her heavy dark hair had burst out from under the little nightcap she wore, and, twining in natural ringlets, had fallen over her shift between her shoulder and bosom. She also wore a short petticoat of green woollen stuff, and slippers on her feet.

At that moment, I must have betrayed my presence by some noise; with a sudden movement of her head she turned towards me a face so haggard with expectation that it would have looked fierce but for the radiance of devotion that streamed from her wide-open eyes and burst like an invisible flame from her speechless mouth. She was inexpressibly beautiful. In a trice the old crone was banished from the room and I was with my mistress. When, in the first rapture of this unexpected possession, I ventured on a few liberties, she shrank from me with an unspeakably anxious pleading both in her look and in her rich, low voice. But in a moment her arms were about me again, and the upturned gaze of her fathomless eyes, straining upon me, clasped me yet more close than her lips and arms. Then again, she seemed to be struggling to speak, but her lips, quivering with kisses, formed no words, and from her pulsing throat there came no sound more distinct than a broken sob.

Now I had spent most of that day on horseback on freezing highroads; later, I had been party to a very annoying and violent scene in the King's antechamber, and then, to overcome my ill-humour, I had both drunk wine and fenced vigorously with the two-handed sword, and so, in the midst of this lovely and mysterious adventure, as I lay with soft arms round my neck and perfumed hair pouring over me, I was overcome by a fatigue that was almost a swoon, so sudden and irresistible that I could no longer remember how I had come into this room. I even, for a moment, imagined the woman whose heart beat so close to mine to be a totally different one I had known earlier in life, and at once fell into a deep sleep.

When I awoke, the night was still dark, but I at once felt that my mistress was no longer by my side. I raised my head, and in the faint glow of the dying embers, saw her standing by the window. She had pushed open one of the shutters and was looking out through the crack. Then she turned round, saw that I was awake, and called (I can still see her raising the palm of her left hand to her cheek to toss back her fallen hair): "It is not day yet—not for a long time." Only now did I really see how tall and beautiful she was. I could hardly wait until one or two steady, long steps of her beautiful, glow-reddened feet had brought her to my side again. On her way, she moved to the fireplace, bent down, took the last heavy log lying in front of it in her shining bare arms, and flung it into the embers. And then she turned, her face sparkling with flames and joy; in passing, she snatched up an apple from the table, and was again in my arms, her limbs still bathed in the fresh heat of the fire, then dissolving, as it were, in the yet fiercer flames that pulsed through them from within. Clasping me with her right hand, she bit into the cool fruit in her left, then held it to my mouth, offering the fruit, offering her face. The last log in the fireplace flamed higher than all the rest. With a shower of sparks it sucked in the flames, then hurled them up again in a furious blaze, and the firelight broke over us like a wave dashing against the wall, flinging our shadowed embrace up and down upon it. The great log crackled, feeding from its heart fresh flames which danced upward, dispelling the darkness with sheaves and fountains of glowing red. Then, all of a sudden, the flame sank; a breath of cold air pushed open the shutter like a hand and revealed the livid, hideous grey of dawn.

We sat up, knowing that day had come. But the light outside was like no day. This was no awakening of a world, and what lay outside was like no street. Things had no outlines. It was a

world without form and void, where only shapeless, timeless
things could move. From somewhere distant as a memory came
the chime of a church clock, and a raw wind, which had no
home in day or night, poured into the room till we clung together, shuddering. She leant back, her eyes fastened on my
face; her throat quivered, something rose in her and surged to
her lips, but no word came, no sigh and no kiss, but something
which, unborn, was like all three. In the growing light the changing expressions flitting across her face grew yet more speaking.
Suddenly, in the street outside, shuffling footsteps and voices
approached the window so close that she bent and turned her
face to the wall. Two men passed; for a moment, the light of a
little lantern carried by one of them brightened the room; the
other man was pushing a barrow whose wheel creaked and
groaned. When the men had passed, I stood up, closed the
shutters, and lit a candle. Half an apple was still lying there, we
ate it together, and then I asked whether I could see her once
more, as I was not to leave until Sunday, while this night had
been the night from Thursday to Friday.

She replied that she certainly desired it more ardently than I,
but unless I could stay over Sunday, she could not see me again,
for she could only meet me in the night from Sunday to Mon-
day.

A number of hindrances flashed through my mind, and I
raised some objections to which she listened without a word, but
with a most painful questioning in her eyes, while her face grew
almost ghastly in its sombre hardness. Then, of course, I promised to stay over the Sunday, and added that I should come
to the same place again on Sunday evening. She looked at me
steadily and said, her voice quite harsh and broken, "I know
very well that I have entered a house of shame for your sake,
but I did it of my own free will, because I meant to be with
you, because I would have done anything and gone anywhere.
But now I should feel like the last and lowest woman of the
town if I brought myself to come here again. I did it for your
sake, because, for me, you are what you are, because you are
Bassompierre, because you are the one human being in the
world whose presence could make this house my house of
honour."

She said "house"; for a moment it seemed as if a more con-

temptuous word were on her lips; as she said it, she cast upon
the walls, our bed, the bed-clothes that had slipped off on to the
floor, such a look that, in the sheaf of light that flashed from her
eyes, all these mean and ugly things seemed to start and cringe
away from her, as if the wretched room had really grown bigger
for a moment.

Then, in an inexpressibly gentle and solemn voice, she added,
"May I die a wretched death if I have ever known any man but
my husband and you, or desire any other in the world," and
bending forward a little, her whole life in the breath of her
parted lips, she seemed to be waiting for some answer, some
assurance of my faith, but not finding in my face what she
sought there, her eager, searching look clouded, her lashes
opened and closed, and in a moment she was at the window, her
back turned to me, her forehead pressed against the shutter with
all her might, her whole body so shaken with noiseless but hor-
ribly violent weeping that speech died in my mouth and I did
not dare to touch her. In the end I took one of her hands, which
were hanging nerveless at her sides, and with the most endearing
words I could command, I succeeded, after long effort, in soothing her until she turned her tear-stained face to me again, and
a smile broke out like a light from her eyes and round her lips,
instantly drying up her tears and bathing her whole face in
brightness.

And then it was the most delicious game to watch her begin
to speak to me again, with endless variations on the one theme:
"You will see me again! Then I will let you into my aunt's
house," speaking the first part in a dozen different ways, now
with sweet insistence, then with a pretence of childish suspicion,
then whispered in my ear as if it were the greatest secret in the
world, then again thrown over her shoulder with a shrug and a
pout as if she were making the most commonplace appointment
in the world, and in the end caressingly reiterated as she clung to
me, laughing up into my face. She described the house to me in
long detail, like a mother telling her child the way when it must
cross the road to the baker's alone for the first time. Then she
drew herself up, turned serious, and bent her radiant eyes on
me with such force that they could have raised the dead to life,
and went on: "I shall be waiting for you from ten o'clock till
midnight, and yet later still, and the downstairs door will be

open. First you walk along a little passage, but you must not stop there, for my aunt's door opens on to it. Then you come to a staircase leading to the upper storey, and there I shall be." And closing her eyes as if dazed, she threw back her head, spread out her arms, and embraced me—and a moment later was out of my arms, fully dressed, strange and grave, and out of the room, for now day had come.

I made my arrangements, sent some of my men ahead with my baggage, and by the evening of the next day was a prey to such vehement restlessness that, soon after vespers had rung, I crossed the little bridge with my man William, whom I forbade to take a lantern, so that I might see my mistress in her shop or in the adjoining lodging and give her, at any rate, some sign of my presence, though I hoped for nothing more than perhaps to exchange a few words with her.

To avoid attracting attention, I stopped at the bridge, sending my man ahead to reconnoitre. He was away for some time, and on his return wore the moody and despondent look which always meant that he had failed to carry out one of my orders. "The shop is shut up," he said, "and there seems to be nobody in it. Indeed there is nobody to be seen or heard in any of the rooms looking on to the street. You can only get into the courtyard over a high wall, and there is a big dog growling in it. But there is a light in one of the front rooms, and you can see into the shop through a chink, though I fear it is empty."

I was put out by this and made up my mind to go home at once, but all the same crept slowly past the house again, while my man, in his eagerness, applied his eye to the chink, which let out a thin ray of light, and whispered to me that the woman was not in the shop, but that her husband was. I was anxious to get sight of this shopkeeper, whom I could not remember ever having seen in his shop, and whom I imagined by turns as fat and shapeless or withered and decrepit. I approached the window and, to my extreme surprise, saw walking about in the well-furnished, panelled room an uncommonly tall and well-built man, who was certainly a head taller than I and who, when he turned round, showed me a very handsome, very grave face with a brown beard, silvered here and there, and a forehead of almost rare sublimity, with temples more spacious than I had ever seen before in a human face. Though he was quite alone in the room,

his eyes wandered, his lips moved, and as he paused from time to
time in his pacing up and down, he seemed to be carrying on an
imaginary conversation with some other person; once he made a
gesture with his arm as if brushing aside some objection with
half-indulgent authority. There was ease and an almost con-
temptuous pride in his every movement, and as he turned in his
solitary pacing up and down the room, I could not but call
vividly to mind a very illustrious prisoner whom I had had
under guard in the King's service when he was held in an apartment in the tower of Blois Castle. The resemblance became still
more complete when the man raised his right hand and looked
down on his upturned fingers with a searching, even grim look.

For it was almost the same gesture as I had often observed my
august prisoner make when gazing at a ring which he wore on
the first finger of his right hand and never removed. The man in
the room then approached the table, pushed the water-globe in
front of the candle, and placed both his hands, with outstretched
fingers, in the circle of light; he seemed to be examining his
finger-nails. Then he blew out the candle and went out of the
room, leaving me with a dull feeling of sullen, angry jealousy,
for my desire for his wife was rising steadily within me, feeding
like a spreading fire on all it encountered, and fanned, in some
bewildering fashion, by this unexpected vision as it was by every
snow-flake that was blown by the raw wind to hang and melt,
single, on my eyebrows and cheeks.

I idled away the next day, unable to bring my mind to bear
on anything, bought a horse I really did not care for, waited
after dinner on the Duke de Nemours and spent some time there
at cards and in the silliest and most disagreeable conversation
imaginable. For it all turned on the plague, which was spreading
rapidly in the city, and there was not a word to be got out of
any of these gentlemen but of the hasty burial of the bodies, the
straw fire that must be lit in the room where anyone had died,
to consume the pestilent vapours, and so on. But the silliest of all,
in my opinion, was the Canon de Chandieu; fat and hearty as
ever, he could not refrain from keeping one eye fixed on his
finger-nails to see if there were to be seen there any trace of the
suspicious blueness which was generally the first sign of the
plague.

Disgusted with it all, I went home early and retired to bed,

but could not sleep; in my impatience, I dressed again and resolved at all costs to go and see my mistress, even if I and my
men had to force our way in. I went to the window to call them;
the icy night air brought me to my senses and I realised that my
plan would mean certain ruin to the whole affair. I threw myself
fully dressed as I was on my bed and at last fell asleep.

I spent Sunday in similar fashion until evening came, and
arrived in the street named long before my time, but forced
myself to walk up and down a nearby alley till ten struck. Then
I soon found the house and the door she had described; the
door was open, as she had said, and the corridor and staircase
were behind it. But upstairs, the second door at the head of the
staircase was shut, though a thin streak of light shone from beneath it. So she was inside, waiting, standing perhaps with her
ear to the inside of the door as I with mine to the outside. I
scratched on the door with my finger-nail; then I heard a noise
within which sounded like the shuffling, unsteady steps of bare
feet. For a time I stood breathless and then began to knock, but
a man's voice replied, asking who was there. I pressed back into
the shadow of the doorway without uttering a sound. The door
remained shut, and I crept downstairs on silent feet, step by step,
then along the passage out into the open air, and with beating
temples and clenched teeth, afire with impatience, walked up and
down a street or two. In the end, I could not resist returning to
the house; I did not mean to go in yet. I felt, I knew, that she
would get her husband away, she would, she must, succeed, and
I should be able to go to her at once. The street was narrow, on
the other side there were no houses but only the wall of a convent
garden; I stood flattened against it, trying to guess which was
her window from the other side of the street. Suddenly, in one
that stood open in the upper storey, a light flamed up and died
down. I seemed to see it all before my eyes; she had thrown a big
log on the fire, as on that other night. As on that other night, she
was standing in the middle of the room, her limbs bathed in the
firelight, or sitting on the bed, listening and waiting. I would see
her from the doorway, with the shadow of her neck and shoulders rising and falling on that invisible wave on the wall. I was
already on the corridor, on the stairs, the door had been opened.
Standing ajar, it allowed the flickering light to pass out. I had
stretched out my hands towards the doorhandle, when I seemed

to hear the steps and voices of several persons inside. But I would not believe it, and took it for the pulsing of my blood in my temples, in my neck, and for the blazing of the fire within. The other night, too, it had blazed noisily. My hand was on the door-handle when it really came home to me that there were people in the room, several people. But now I cared no longer, for I felt, I knew, she was there too, and as soon as I had opened the door, I should see her, take her in my arms and, though I should have to wrench her out of the hands of others, hold her to me with one arm, cutting a way for her with my sword, with my dagger, through a mêlée of shouting men and women. The one thing that seemed quite intolerable was to wait longer.

I pushed the door open. This is what I saw.

In the middle of the empty room I saw a few people burning bed-straw, and in the flames whose light flooded the room, scaling walls whose plaster lay on the floor, while against one wall there was a table, on which two naked bodies lay stretched, one very big, with covered head, the other smaller, lying against the wall with the black shadow of its outline rising and falling beside it.

I reeled down the stairs, and in front of the house encountered two grave-diggers; one held his little lantern up to my face, asking me what I wanted, the other pushed his creaking, groaning barrow against the door. I drew my dagger to fend them off, and went home. There I at once drank three or four glasses of heavy wine and, having slept, set out on my journey to Lorraine.

All my efforts to discover something about the woman after my return were vain. I even went to the shop with the sign of the Two Angels, but the people who kept it did not know who had kept it before them.

BIOGRAPHICAL NOTE

Hugo von Hofmannsthal was born in Vienna on 1st February 1874 and lived all his life in or near the city. His was a precocious talent, and he attracted attention with poems and essays published while he was still at school. His lyrical dramas *Der Tod des Tizian* (1892), *Der Tod und der Tod* (1893), *Das kleine Welttheater* (1897) and the verse plays, *Hochzeit der Sobeide* (1899) and *Der Abenteurer und die Sängerin* (1899) already show to the full Hofmannsthal's philosophical concern with the nature and destiny of man. His imaginative view of the condition of man and society is more elaborately dramatised in the allegorical mystery plays, *Jedermann* (1911), *Das große Salzburger Welttheater* (1922) and the adaptation from Calderon, *Der Turm* (1925). Hofmannsthal is perhaps best known outside Germany through his collaboration as librettist with Richard Strauss in numerous operatic works : *Elektra* (1909), *Der Rosenkavalier* (1911), *Ariadne auf Naxos* (1912), *Josephslegende* (1914), *Die Frau ohne Schatten* (1919), *Die Ägyptische Helena* (1928) and *Arabella* (1933). The poet's correspondence with the composer is a major contribution to the aesthetics of poetry and music. In his comedies, of which probably the most distinguished is *Der Schwierige* (1921), Hofmannsthal shows a psychological subtlety that is perhaps typical of his race and native city. He analyses with melancholy, but wryly humorous acumen the decay of the cultured society of Vienna after the First World War. His prose works include, besides *Bassompierre*, the short stories *Reitergeschichte* and *Lucidor*, and a *Bildungsroman, Andreas,* that was never completed. Hofmannsthal also wrote a number of penetrating literary studies, as well as the remarkable *Brief des Lord Chandos*, which describes a mutation of the artistic imagination verging on a mystic experience. Hofmannsthal died of a cerebral stroke in July 1929 after hearing of the suicide of one of his sons.

Many of Hofmannsthal's works have been translated into English, and a list of these, along with secondary literature, may be found in V. Lange : *Modern German Literature,* Ithaca, New York, Cornell University Press, 1945, pp. 165–67. Two useful studies of the poet in English are by H. Hammelmann, *Hofmannsthal,* Bowes and Bowes, London, 1957, and B. Keith-Smith, *Hofmannsthal,* in *German Men of Letters,* Series I, London, Wolff, 1961, pp. 253–73. A volume of commemorative essays has been published by the Institute of Germanic Studies : *Hofmannsthal: Studies in Commemoration,* ed. F. Norman, London, 1963. This includes a very full bibliography of "Hofmannsthal in England and America".

Werner Bergengruen

Translated
by
Lawrence Wilson

WERNER BERGENGRUEN

EXPERIENCE ON AN ISLAND

An elderly Russian painter told this story to his friends in a café in Paris.

Around the turn of the century—at that time I was attending one of the upper classes in a secondary school in St. Petersburg—I spent the summer holidays with my family at a small seaside resort in Esthonia.

We led the usual sort of life on the shore, bathing and making friends; there were trips, picnics, boating expeditions and we danced. Often I kept away from these pastimes, reading, sketching and painting.

But as I was at that time, all this could not satisfy me. I did enjoy cheerful company and I also like meeting girls. But for me the hazard, the adventure of solitude had suddenly acquired the stronger lure; and I felt the need for a deeper isolation than, occasionally and on the fringe of social life, I could obtain there. One day I told my parents I wanted to hike along the coast for a number of days, so as to explore the scenery and do some sketching. This was certainly part of my intention, but the most important thing for me was to confront the world alone, its emanations, its thrills and its overwhelming surprises.

A project of that kind was considered unusual in our family and at first my parents raised objections. But in the end I had my way, and I did not even have to take my younger brother with me, as my mother had at first suggested.

You can judge for yourselves how I felt. At that age, as you know, one expects to be confronted on every journey with the unusual, even with fate itself. Well, in this case I was not so far off the mark, as you shall see.

So I set off. It was a strange land, that I can tell you! I had hardly left the area of the coastal resorts when I found myself in lonely, primeval surroundings which, as a city-dweller, I found well-nigh bewildering.

The word "glint"—I do not know whether it is German, Swedish or Esthonian—will be strange to you. It refers to the steep, rocky cliffs in those parts which are torn by deep clefts and crevices. In some places they directly overhang the water, in others there is a strip of shore between the *glint* and the sea, generally narrow, but broadening out at times to a few hundred paces. This stretch was my highway. But often, when I came to a path or a means of scaling the cliff, consisting sometimes of rotting wooden ladders placed one above the other, I scrambled up and continued along the top, allowing myself to be lured down to the sea again as soon as the possibility of descent occurred.

At that age, you must remember, one is tireless and insatiable, like a small dog which on walks with its master keeps rushing on ahead, running back and out to the side, so covering the actual route many times over. What attracted me to the top was not only the open view, but the riotous luxuriance of the vegetation : flourishing limes, alders, ash, oaks, poplars, birches, pines, larches—all jumbled together ! Thick on the ground grew deadly nightshade, willow-herb, basilweed and bellwort, and, higher up, hips and hazel bushes, giant ferns, wild raspberries and hops (which in the North do duty for ivy) twining round the tree-trunks. Suddenly I came across the fallen and mouldering trunk of an elm, sixty feet long or more, covered with moss, lichen, fungus and wound round with some little flowering creeper. That would be a novelty to you, no doubt. In Western Europe, after all, the countryside is basically all parkland and every tree is registered with the forestry commission. One day they will start putting squirrels, hedgehogs and partridges on lists and residence permits will be issued to owls only on condition that they allow the wild pigeons to sleep with them at night. Well, that's as may be.

Down below, the picture was different, although in some places the woods stretched right down to the water. There, the surf pounded against cliffs and fallen rocks, flinging the spray vertically upwards. But there also lay the still sand with its silken sheen, crossed in places by elk tracks, with patches of bright violet flowers, stone-crop and sand-barley. And the colours of the sea, the sky, the sails, the gulls, the velvet scoters and the sawbills—but what point is there in describing them ? You all have imagination, and I am not concerned with the scenery but with my state of mind at the time and with what, thus subconsciously prepared, I experienced towards the end of my journey. I bathed a lot, sometimes twice or three times a day, I swam out to sandbanks or rocks in the sea, I found snow-white skeletons of animals, skulls of fishes and birds, and occasionally, in a bay sheltered from the wind, white water-lilies lay motionless between blocks of coloured granite, or the shallow sea-bed was completely covered with water-plants, among which herons, ducks, sand-pipers and snipe were splashing around.

I spent the nights as opportunity afforded, sometimes in fisher-men's huts or among the hay at a farm; once I slept in the open air. I saw hardly any inns—in that respect the East is different from this country. You could go a long distance before coming across small, poverty-stricken settlements, derelict fishermen's huts, or "shore rider" posts. The shore riders were a kind of military corps, except that they came under the Ministry of Finance and not the Ministry of War. Their job was to patrol the coast and prevent smuggling. Their little houses, built to Treasury specifications, were clean and bright and looked like toy barracks. But in that landscape they struck me as alien. They had a certain importance for me, for it was there that I could be sure of finding people who spoke Russian.

To the strange state of enchantment to which I had succumbed the difficulty of making myself understood contributed: often, in fact, it was an impossibility.

I wonder if you know that feeling of being cast without com-panions amongst people of a totally different tongue? It cannot be called loneliness, because there is something pleasantly daring about it, as though you cannot be reached or got at. Esthonian, you must know, is as strange to the likes of us as Arabic. With Poles, Serbs, Czechs, and with all the Romance peoples I can manage to get along, one can always pick up familiar words and turns of phrase, though I am not really fluent in their langu-ages. But here I felt I had fallen into the ocean depths, yet the distance to St. Petersburg was no greater than from Paris to Vichy or Dijon. Only men who had served in the army could speak a little Russian. That sort of thing was not uncommon with us: peoples or tribes who had their own languages and kept a smattering of Russian for dealings with the authorities. And unless you were a Pan-Slavist you found nothing wrong in that, and it was even a quaint and colourful curiosity. On the small

islands off the coast, where only a few fishermen or seal-hunters
lived, Swedish was spoken as well in many cases, but such old-
fashioned Swedish, so I was told, that travellers from Sweden
had some difficulty in conversing with the local folk.

I felt drawn to those islands. I love islands of any kind, but in
their remoteness these seemed to me more insular than any
others, and I resolved to pay them a visit.

I had long since lost all idea of time. You know how quickly
that can happen on a journey. Every day seemed to be endless,
and life at the seaside with my family, let alone school life in
St. Petersburg, seemed to have dropped into a bottomless anti-
quity.

The day when I should have been back with my people had
passed. But what was I missing? And perhaps it was merely fantasy that told me I had parents at all, brothers, sisters and girl-
friends at a seaside resort swarming with Petersburgers, where
Russian was spoken and spa concerts were held. I had had so
little opportunity of spending money that there were no obstacles
on that score to my extending the trip. So I wrote a postcard that
I would be away a while longer, though I found it hard to imagine that the news would really reach the populous, tradition-
bound world of the holiday visitors. Incidentally, I discovered
later that the card reached my parents two days after I sent it
off.

I had a map with me and on it I examined the confused mass
of small islands. It looked as though a sack had been opened and
its contents scattered all over the place.

The map did not show much more than the names of the
islands and their shape, but one of them I found especially
attractive. I cannot now say for what reason : perhaps it had an
intriguing outline, perhaps a name which appealed to me. The
name, too, has slipped my mind; for strangers, such names are
easy to forget. It was by no means the nearest, either, but the
urge to explore it had somehow taken hold of me. You will
remember from your schooldays how these sudden passions can
arise. In a dull geography lesson you become convinced that
some day you will have to get to Trinidad or Janina, there will
be no peace until you do. You become absolutely obsessed with
the idea! Probably desires of quite another sort underlie such a
wish, particularly the one that I have already mentioned, namely

to come face to face with the extraordinary, with fate, with the key to the meaning of one's existence, or whatever you care to call it.

I made my headquarters at one of the "shore rider" stations, that is to say, I left my rucksack behind so that I could wander around with more freedom, and I also spent two more or less comfortable nights there.

The shore riders took me in with a kind of friendly indifference. They were comparatively old men, for only ex-soldiers were employed in the service and most of them had to have reached non-commissioned rank. Life was more sedate with them, not so gay and rowdy as with really young soldiers. Today, admittedly, I would tend to look on these "old" men as themselves young.

I watched them polishing their weapons and harness and playing cards. As far as I knew how, I enjoyed helping to look after the horses. They also allowed me to go with them when, early each morning, the horses were ridden into the sea. The powerful naked bodies of the men flamed in the light, and I felt as though I had been allowed a glimpse of a Homeric world.

My sketch-book was still almost empty. This was the exact contrary of my intention when I had started out, but I had been in such a state of receptiveness and absorption in face of all I had encountered that activity on my part was difficult. To please the men, I now forced myself to do a few drawings in pencil, as well as in pen and ink : sketches of horses and views of the station with the *glint* or the sea as a background. I presented them to the men and even aroused their admiration.

In those two days with the shore patrol I soon felt I had been one with the place and its inhabitants for years. I attached myself mainly to an older man, an Esthonian, who spoke Russian so badly that I could not always understand him. He wore his fair hair very close-cropped, had a bushy moustache and was of impressive build. His clean uniform, white summer tunic and blue breeches with green piping, suited him well. He showed, it is true, the reserve I have often noticed towards us Russians among the Esthonian population, but I liked his serious though not unfriendly manner, and I quickly got used to his laconic conversation. He knew the area better than his comrades, who for the most part came from Central Russia, and so I could get him to tell me all sorts of things and supply me with a great deal of information.

I showed him my map and said I wanted to have a look at the islands, that particular one especially. He looked at me with surprise, as though it were an incomprehensible whim. He even tried to dissuade me : what did I expect to find there, anyway ?

This man took a marked pleasure in watching me draw. I sketched his portrait, achieving a tolerable likeness of his features, and presented it to him. He accepted this modest, not to say dubious gift as something of great value; there was a touch of something approaching awe in his manner. From then on he was more forthcoming. He took up my plan seriously and promised to find someone who, for a small charge, would sail me over.

But this was of less importance. Of greater interest to me was what he told me about the island. This island, he said half reluctantly, had at one time been much talked about. When I asked for details he was evasive, but finally I persuaded him to give me a halting account.

I heard of an old woman who lived alone, an object of sympathy and pity, but also of some dread. From the account delivered in faulty Russian I could not obtain any more detailed impression of her.

Then he spoke of a fatality that had occurred a few years before. He also used the word "murder", but not as a definite assertion.

The woman, as I understood it, had had two sons, fishermen by trade, poor people. Her husband had lost his life in a storm a long time ago. Then her elder son, to whom she was very attached, failed to return from a fishing trip. There was reason to think he had been murdered. The mother's grief had been desperate, and probably still was.

I asked about the circumstances of the death and the reasons for suspicion. But whether he deliberately exercised reserve or his Russian vocabulary let him down, he began to slip into Esthonian words and I heard nothing revealing.

I asked whether the woman had no other children or why, otherwise, she lived alone. He replied that after the death of the elder son she had only the one younger son. When the disaster happened, this boy had been at home, on leave from the army.

Later, after his period of conscription had ended, he was said to have stayed on as a soldier.

I inquired of my friend whether he had known the dead man.

He nodded, then said shortly: "And the mother, and the brother."

He now paused for a while, as though in hesitation. But when he noticed how his story interested me he told me more in answer to further questions. It was said, he declared, that the old woman had been granted gifts not possessed by other human beings, and she had, moreover, lived in a particularly close association with the dead man. Who would want to delve further into that? But the people on the island maintained that by arts and conjurations she had persuaded her dead son to appear: almost every night he came and had talk with her.

This lurid and sinister story gripped me. I was immediately determined to visit not only the island but also the old woman. Was it curiosity, was it thirst for adventure? It must have been more than that. Here, as it seemed to me, there was moving towards me that experience for the sake of which I had undertaken the whole journey.

Not that I really believed the story of the patrolman. After all, we were enlightened in those days. Or were we? It was our fathers who were enlightened. But we were in opposition to them, and so wanted to be even more enlightened and more radical than they, who always kept a few bridges open for retreat—at least to that half-belief in miracles which the State, allied to the church, expected of its officials; or pretended to expect, for of course for some time it had been expecting nothing at all, but simply letting things slide. But sometimes we wanted to be more believing, or let us say more superstitious, than our fathers, and wanted to regard as at least possible those things which our grandfathers and great-grandfathers—or at least their nursemaids—had considered possible. At the same time we youngsters loved Nietzsche, or Renan, or David Friedrich Strauss, or even Haeckel; we discussed Ibsen, and Dostoievsky we held to be a sinister reactionary and a crack-brained idiot. At that time I had long since turned away from the church.

My shore rider helped me find a sailing boat, and as for the return journey, I was told not to worry, as a fair lasting several days was due to begin at a place on the mainland, many of the islanders would be going there, and I could come back with them at any time.

So I said farewell to the shore riders. What shall I tell you about the island? It was magnificent, it was so empty of human beings. In the woods it seemed to me that no human foot had ever trodden. I spent the day wandering around, picking berries, bathing, lying on the shore. But I was not greatly inclined to surrender myself to the influence of the landscape, the season and the progress of the day. For the first time on this trip, an impatience not far removed from ill-humour assailed me. The island had now no other significance for me than that of a setting —the setting of an extraordinary event I was expecting. And I forgot that, throughout the days of my journey, I had been experiencing the extraordinary in small things. That, incidentally, is a forgetfulness that seems rooted in human nature.

But what guarantee was there that I would in fact have an experience and an encounter? It might be all peasants' gossip, and it was also possible that I might not succeed in meeting the old woman and being accepted by her. All the same, I had made a plan that would, in all probability, lead me to the goal. My shore rider had described the position of the hut exactly, and as darkness fell I meant to turn up and beg shelter for the night. In a sparsely populated area that is a request which is hardly ever denied. I also intended to feign exhaustion, so that I could not be expected to seek shelter further off.

I found it difficult to while away the time. Once or twice I lost courage and called myself a fool. Then I thought my best course would be to find my way to the nearest settlement, ask for a bed and a means of returning to the mainland next day. But, having got so far, I felt it would be ignominious to abandon my plan.

Towards sunset I was on the spot. The hut lay on a narrow wooded tongue of land. Here, the shore was backed by cliffs, and sandstone boulders that lay about in confusion were covered with livermoss which shone emerald green in the slanting rays of the sun. It seemed too early to go any closer. I sat down on a rock and listened to the surf. Below me, the waves, in shapes almost like hemispheres, crashed on the stony beach. Hissing white masses of foam shot up continuously.

I waited a long time, suddenly free of all impatience.

The blue-black surface of the water lay motionless and the sky above it had assumed almost the same hue, though a fraction lighter.

Above the horizon stretched a narrow strip of glowing red, reflected in pale rose by the dark water.

It seemed that the time had now come; I got up and went to the hut. It was low and small. Beside it stood a dilapidated stable or shed.

Suddenly, as though out of nowhere, nightjars rose into the air, soundless and swift as lightning; down they came again like falling stones, crossed paths, and vanished. From the wood, looming up as a dark mass, came the long drawn out, melancholy cry of the long-eared owl, very clear above the sound of the sea, which was muffled now that I had left the shore. I shivered, although in the evening cool a warm current of air unexpectedly passed over me.

No one replied to my knock. I opened the unbolted door. There was a sour, stuffy smell. I went in, and said in Esthonian : "Good evening", for so much I had learnt during my trip. There was no answer.

I had an electric torch with me; that was a new invention in those days, much valued and admired. The first thing its beam lit up was a small photograph fixed to the rough wooden wall above the wretched bed. It showed a young man in N.C.O.'s uniform with a diminutive moustache. He looked handsome, empty and vain. From the printed address of the studio I saw that the photograph had been taken in a Siberian garrison town.

There was something very striking about the picture. At first I did not know what. It was not merely that it was the first object my torch had shown me. Then I realised what it was : the photograph was the only thing in the room that had any relation to our own times. Everything else was just as it might have been decades or centuries ago. The crude furniture was home-made, the hearth had been built of rough stones, the cracked cooking utensils might have come from a village potter. The bed-coverings and the article of clothing seemed to have been spun and woven by peasants. Everything was untidy and neglected.

I took off my rucksack and sat down on the bench by the

hearth. To save the irreplaceable battery, I switched off my torch. Suddenly, I was overcome by drowsiness and fell asleep.

I was awakened by light and noises. The mistress of the place had come in.

She was a tall, sturdy figure, and her hair was of that absolutely pure white seldom found even among very old people. Its whiteness reminded me of the water-lilies in the sheltered bays and of birds' skulls, bleached by the sun, lying in shallow water by the shore. She had bright, sharp eyes. I thought, this was how the mothers of medieval pirates must have looked. Her clothes were in rags; it was impossible to tell from them whether they concealed the body of a woman or a man.

I notice that my memory gives no clear conception of her age, and her sons, it had been said, were comparatively young. But in youth one is lavish with the description "old" and lacks the ability to estimate the number of years that older people have lived. It may be that she was younger than she seemed and that the signs of age had marked her prematurely.

For a while she pottered about the room, mumbling monotonously to herself, as old women do. Then, sticking a bare candle on a stool beside her, she sat down on the low bed and began to mend some clothes.

I had thought out exactly the gestures I would use to convey my state of exhaustion and the impossibility of continuing on my way. But as the old woman still took no notice of my presence I found no opportunity to put this pantomime into practice. She seemed completely absorbed by some internal preoccupation which, doubtless, was the only thing that mattered to her.

The thought occurred to me that she might be deaf or hard of hearing. Perhaps her sight was bad as well. But the powerful expression in her glance contradicted any such idea, apart from the fact that her sewing presumably required sharp eyes, and she had previously moved about the room with complete assurance.

I began to feel like an intruder and was embarrassed. I felt ashamed of the dishonest trick by which I had thought to gain a footing in the hut. I went up to the old woman again and said my "Good evening". She did not look up from her mending. I bent forward, so that my shadow fell on her hands and the clothes she was working on. Then I touched her sleeve. But that, too, made no impression on her.

I went back to the bench. I realised that her mind was not with her, or, rather, that it was only with herself and not with her surroundings.

During the day I had eaten what food I had with me and I was now hungry. I had counted on finding at least tea and bread in the hut and those dried, salted fish which are cut in strips, skinned and then cooked in boiling water, or roasted over the fire. They smell unpleasant, but by this time I was used to them.

On the table in the middle of the room lay a loaf of black bread. I cut myself a thick slice and put some money on the table in payment. Childishly conscientious, I tried by sounds and signs to draw the old woman's attention to this exchange, but even now, of course, I did not succeed in making her look up.

I chewed the coarse, dark bread. Then I took out my sketch-book and tried to draw from memories of the past few days. In this way I hoped to keep myself awake, for I still could not free myself from the idea that something was going to happen. But the light was too feeble, and I had to abandon the attempt. I had also thought of drawing the old woman's portrait, so as to provide some means of contact with her. But when I handed over the result she certainly would not have understood and would have ignored it.

So I waited with nothing to do, and my sleepiness increased. Finally, it overpowered me. When I jerked awake again, I saw the old woman still sitting on the bed, but she also now seemed to be asleep, with her head drooping over her lap. I looked at my watch, and then realised that I had forgotten to wind it. But only a short time could have elapsed, for the candle was still burning and seemed only slightly shorter than before.

Suddenly, she was awake again. She sat up straight, raised her right hand and passed the outstretched fingers very slowly over her face, as though brushing away a cobweb. Then she slipped off the bed and went down on her knees. She folded her hands and seemed to be praying, and now I could see only her shining white hair, for she kept her head lowered, so that her face was not visible.

She raised her clasped hands as high as her chest, as though in supplication, then she also raised her head. Her eyes had grown so wide that the whole of the rest of her face seemed to be swallowed up by them. I felt icy cold. I remembered the long-eared owl, and its sinister call again sounded in my ears.

I felt that something had happened.

I turned my head half-left to look over my shoulder. In front of the table on which lay the bread I saw a figure, half leaning and half sitting. I can still see it clearly before me at this moment. It was that of a tall man and was shrouded in coarse, whitish cloth. The head, too, was wrapped in a cloth of the same material which was pushed up over the forehead. In places where the skin was not covered—on the face, the neck, the hands, the legs and feet from the knees downwards—it showed a whitish yellow colour. The expression was rigid, as though something lay over the face and prevented the features from moving. The facial similarity between the apparition and the woman was unmistakable, and this was particularly true of the eyes.

The old woman unclasped her tensed hands and stretched them imploringly towards the figure. Her face showed an anguish that seemed to blot out all its normal characteristics, leaving room for nothing but naked, all-embracing motherly grief.

I kept on looking from one to the other. The eyes of the man seemed firmly fixed on the woman. But was I mistaken when I thought I saw them shift once or twice towards the photograph over the bed?

Suddenly, he began to speak. It was not, at first, the kind of voice that human beings use, but rather a harsh, monotonous howl, though not as resonant as normal speech. There was no rise or fall in this monotone, no accentuation. But repeatedly, when he had spoken in this terribly lifeless way for a while, he paused, then uttered a single, short sentence, always, as it seemed to me, consisting of the same words, full of passion and urgency, as though he wanted to assert something and persuade his listener to accept it.

Each time, for the duration of this sentence, he raised his voice. It was like a litany in which the response "Lord, have mercy" recurs with emphatic entreaty after each invocation. But the complete lack of movement in his features, even in these more animated passages, was terrible. Skin and muscles seemed to be made of some inflexible material. Not once did I see that rise and fall of the eyelids, the flicker in the human face which has always seemed to me like the stirring of the water even when the sea is calm; I have always thought of it as a fundamental sign of life, and also as indication of man's dual nature, which reveals itself in waking and sleeping, in action and reflection, in life and death. From this duality the man by the table had withdrawn; he had been obliged to choose instead a terrible singleness of mind. But this was the lesser horror; for the lips did not move either. It was not clear how the voice was produced, and the assumption almost seemed justified that it came directly from the interior of the body, from its centre, without the use of vocal organs. In all this rigidity it seemed all the more significant that the man pointed once or twice to his white-bandaged head and also, as I thought, to the photograph on the wall.

Naturally, I did not understand a word of what he was saying. I did not even know whether he was speaking Esthonian or Swedish. But I felt I no longer needed to understand. I was convinced that his argument was irrefutable and that I must blindly assimilate the content of his sentences, incomprehensible though they were.

I could see from the mother's attitude that she was taking in every syllable, absorbing the words with an anxious and fanatical greed. Clearly she was not hard of hearing, let alone deaf.

Sometimes it looked as though she wanted to interrupt him with a contradiction; but then she heard him through to the end.

He fell silent; she replied. But if he had spoken without moving a muscle, then she spoke without making a sound. Her lips moved violently, her whole face quivered, her eyes protruded, her hands and arms were in desperate agitation. But not a sound could be heard. Suddenly I recalled the expressive, but completely soundless movements of the nightjars.

What significance was there in the fact that each of them used the opposite means of communication? Did the mother know that return to the audible world was barred to her son and that only the visible was still open to him? And what terrible congealing law prevailed over this soul, restored for a few hours to earthly things and allowed to assume a voice, but not the truest characteristic of human beings, namely the play and changing expression of the features?

Here I was brought to the extreme, the most fearful degree of that incomprehension which, in a provoking but not unsalutary manner, had filled the last few days. My journey had brought me among people with whom there was no possibility of understanding, and I now felt that this fact should have prepared me for this most horrifying scene; the impossibility of agreement between mother and son, it seemed to me, though different in kind and cause, was merely an indication of a secret imposed on both worlds, a secret which I could not unravel.

Each of the two strove with the utmost effort to urge persuasion on the other, the son remorselessly maintaining his assertion, the mother making persistent but weakening attempts to dissuade him from it. She positively begged him to spare her the ultimate, namely the acknowledgement that he was right.

This strangest of all conversations ended abruptly. Suddenly, the mother rushed forward with outstretched arms. At the same moment the figure vanished. The old woman had probably meant to clasp her son's knees, but now she found herself kneeling with both arms round the table-legs nearest to her. Perhaps she had wanted to speak to him, and she did utter a sound, but it was a desperate groan. I hurried over to her.

I had to release her hands from the table by force. I helped her to the bed and laid her down. I brought water, and when I held the cup to her lips she drank obediently. But she still seemed unaware of my presence. I talked to her, as one does to a sick or frightened animal, hoping for effect through the tone of what is said rather than through the sense.

There was no sign that she heard me. But she grew calmer. She closed her eyes and at last began to breathe regularly, as though she had fallen asleep.

All this, I think, had taken an hour. I myself was too agitated to doze off. I looked at the old woman, and again glanced at the photograph on the wall. Behind the vacant good looks of the young man I now seemed to detect an ice-cold egoism. Soon I was caught up in many trains of thought.

I gave a sudden start. The old woman had sat up and was stretching out her arms. Her face was corpse-like and rigid.

I had the feeling that it had gone very cold all of a sudden. Involuntarily, I looked round.

The figure had come back, soundlessly risen from the unfathomable, like the nightjars. Once again it took up a half leaning, half sitting posture, but this time in empty space, away from the table and perhaps two paces in front of me.

And yet, although I was still sitting on the bed, it did not seem to see me. The eyes were directed at the old woman—past me or through me. And perhaps it was part of the restrictive conditions of its return that it could be aware only of things directly connected with its former earthly life or with the events that had brought about its end.

But once again I learned how little I knew of the laws that obtained here. For the behaviour of the two underwent a marked change. His former rigidity had fled from the son: his face twitched and changed expression from one moment to the next. The gibbering lips seemed to be foaming. Head, arms and hands were in the wildest motion. But now no sound came from the mouth.

The mother had lowered her arms again. She held her head craning forward, as though listening intently. Suddenly a cry burst from her lips.

It was the first sound I had heard from her. What did it express? I can only reply—although this may cast a ludicrous light on my capacity for cogent description—in the one word: "Everything." And that means that, at this moment the last, perhaps flimsy barrier between the two was torn away, the same circumstances embraced them both, and so agreement was reached on the one matter that still divided them.

The old woman's cry was followed, I think, by a series of sounds, perhaps even of words. But I did not hear them. Such terror had seized hold of me that I rushed blindly from the hut.

I threw myself down in the grass, I sprang to my feet again. I wandered round in the darkness—up there, at that time of the year, it is hardly ever total darkness. For a long time I sat by the shore. It began to grow lighter. The vast surface of the sea lay motionless, a deep steel-blue, almost black, divided from the dark wall of the clouded sky by a barely perceptible line.

I pulled myself together and went back to the hut. The candle had burned out; the early light was filtering through the two small windows. The apparition was no longer visible. I went over to the bed and found that the old woman was dead.

I took out my torch and looked at her face. It wore an expression of sublime peacefulness.

I know one says in such cases that the eyes turn "glassy". That may often be so, but not here. I would rather say that these eyes had only achieved the power and the limpid clarity they were meant to have. It was as though, perhaps at the very last and supreme moment, they had beheld everything that it is given to man to behold—and that is nevertheless withheld from him.

I took my rucksack and went. Perhaps it would have been my duty to hasten to some headquarters and there to report the old woman's death. But that never occurred to me, and anyway, what have the like of us to do with the authorities? Was I to spend hours looking for an office, which might be God knows how far away, or search around until I came by chance on one of the Russian powers-that-be?

Next day, once more back on the mainland and on the way back to my family, I made a few sketches from memory, in which I tried to recapture the events in the hut. They did not quite satisfy me, although they may have given a tolerable idea of the outward happenings. I no longer have them; as an emigrant, it is not easy to keep souvenirs.

At home, I said nothing of my experience; what point would there have been?

When I thought back to the photograph of the soldier, I felt sure that the dead man lay on his soul. And today I still think that he was the murderer. May God not hold it against me, if I am doing him an injustice. Of course, I do not know the slightest thing about him. Perhaps he was killed in the war while he was still a young man; perhaps he now has hair like his mother's and is a general in the Red Army. In any case, this man is not important, and whether he sullied himself with his brother's blood, perhaps from envy or jealousy over some girl, is a matter of complete indifference. And although it looked as if the conversations between the older brother and the mother were solely about this son's death, its cause, and so on, in reality, I am sure, they were concerned with something quite different, namely with the secret of the world.

Literature, you know, nourishes itself to a great extent on the fiction that men undergo experiences which produce profound changes and upheavals, and that their lives are thus given a certain direction for ever—and this is supposed to happen above all in youth. (As though one could experience or discover anything whatever that is not already within oneself : every experience merely confirms and clarifies, it does not introduce something quite new.) No, I do not believe that; I think one discovers the truth about these things for oneself in later years. If this opinion derived from literature were true, the experience on the island would have been bound to have immense significance for me. Well, in one way they did, but differently from what one might imagine.

Admittedly, I cannot resist, even today, the thought that I would have received an intimation of the very greatest importance, had I only been able to communicate with the old woman. But here I myself am falling into the error of those literary gents and their credulous readers. And perhaps in the very impossibility of understanding lay the most significant fact of all, only I have been unable to grasp it.

Finally, what I received on that island was an inkling that the scope of human life is much larger than, for instance, was assumed by my father, who taught chemistry at various institutes in St. Petersburg and waited patiently for his Order of St. Anne, third class: an inkling that beneath the surface of the regulated world, in the inviolable existence of which we young people believed, in spite of our sceptical mania, lies something that appears completely unregulated; an inkling that, not only in human life but in all life, lightly covered by vegetation of various kinds, yawn clefts and crevices such as I saw in the *glint*, but clefts of a depth which no one can fathom, crevices, which, one may well think, lead directly to the centre of the earth, which no one has ever set eyes on.

When I look back today, after half a century, on all that I have lived through since then and all that the world as a whole has lived through, it seems to me, although the connection is obscure, that it was all foreshadowed then on that small island. And I could almost bring myself to believe that there would have been no need of all the events that have since occurred, if only I had managed to attract the old woman's attention, persuade her to speak and grasp what she had to tell me—and if only I had possessed or acquired the ability to pass on what I had learnt. Then the secret of the world would have been revealed and everything else would have been superfluous. For all the convulsions, upheavals and catastrophes that occur on this earth,

can they, I ask you, have any other meaning but that the secret
of the world is in process of being made manifest?

Or perhaps the exact opposite is true : that it is being concealed? What do you think? Everything is so uncertain! But to
have an answer to these questions—that would be important
indeed.

BIOGRAPHICAL NOTE

Werner Bergengruen was born on 16th September 1892 in Riga, a
city that was then under Russian rule. He studied in Marburg,
Munich and Berlin before serving in the First World War and in
the confused fighting in the Baltic states which followed the armis-
tice. In 1919 he married Charlotte Hensel, and in 1936 became a
convert to Roman Catholicism. Bergengruen has a natural relish
and talent for story-telling which is perhaps part of his Baltic heritage. At the same time, he was strongly conscious of the spiritual
tradition of German literature and of the poet's mission in the
revealing and sustaining of abiding human values. It is not only
in the Baltic settings of many of his tales that Bergengruen reminds
us of his origins : a predilection for the supernatural that
verges on mysticism is perhaps characteristic of a homeland
on the twilight fringe of the Slav countries. It is not without
significance that Bergengruen wrote a sympathetic study of
the great Romantic writer of ghost stores, E. T. A. Hoffman.
Bergengruen's lyric writing is concerned mainly with man's place
and development in history, and with Nature. The two collections
of poems, *Der ewige Kaiser*, and *Dies Irae*, some of which circu-
lated anonymously during the Nazi period, are eloquent protests
against the regime. History is, in fact, the element of many of
Bergengruen's best works. His short stories are too numerous to be
mentioned individually : the best of them—*Die drei Falken* (1937),
Der spanische Rosenstock (1940) and *Das Beichtsiegel* (1946), to
name only three—have the formal perfection that marks the best
tradition of the German Novelle. Two of Bergengruen's more significant novels, *Das große Alkahest* (1926) and *Der Großtyrann und
das Gericht* (1935), take as their theme the conflict of integrity and
worldly power; the latter was widely read in its time as a disguised
attack on the arbitrary rule of the Nazis. *Am Himmel wie auf
Erden* (1940) is a long and complex historical novel set in sixteenth-
century Berlin which again involves the problem of the ruler's
responsibility towards the ruled. Bergengruen's trilogy, *Der letzte*

Rittmeister (1952), *Die Rittmeisterin* (1954) and *Der dritte Kranz* (1962) is of unequal quality. The first volume is certainly the best: it contains twenty-four tales told, allegedly, to the author by the old cavalry captain, an exile brought up in the chivalrous traditions of the old Russian Empire. The mellow and urbane Rittmeister gives an artistic unity to the book, which looks back with nostalgia and gentle irony to a vanished age. The later volumes, lacking this unifying personality are somewhat prolix and diffuse. Like many German authors, Bergengruen was attracted to the Tyrol and Italy and many of his stories have the landscapes of Italy rather than his native Baltic shores. From 1946 until 1958, Bergengruen lived in Zürich, before moving to Baden-Baden, where he died on 4th September 1964.

Gertrud von Le Fort

Translated
by
Isabel and Florence McHugh

GERTRUD VON LE FORT

THE JUDGEMENT OF THE SEA

WHEN the royal ships were sailing across the Channel to Cornwall, the raging storm against which they had been struggling in
the beginning was smothered with fantastic suddenness by a
soundless calm, whereupon the little Prince was taken ill with
a most extraordinary malady, the like of which had never before
been observed in a child of such tender years. While the sea
seemed to sink deeper and deeper into the drowsy intoxication
of a leaden slumber, the poor little child was seized with absolute
sleeplessness. In vain did his young wet-nurse sing him the usual
lullabies, in vain did she offer him her breast, on which he normally fell asleep contented; he refused all nourishment, craving
only for the sweet milk of slumber which no one could give him.
And while the wide-open eyes in his pale solemn face grew larger
and larger, his little body wasted away as if consumed by the
hunger of those over-large, over-watchful eyes, which would not
close for a single moment.

The physicians on board the royal ship were at a loss; they
could give no counsel. The coasts of Normandy, from which the
ships had sailed, seemed as hopelessly out of reach as those of
Cornwall, towards which they were trying to sail, for not the
faintest breath of wind touched the limp sails.

Finally, seeing that the child's condition was becoming more
and more disquieting, those who were with the royal parents took
courage to remind them that the hostage Anne de Vitré was
aboard one of the escort ships, and that her countryman Budoc
asserted she was one of those who could still sing the old Breton
slumber song.

King John was alarmed at this suggestion; he feared to have
Anne de Vitré called, for he thought of his last raid on the
Bretons, of their burned towns and trampled fields. But most
of all he thought of the young Duke, the gentle boy whom he
had carried away in that raid and murdered with his own hand
at Rouen. And so he replied that he had known long since that
the Bretons were still heathen magicians but he himself was a

good Christian and did not wish to have anything to do with their evil cradle songs. Had they forgotten Anne's grandmother, the woman called Avoise, who had gone through the Castle of Reaux by night singing as the English troops lay in their beds there? Not a single man of them had risen the next morning.

So the little Prince continued to suffer, his over-large, over-watchful eyes wide open while the sea continued to sleep undisturbed. But after a few days, when King John had fled to the Seneschal's ship to escape from the sleepless eyes of his child, the Queen, in desperation, sent for Budoc and ordered him to row one of her serving women over to the Breton woman under cover of darkness.

Anne de Vitré had not yet lain down to rest, but was sitting on the deck of her ship under the starry tent of heaven, and questioning the sea, as her people were wont to do when they knew of no other counsel. It gave Anne a deep calm confidence to know that she could turn to the sea; it gave her a feeling of assurance such as her heart had not known for a long time. In Rouen she had always felt so helpless; there everything had seemed frightening and uncertain to her, but on the sea she felt secure. On the land there were woods and caves, and dark castles with dreadful dungeons; places where evil secrets can easily hide —but on the sea all things reveal themselves as they are. Anne thought of the times when men were tried for their lives in her country, of how the people entrusted themselves to the sea and submitted to its judgement, and how the sea recognised the guilty and kept them in its clutches, but set the innocent on land. And it never erred in its judgement. After all, the sea was not like finite, short-sighted man; the sea was God's greatest and most powerful creature, it came nearest to Himself in omnipotence, it was very close to His heaven—it was almost like God. You had to ask the sea if you hoped to hear the voice of God, and what voice could Anne de Vitré still hope to hear but His?

All the people around her shrank back timidly and wrapped themselves in impenetrable silence whenever she tried to find out about the young Duke of her country; it was as though his name had been completely wiped from their memories. And after all Anne de Vitré had a right to ask about him since it was for her young Duke's sake that she had been delivered up to this foreign king: she was held hostage for the oath of allegiance which had been wrung from the Duke. It was for him that she had had to leave her devoted parents and her loving brothers and sisters, and all the beauties of her sorrowful country. If she had not left her people he would have had to go—but a Duke must not desert his people. This was what her father had impressed upon her when parting from her, and thus Anne repeated his words in her heart again and again each day. Otherwise she would long since have died of grief and loneliness among the Britons. But she had been able to go on living, for if she had gone into a strange land for the sake of the young Duke of her people, he had remained in the homeland for her. If she had to be a prisoner for him, then he had freedom for her: he was at home in her place; he was her freedom. Her real life was not here among this hard alien race; her real life was the life of her young Duke. Surely Anne must have a right to ask about this, her real life! But even though she might get no answer from man, the sea would not refuse her an answer. The sea was just; the sea was almost like God. Anne de Vitré listened.

No sound arose from the motionless water. The ships lay upon it like dead black swans, almost as if they had been frozen on to it. Never in her life had Anne seen the sea so calm. One would really have thought that it was sleeping. But the sea did not sleep, as these Britons thought it did; it was only silent, as God too is only silent when He seems to be sleeping. And when God has been silent for a long time He will speak. Anne de Vitré listened once more.

Suddenly she seemed to hear a faint sound like the beat of a wave close by the bow of the ship; it was as though the sea were about to open its mouth. And as Anne rose to her feet—for it is but seemly to listen to the answer of the sea standing—she saw the dark outlines of a man rise up above the water like a creature of the deep. She heard a short, subdued cry such as the seafarers of her country use when their boat is putting in somewhere. And now Anne de Vitré could see the boat silently gliding towards the ship. She recognised the man in it. It was Budoc.

Anne was disappointed, for Budoc would only disturb her as she questioned the sea—Budoc was a turncoat and a traitor. He had long ago forgotten that, like herself, he was here among the Britons as a hostage for the young Duke of their people. Budoc

dwelt among the Britons as if he were one of them. Anne despised
and avoided him although he had once been a close friend and
a guest in her father's house. Yet sometimes when their eyes met
unexpectedly, she was overcome with homesickness as if she saw
her distant country before her. But that must surely be an illu-
sion.

Meanwhile Budoc had tied his boat to the ship and helped
the serving woman on board. Anne could not imagine why the
Queen should send for her at such a late hour, but she was too
proud to ask because she would of course have had to use
Budoc's help as the serving woman did when delivering her message—the woman did not understand the Breton language, and
Anne did not understand the hated Briton tongue. She had
never tried to learn it; but of course Budoc had learned it!

Anne followed them in silence. But now, as she sat opposite
Budoc in the little boat, close above the water, very near to the
deep, clear, omniscient eye of the sea, it suddenly seemed to
her that he was beginning a mysterious conversation with her in
the darkness, not with the voice of his mouth but with the voice
of his blood, that ancient Celtic blood which flowed in the veins
of both of them, deep as the beautiful springs of their country
and dark as the woods of the sorcerers, and wild as the wave-
lashed rocky coasts where the "Woman of Death" croons the
slumber song of their mothers in the ears of drowning seafarers.
Although it was too dark to see Budoc's eyes she seemed to see
through them into the abyss of an unshakable fidelity; not the
tender, noble fidelity of her own love, but the fidelity of hatred,
the daringly cunning fidelity which does not shrink from playing
the turncoat to the enemy in order the more surely to betray
him. Anne felt that the same pain was quivering through both
of them; and she felt that at any moment she would have to
listen to the voice of his mouth speaking of the young Duke
who was the lord of them both. No, Budoc would not dare to
speak before the serving woman; it was so alarmingly silent out
here on the sea that even the softest whisper would resound to
the horizon.

Only when the small boat, rocking slightly, lay close by the
bow of the royal ship and the serving woman had already
climbed aboard, did Budoc bring his dark face close to hers and
whisper in her ear, "The Duke is dead. The King himself was

his murderer. The sea has judged him, and you ... you ... you ..." It was as though a wild feeling of triumph robbed him of speech. He raised her up in his naked arms—for a moment she did not know whether he was going to fling her up in the air like a jubilant shout of revenge, or cast her into the sea. But no, he had already set her down on the deck.

Bewildered and dazed, Anne entered the pavilion of the royal ship. The interior was in semi-darkness; only from the entrance, where the sailcloth was turned back and bound to two carved pillars, a glimmer of the sea was visible, white as the stars.

The young Queen was standing there, straight and graceful, but her little insignificant face under the golden winged cap was tear-stained. She addressed Anne in hurried, timid words. She spoke so anxiously that one might have surmised that she, as Anne, was thinking of the murdered young Duke, but she was thinking only of her small sick child. Anne did not understand her, Budoc's words were still ringing like a peal of bells in her ears; the frail boyish shade of the murdered Duke seemed to absorb all her attention. She did not even realise that the Queen was speaking to her—she took no notice of her. But then she heard Budoc's voice again. "Anne de Vitré," he said, "Madame the Queen wants to know whether you would be able to sing the Breton slumber song to her sick child?"

Anne understood Budoc just as little as she had understood the young Queen. It was as if he spoke to her in the language of these strangers, and she made no answer.

The arched eyebrows of the young Queen moved a little, as if they wished to threaten Anne. But then her little insignificant face became quite helpless again. She tore off the golden chain from her neck and laid it over Anne; she stripped off her bracelets and offered them to her; she kissed Anne on both cheeks. Anne felt the weight of the chains and the bangles on her body; she perceived the wetness of tears on her face, but still she did not understand. All this while Budoc stood there, quietly waiting, his dark face detached and impassive.

Now the Queen turned to him again. "Ah, Budoc," she sobbed, "I believe Anne has forgotten the song. Do please ask her to remember it. Beg her to; you see she doesn't understand my words."

"Anne de Vitré," said Budoc, "Madame the Queen is afraid

that you have forgotten the song, but I know that you have not. You were already old enough when you heard your mother sing it by the cradle of your little brother Alain—the little Alain who drowned in the sea afterwards. I remember you exactly in those days : you used to lie in the lower part of the old trunk-bed singing with her, singing like a little bird in its nest until you fell asleep."

Anne remained silent although she now understood Budoc; her eyes filled with tears. How could Budoc think that she would sing to the child of the royal murderer the cradle song, the sweet cradle song which her mother had sung to her little brother Alain? Was Budoc a traitor after all? Her child-like face became quite stern and pitiless. The young Queen looked at her with dismay; like a poor woman of the people begging alms. "Oh, God, she will not sing to my child!" she wailed. "She will not do it! Ah, Budoc, do please speak to her again! Persuade her, tell her she must have mercy on us!"

"Anne," said Budoc, "you understand now what the Queen means, but you don't understand what I mean. You will not sing the cradle song to the child because he is the child of the royal murderer. But you can sing it to him, and for that very reason! Just think once more of your little brother Alain—little Alain who was drowned in the sea afterwards. To all who are drowned in the sea the 'Woman of Death' sings the song which she has heard their mothers sing by their cradles. It is the same song, Anne, exactly the same song. Your grandmother Avoise knew it, and you know it too : the child to whom the beginning is sung falls asleep, and the child to whom it is sung to the end never wakes again. You must sing it to the end for the child of Madame the Queen! You know the beginning—the beginning and the end—cradle and wave are one. Now do you understand at last that you . . . you . . . you . . ."

Once more the note of jubilation, which choked his words, had come into his voice. But now Anne understood : the sea had answered, the sea had passed judgement, the sea demanded this child. Truly the sea was just; the sea was almost like God. She remained quite still for a moment like one praying; then, slowly, she removed the Queen's chains and bangles from her neck and arms, walked up to the rail of the ship, and threw them into the sea. Her face was as white and impassive as the sea. She did not look at the Queen. She kept her eyes turned only towards the sea. "I will sing the cradle song," she said.

But now the young Queen became uneasy. "Budoc, why has she taken off my jewellery?" she asked, tremulously. "Chains are fetters—I wanted to bind her to me with my chains. Why did she give them to the sea? Does she seek an alliance with it?"

Budoc replied lightly that he thought custom required it of those about to sing the Breton slumber song. But the young Queen was not reassured. "So she is in league with the sea when she sings!" she cried, beside herself. "But the sea is our enemy! The sea is cruel! It is holding my little sick child fast and preventing us from bringing him to land! What kind of a covenant is it that she has with the sea?" And she looked searchingly into the eyes of Anne de Vitré.

Anne had now turned back from the rail of the ship and was standing in the dimly lit opening of the tent. The whitish radiance of the motionless water outlined her figure from behind as if with a silver pencil; it was still as slender and as touchingly unrounded as that of the young girl who had been delivered up a hostage to the Britons a year and a day before. It was as though Anne had not yet blossomed fully into womanhood although she was already in her first tender maturity. But after all, Anne could not flower in a strange land; her life was as a motionless shadow.

The Queen's eyes in that small face of hers, suddenly took on an odd visionary expression : it seemed to her as though she were really seeing Anne de Vitré for the first time at this moment.

Budoc had motioned the ladies and serving women to leave the pavilion and to escort their mistress from it if Anne began to sing. But the young Queen hesitated. "No, no!" she protested. "I will not go out. I will remain here while Anne is singing. I will not leave my child alone with her if she has a pact with the sea!" She sounded very much afraid of Anne de Vitré.

The women tried to smile reassuringly. The eldest of them, a kinswoman of the royal house, went to encourage the young Queen : Anne was only going to do what had urgently been requested of her; now they must trust her and act as Breton custom prescribed. Anyway, they would have to leave the pavilion if they did not want to be put to sleep themselves.

At the word "trust" the young Queen suddenly began to

tremble. The little silver discs with which the edges of her golden
bonnet were decorated began to whisper and flutter like the
leaves of an aspen. She stared into Anne's lonely young face as
if her eyes were feeling their way through its sorrowful loveliness
to the countenance of a Medusa within. "But I cannot trust
her!" she cried. "Just look at her! We have never really looked
at her before!"

Once more the women tried to smile reassuringly. The aged
cousin of the royal house renewed her persuasions. Anne held so
tender and innocent an expression, why would the royal cousin
not trust her child to her? After all, Anne herself was hardly
more than a child!

"But that's just it! That's just it!" stammered the Queen.
"Do you not understand? Of course she doesn't understand what
a little child is. She has neither husband nor child. She has no
life at all, and she doesn't even desire one. She has given away
her life to someone else...to someone who is no longer alive."
The last words came like a mere breath from her lips. No one
understood what they meant.

Now the Queen became completely beside herself. "But you
must understand me," she cried. "You must! We know, don't
we, that the Bretons can kill people with their slumber song—
have you forgotten about the British soldiers in the Château of
Reaux?"

At these words the courtly aristocratic faces of the women
suddenly forgot their smiles. The aged relative made a motherly
movement: how could the royal cousin speak so? We must not
offend Anne de Vitré like that! Kill a child? No one would
have the heart to do that!

The young Queen, barely whispering, continued: "Oh, yes,
indeed, yes indeed, people do find it in their hearts to kill children," she breathed. "These days people find it in their hearts
to do anything—anything at all. You know as well as I do ...
the whole court knows it ... everyone in Rouen knew it ... don't
keep on pretending! Oh, God, I cannot say it! Why do you
question me?"

The women had turned pale under their paint and powder.
Did Madame the Queen perchance mean the young Duke of
the Bretons? He was still a boy, almost a child. They did not
dare to look at each other, for no one of them knew how much

the other knew, so efficiently had every rumour of the crime been silenced.

For a few moments it was as though even the sea outside were holding its breath. Suddenly the ladies began to feel uneasy; their smooth suave courtiers' faces assumed an expression of helplessness; they turned around timidly as if they feared someone might be listening outside the pavilion. Only the good simple eyes of the royal cousin looked guilelessly unembarrassed, for the old generation cannot imagine the horrors of modern times. What did the Queen think they had been asking her about, she inquired placatingly? None of the women had uttered a single question; neither had Budoc nor Anne, and there was nobody else there. The Queen was making a mistake.

"But someone keeps questioning me all the time," murmured the Queen. "Do you not notice it? It's as if we were on trial here, being cross-examined before a court. And before a court one must confess if one wants to obtain mercy. But I have nothing to confess. I don't know why my little baby cannot sleep, and I don't want to be asked about it any more. It is a terrible thing when little children cannot sleep any more—only criminals are sleepless! But my little child has committed no crime. There must be some mistake. Why should he suffer? Budoc, tell Anne there's been a mistake. She needn't sing—I'll do it myself!"

"Anne," began Budoc, "it seems that the sea is demanding the confession of Madame the Queen before it can carry out its sentence. But she cannot bring her lips to utter it. Do not be annoyed, you will have to wait a little longer."

Anne had been standing there the whole time, completely lost in her own thoughts, intent upon recalling the song which she was to sing. It was such a long time since she had heard it; she had to summon up all her powers to remember it; she dared not take any notice of what was happening around her. At Budoc's words she looked up for the first time. An expression of astonishment came into her impassive face. Where now was the graceful Queen who had held such gay court in Rouen at the time when that great impenetrable silence had arisen concerning the young Duke of the Bretons? Where now was the painted, bejewelled woman who had always smilingly evaded Anne's trembling questions about him? Where was the flatterer who had pretended to be so kind to her, even here on the ship? Now, all of a

sudden, there was only a little wild desperate face, mirror-clear
as the naked stones of the strand washed by the sea. Yes, truly,
on the sea everything is revealed.

Anne did not venture to speak a word. She nodded to Budoc
signifying that she would wait. How could she refuse to do so?
The sea was waiting too; the sea was in no hurry; it had the
breath of eternity; it was almost like God. No one could escape
God and eternity.

A soft breath of wind came from outside—the waters must
have begun to stir. It was as though the sea were mounting its
judgement seat. To Anne de Vitré it seemed suddenly strangely
bright for the middle of the night.

Meanwhile the Queen had sat down beside the cradle and
begun to sing in her small thin voice. As she sang the melody
became confused, the words became senselessly jumbled and she
sang the wrong notes. It was as though the little song which
she had started were going quite mad in her mouth. Suddenly
she stopped and said in a faint, gasping voice: "My God!
What's this? It's getting so bright, and the little Prince must
sleep! The tent will have to be closed!"

Her eyes fell on Anne, who was still standing in the entrance,
now no longer as if drawn with a soft silver pencil but rather
as if enveloped in radiance from a star: the sea behind her had
begun to shine. At the sight of her the Queen uttered a cry and
threw herself over the cradle as if to protect the child with her
body.

"Why is she still there? Why is she still there?" she sobbed.
"Have I not said to tell her that the little one will be able to go
to sleep himself? Yes, I believe he's already asleep—just look . . .
look . . ."

With a trembling hand she raised the curtains of the cradle.

Suddenly it had become so clear it seemed as though the
brightness of the sea had come on board and were sweeping into
the middle of the pavilion. One could see every corner of that
tented space; and one could recognise in the half-light of the
open cradle the solemn face of the little Prince. The young wet-
nurse suddenly began sobbing loudly and could not be consoled.
The Queen's ladies were weeping too, but the Queen herself sat
there as if turned into a pillar of salt with her tearless eyes staring
into the wide-open eyes of her child.

At last the aged relative touched the Queen on the shoulder and said compassionately: "Dearest cousin, Anne de Vitré is still here, will you not open your heart and have confidence in her? For it's not just by mischance that the little Prince cannot sleep."

The Queen made no answer but began murmuring in a low voice. No one could say to whom she was speaking—it was as though she were rendering an account to an invisible father-confessor. "No, it is not by a mischance that the little Prince cannot sleep," she whispered, "and I know why it is not. It is because there is nothing on earth more frightful than to murder a child—and we have murdered a child. When you are silent in the face of a crime, you give your consent to it. And I have kept silent about it—every one of us has done so—the whole Court has done so. We have kept silent, and our silence has cried to heaven. We have eaten and drunk, we have dressed ourselves up and adorned ourselves as if nothing had happened; we have laughed and danced. And yes, we have even slept soundly although one would have thought that no one could have slept any more at Rouen. But we could . . . we did. Why should we not have slept? There was no judge who could have wakened us, for the judges were also asleep. Of course they had to sleep —they were ordered to do so. Only my little child can no longer sleep!" And she looked round her with the air of someone who had completely forgotten where she was.

The women had slipped out of the tent one after another. Even the Queen's cousin had withdrawn, perplexed. Only Anne de Vitré was still there, and in the background, Budoc. His face seemed the only dark thing left in the light-filled room. The Queen took no notice of him; she leaned back her head again as if she would cry out in sheer anguish. As she did so her golden winged cap slipped back on to her neck, and her golden hair came loose and fell into her face like a lion's mane. She stood up and walked a few steps towards Anne. It seemed as though she wished to throw herself on her knees at Anne's feet, but that her whole being clamoured in its depths to struggle with the girl. Her small, doll-like face, so pitiable without colour or adornment, was wiped out, completely overwhelmed and blotted out by its own prototype. She was now no longer herself. She was only a part of the vast elemental forces from the nameless mother's womb of Nature.

"Anne," she cried, "I know that you are in league with the sea which you Bretons say is just, and almost like God. I submit myself to its judgement. But a person is surely at liberty to plead for mercy before any judge. And so I plead : Kill me but save my child! I swear I will surrender myself to you when we land in Cornwall. Sing there if you like, and where you like. I will give you the key to Bristol Castle. You may go through all the passages there in the night as your grandmother did through the Castle of Reaux when the British garrison lay there in their beds. And when I hear your voice outside my room I myself will open the door to your song and listen to it willingly until I can no longer hear. No, do not fear that I will flee from you! Ah, Anne, you have no child! You cannot understand me—but you must believe me, it is not difficult to die for this little child. I know it—once before, I nearly died for him—the time I brought him into this world. Ah, Anne, believe me! I pray you, believe me!"

She had quite forgotten that the Breton girl could not understand her language.

Anne felt vaguely that the other woman was struggling with her for the life of her child. Once more her noble young face took on an unyielding expression and she shut her eyes to the Queen. She was concentrating completely on the song which she seemed to hear from afar, from the beautiful springs of her homeland and the woods of the sorcerer Merlin, and the sea-lashed rocky coasts where the "Woman of Death" crooned the cradle song of their mothers into the ears of drowning fishermen. And now Anne walked into the great twilight chamber of the Castle of Reaux, softly, as her long dead ancestress had once walked there; no, as the "Woman of Death" had entered when she came to listen by Alain's cradle. Anne heard her singing the sweet lullaby of her mother—and her heart began to beat faster. It seemed to her as if she were reawakening with terrible suddenness to her own, her real life. And now she would see Alain again too—her resolute young face became indescribably tender at the thought.

The Queen never took her eyes off her. Suddenly something like a breath of relief passed through her whole body. She grasped Anne by the hands and drew her over to the cradle. Anne felt a sisterly kiss on her lips and heard the fading rustle of a dress. For a few seconds she remained like a sleeper who resists wakening at the end of a dream. Then she realised that the Queen had left her alone with the child. The hour had come. She did not dare to open her eyes. With her hands folded fervently, looking like the picture of one in prayer, she began to sing.

At first her voice sounded very shy. She sang without words, only humming the notes, murmuring them tenderly, and beginning at the beginning again and again with the first ones, which sounded like little waves breaking on the strand and gently rocking a small boat back and forth. But then the words leaped out from the melody as if of themselves—gracious innocent words in childish rhymes. To Anne it was as though her mother were singing them aloud to her; she did not notice that her own voice had become like her mother's. Since she had been with the British, Anne had never once sung; she no longer knew her own voice; she thought she was listening to her mother's : now she was lying once more in the big trunk-bed in the Château of Reaux and needed only to join in as her mother sang her little brother Alain to sleep.

As soon as Alain fell asleep her mother went out to call the old maid-servant Enora to come in and sit with the children. Until Enora came Anne was alone with Alain; she could be his little mother for a while. Alain needed that because he was so very tiny. Every time she looked at him she was filled with tender compassion, although he really was a rosy faced healthy child. But something could easily happen to such a tiny child; Anne dared not let him out of her sight; she would have loved to take him in her arms and press him to her heart, but her mother and Enora had forbidden her to do that; Anne herself was still so small she could have let Alain fall.

"But when I'm big, may I take Alain in my arms?" Anne had begged.

"When you're big," Enora had replied, "you'll take a child in your arms—a child to whom you yourself have given life."

It was often a long time before Alain fell asleep and one had to begin singing again and again, tirelessly, just like the little waves on the shore when they rock a little boat.

Anne imagined she could feel the gentle rocking of the cradle which stood beside her on the trunk-bed. By now it should be time to hear the gentle, steady breathing of the sleeper; that soft heavy breathing of a child always filled Anne with such tenderness. She stopped singing and listened, and she became aware that only she had been singing; her mother must have gone out already to call Enora—she was alone with Alain. When she sat up straight in her own half of the high-backed bed, she used to be able to look down into the other half of the bed, right into Alain's face as he lay there in his cradle, sleeping so peacefully, his two sturdy little fists clenched one at each side of his rosy face as if in touching ignorance of his strength. Anne had to smile at the memory—it had always been such a joy to look at him and to know that she was protecting him.

Anne opened her eyes and bent down. There stood the cradle right in front of her, white as whitethorn. Alain was lying in it, but he was not rosy, and he hadn't his little fists clenched either. Alain—oh God, it was not Alain at all—it was the little Prince who couldn't sleep and whose life the sea was demanding! Anne stared at him in horror. His tiny face was as white as the flowers on the cradle; his hair was stuck to his forehead, wet with fear and perspiration; and the corners of his mouth were drawn down by suffering. But in spite of all this there was something easy and comfortable about his little face; his breathing was barely audible, but gentle and peaceful. He had shut his eyes, he was asleep : Anne had sung him to sleep.

She felt a strange confusion, and suddenly a feeling of tender compassion, the same feeling which used to overwhelm her when she looked at Alain. She forgot completely who this child was, she saw only that he was even tinier and in greater need of protection than her little brother had been : the longer she looked at him the more touching he seemed to her. She would love to take him in her arms as she had always wanted to take Alain. Then why did she not do so? No one could stop her doing so now for of course she was grown up. "When you're big," Enora had said, "you'll take a child in your arms, a child to whom you yourself will have given life."

Anne felt a piercing grief, a grief as of being dragged away a second time from her harsh yet beautiful homeland—no, rather, from the primitive essence of her own deepest being. For was she not standing here to deliver a child up to death? Shuddering with horror she looked at the infant. It would not take long—not as long as it had taken her grandmother Avoise to sing the slumber song to the Britons who had occupied Château Reaux—for of course the little Prince was so weak and sickly! If Anne sang just a little longer his breathing would become inaudible, and a little longer still and it would begin to falter, and yet a little longer and it would cease, lulled to sleep and then washed away by this gentle dreamy melody, which sounded as childish and innocent as those soft waves on the shore as they rock a boat and yet was as near to the abysmal depths as these—yes, as near as sleep is to death—and that is so near that both can be called by the same name.

Now the child suddenly started crying—Alain too would often start crying loudly in that frightened way in the midst of the sweetest slumber—one could have thought that he had seen upon him the eye of the "Woman of Death", who had stood by his cradle. Involuntarily Anne stepped back a pace. As she did so she became aware that the coverlet had half slid off the cradle; she came nearer and drew it up carefully. Again the child cried out. Anne had to be careful not to waken him. But there, he had wakened after all: for an instant her gaze was held by the over-large, solemn eyes of the child—it was as though this tiny creature knew the fate awaiting him. Suddenly she thought of the young Duke of her people: he had probably looked at his royal murderer just like that in the last moment of his life. Growing pale, she turned towards the sea—it was as though she wanted to wipe from her sight the picture there in the cradle just as she had removed the Queen's jewels from her body a little time before.

Once more she clasped her hands and began to sing.

Now her voice was even softer than before; it had taken on an ardent and imploring tone, in fact, an almost adjuring note. She seemed to be appealing to the sea to support her, but she could not look at it while she sang; she had to close her eyes once more.

She was back in the half-dark chamber of her parental home, but she no longer heard the sweet singing of her mother. Instead she heard the voice of her grandmother Avoise singing as she had sung in that night to the British soldiers who had taken possession of the Château of Reaux. Anne had been awake at the time although the old nurse-maid Enora had stuck wax in her ears. All the family and servants of the Château Reaux had had to do so that night so that they would not fall into that sleep with the Britons. But Anne had loosened the wax a little bit, and every time Dame Avoise had passed by her door on her way through the Château, she had been able to hear her voice for a moment: it was thin and clear like the silver hair on the old lady's head; it seemed incomprehensible that this gentle voice could have overcome all those many, many strong men.

Towards morning Enora had opened the door a little way; in the pale light of dawn Anne had seen through the narrow opening the naked arms of the men who had slipped behind Dame Avoise, their swords in their hands—to strike down any of the Britons who should stagger up from their sleeping-places —but none did. Those men had a wild sombre joy on their faces as if they were finding it hard to hold back shouts of victory; but there was no jubilation in the face of Dame Avoise. It was quiet, mysterious and open, yet it seemed to Anne much more horrifying than the faces of the men; at that time she did not know why. But now she knew. A woman cannot give herself up to being an instrument of death—woman exists to give life. Anne could feel a yearning rising from the very depths of her being and the remotest sources of her blood, a soft and tender feeling, yet nonetheless strong and powerful and in fact compelling.

Trembling, she shrank farther and farther away from the cradle and towards the opening of the tent; so far that she tasted the salt of the sea on her lips. But the nearer she came to the rail of the ship, the more demanding became her desire. It seemed to her as though the sea were searching through her closed eyes into her innermost being; it became as translucently clear in her as it had been just now under the tent when the Queen had made her confession of guilt—Anne could see into every fold of her own heart: suddenly she could no longer sing. It was as though the sea had drawn her too before its judgement seat. She wanted to fall on her knees and implore its mercy, but she could no longer do even that, so greatly did she fear for the child—she could only escape now into her own mercy, she could only save herself by the cradle.

The child lay in a terrifying quiet. Anne had no choice; she had to take him in her arms to assure herself that he was still alive. As she did her hands trembled : he was light as a new-born infant. Anne had never held a small child in her arms before and she shuddered as she felt the warmth of the tiny body against hers. The infant was breathing, it was sleeping, but more deeply than before. Anne felt as overjoyed as if she herself were recovering from a mortal illness. "It must feel like this," she thought, "to have given birth to a child. It must feel like this!" At the same moment Enora's words came back to her mind, but now a mysterious sweetness mingled with the memory. "I have given him life," she thought, "I have given him life—he's sleeping, he's well again, he's saved." And all at once a deep peace came over her as if she had now fulfilled the meaning of her own life. Again and again she repeated the words, "I have given him life—I have given him life." In her joy she had forgotten everyone and everything else and she felt as if she were alone in the world with the child.

But she was suddenly aware that this was not so; the thought of Budoc occurred to her. And now she actually saw him emerging from the back of the tent. He spoke no word; but he looked at her as though he had never let her out of his sight the whole time. She tried to ask, "What do you want of me?" but she knew that already. Again she looked into his eyes—through his eyes—into the depths of a fierce unswerving fidelity. These eyes asked her : "Will you sing to the end?"

She shook her head in silence and pressed the child to her breast. Budoc's dark face paled with pain and anger. He stepped up to her, so close that she felt his breath on her face. "Anne," he whispered, "you know that the 'Woman of Death' stands by the cradle of all who drown in the sea—you were a child when she came to your little brother Alain. Are you really sure that she came for him alone?"

There was a veiled threat in his words. Anne understood it instantly. She looked at his naked arms which had lifted her out of the boat a short while ago when she did not know whether he wanted to throw her up in the air like a jubilant cry of vengeance, or fling her into the sea. But now—curiously—she felt no fear; it seemed to her that Budoc no longer had any power over her. She smiled at him. She no longer believed in the "Woman of Death".

He looked at her fixedly. "Will you sing to the end?" he asked; and she knew within herself he was asking for the last time. Again she shook her head in silence and pressed the babe to her breast. Budoc became yet a shade paler; never would Anne have believed that this swarthy face could turn so terribly white. Slowly he turned to the opening of the tent and let the drawn up sailcloth drop behind him.

Now the two were almost in darkness. Anne could no longer make out Budoc's form, but the nearness of his naked arms seemed terrifying: involuntarily her thoughts went back to the men who had crept along behind Dame Avoise. Like lightning the certainty flashed through her mind: those arms are seeking the child. Uttering a faint cry she pulled back the curtain and with the child pressed to her heart, rushed out on to the deck. The next moment she was surrounded by the Queen's ladies.

They took the little prince out of her arms. She heard the young Queen's faint cry of joy at the sight of the sleeping child; she heard the happy excited chorus of whispers. In the rejoicing none of them took any notice of her—after all, it was not her child to whom she had given life, it was the child of the foreign woman, the child of the enemy woman and of the royal murderer. Anne watched them as they laid the babe on the breast of the robust young wet-nurse, who carried it triumphantly back into the tent, followed by all the others. Anne was alone once more under the starry dome of heaven—alone as she had been shortly before, when she had questioned the sea about her young Duke. . . .

But the sea was now questioning her about him! And Anne had to render an account of herself; she had to render an account to this holy, this dread element from which she had fled just now in her mortal anxiety for the child. There it lay, looking as white as if all the stars of the constellations had been drowned in it; as stern as the mirror of an iron law; as motionless and fixed as an all-seeing eye. Once more it seemed to Anne as though a great light was searching through her very being. She did not try to hide. Where should Anne have hidden herself from the sea? The sea was like God! Anne had questioned it, and it had answered her, it had entrusted to her the execution of its judgement—its holy and just judgement. Anne did not think of questioning the judgement: murder cries out for atonement!

She felt that she was guilty before the sea, but she felt no re-morse. It was as though she had been brought before a different Judge, almighty and holy as the sea, but not only as just but, like her heart, merciful as well. Henceforth she could only accept this god become man as her Judge.

But at the judgement seat before which she stood how was Anne to explain this knowledge? How could she dare hope to make the sea, that great, that terrible power, understand this? How, when she could not even understand it herself! And what should she offer to her young Duke as atonement for his murder? She did not know. In the pious simplicity of her heart she could neither take the responsibility for her action nor explain it—she could only surrender herself in expiation. In childlike faith she bowed her head.

At that same moment she caught sight of Budoc's dark form rising over the edge of the ship some distance away. Again he appeared to her as a creature of the deep; a messenger of the sea as he had come a short while before. He climbed on board and came to her. "Come, Anne de Vitré," he said brusquely. "The boat is ready!" His face was sinister and domineering, but his voice sounded quite calm, almost indifferent. Anne felt with-out fear once more; once more it seemed to her as though Budoc had no power over her. She followed him willingly to the bow of the ship where the boat lay in the water. It was rocking gently in a sea that seemed suddenly—but gently and joyfully—agi-tated. Anne felt the breath of a light wind caressing her brow. Dawn was breaking but on the ships all around it was deathly silent. Only from the royal pavilion did there still come the sub-dued but cheerful murmur of the women's voices.

Budoc bent down silently to help Anne into the boat. She felt his naked arms clasp her knees. He raised her up, high up, as if he were again shouting a jubilant cry of vengeance. It was indeed a cry of vengeance: he was tasting its sweet power to the full. For a few moments Anne hung suspended, motionless, held fast by his arms, over the waves: she had just time to see the much too early rosy glow of sunrise which wreathed the hori-zon; she could see a sail being hoisted on the distant escort ship which had carried her away from Brittany; it looked like the wing of a swan rising over the waters. Then Budoc let her drop. The waves broke over her with a roar as Anne fell into the sea—

down, down into the bottomless depths, where all things can be called by the same name. Then there came the agony of drowning.

In the depths suddenly someone clasped her in his arms again. She was saved, she was given life—and the roaring lashing waves became quiet as the gentle waves on the strand when they rock a boat. Close to her ears Anne heard a sweet voice, a voice like that of her mother by the cradle of her little brother Alain; it was singing the same song that Anne had sung to the child of the royal murderer. But it sang it to the end.

BIOGRAPHICAL NOTE

Gertrud von Le Fort was born in Minden on 11th October 1876, the daughter of a Prussian army officer of Huguenot descent. She showed a precocious interest in history and religion and it seemed natural that she should study these subjects in the Universities of Heidelberg, Marburg and Berlin. After the death of her father she travelled widely and spent a considerable time in Rome, an episode which is closely connected with her conversion to Roman Catholicism in 1926. It was about this time that her first major works were published : a series of *Hymnen an die Kirche* attempts to explain the total relevance of the Catholic Church to the present age of doubt and disillusion. A companion cycle of poems, *Hymnen an Deutschland* (1932) is inspired by her idealistic patriotic vision. Her longest prose work, *Das Schweißtuch der Veronika*, is in two parts: *Der römische Brunnen* (1928) and *Der Kranz der Engel* (1946). The heroine, who clearly has features of Gertrud von Le Fort's own personality and experience, finds her way through devious distractions to an intellectual and emotional commitment to the Church. The second part of the novel is concerned with the theological and personal difficulties involved in marriage between believer and non-believer. The heroine demonstrates in a manner reminiscent of certain characters in the novels of Graham Greene her willingness to run counter to orthodox theology, and to forego even the sacraments of her Church for the sake of a spiritual love that transcends dogma. This readiness for self-sacrifice as part of woman's divine mission points to a most characteristic theme in Gertrud von Le Fort's work : the place of woman in God's creation and her changing functions as virgin, bride and mother. This issue is specifically dealt with in the essay *Die ewige Frau* (1934), and it informs many of the short stories : *Die Letzte am Schafott*

(1931), *Die Tochter Farinatas* (1941), *Plus Ultra* (1950), for instance, as well as the story in the present volume, *Das Gericht des Meeres* (1941). In this last story we may perhaps detect a veiled protest against the tyranny of the Nazis and the silent acquiescence of the mass of the German people. Gertrud von Le Fort was certainly critical of the Hitler regime, and soon incurred the prohibition that was imposed on so many liberal and Christian writers. The war years she spent mainly in Switzerland, but she returned to Germany soon after 1945 and now lives in Oberstdorf in the Allgäu.

An authoritative interpretation of the poetess, together with a bibliography, is offered by N. Heinen : *Gertrud von Le Fort*, Luxembourg, Editions du Centre, 1960. An essay in English by I. Hilton is included in *German Men of Letters*, Series II, Wolff, London, 1963, pp. 277–98; this has a select bibliography.

Kasimir Edschmid

Translated
by
R. P. Heller

KASIMIR EDSCHMID

THE HUMILIATING ROOM

I was spending the evening with a friend. We were alone. We
had been furiously discussing politics. We had drunk tea that
smelled slightly of ... camel hair, I think. He had been telling
me about a hunt in Turkestan, and I had talked about some
winter days I had spent near Utrecht. After that we talked for
a long time about Paris once more. I had just mentioned the
shadow-plays of the Connards, and was going on to tell him
about meeting Wolfsberg in the Square de Vaugirard without his
beard, and what a curious effect this had on me ... when my
friend, who had been sitting quite still, leapt to his feet as though
impelled by some long suppressed resolve. He led me through
his bathroom into another room which, until then, I had not
even known existed.

He raised his arm. Slowly a brilliant light began to flow into
two lamps at the base of the walls; its warm waves streaked up
their honey-coloured sides. Then he opened the large window
on to the street and drew a blind across the gap. The profile of
his adventure-torn yet benign face sprang up against the bright
fabric ... and then there were only his hands. Now they
alone were bathed in light, grotesque in their ruddiness and looking more than ever like a sailor's hands. His every movement
exuded strength tempered by gentleness. On the other side of the
room, flanked by two cupboards, there was a sash window giving
on to the garden. He went over and opened it. The summer
night streamed in. The curtains billowed out from the frame.
Shadows swung across the carpets and a rattling noise travelled
along the walls. It was a melancholy, unpleasant sound. Looking
up, I saw my friend smile and his half-turned hand point to the
pictures strung across the width of the high wall like a belt, so
that an equal area of gleaming wall-paper was exposed above
and below them. They were hung on strings, ribbons, silken
cords and lengths of rope. Some were almost entirely obscured
by pictures which covered them, the frames of others overlapped
and all together formed a strange, multi-coloured mosaic.

Pointing to the pictures, he said : A piece of my life has dug itself deep into each one of these. Call it a whim or an experiment. I must wait and see. I hung them in here indiscriminately, at random, just as I happened to come back here and as the fancy took me. Years are buried in some of them and radiate their memories.

Often my room here is full of spring in Paris. This picture is Fragonard's "Lady on a Swing". She has pulled back one leg; the other is boldly thrown upward and traces the curve of the discarded slipper sailing through the air. And round this charming exposure floats the fullness of her robe and the fragrance of the colour that hangs above it like a cloud.

I bought it one evening after we had spent the day at St. Germain. It was the first of those captivating days that well up from an indifferent night and are full of the tenderness of blue skies and the warm stillness of promise. We stood on the soot-caked roofs of railway trucks. In the garden almond buds were bursting. We scampered across the park like young puppies. At such times there is but one bliss : the joy of movement, the play of awakening muscles. We laughed and raced about, leapt over hurdles, opened a wooden door carved with lilies . . . and only when we entered the circular enclosure did we realise that we were intruding.

A swing was coming down through an archway. On it sat a lady. She was wearing a flimsy dress of bright pink. We saw her from behind. Her arms hugged the two cords and pulled them together in a lazy curve, and in doing so she leant slightly to the right. Her head was lowered over something she seemed to be clasping in her cupped hands. It was so still that you could hear the squeak of the swing when, on each forward run, the lady quickly pulled back one leg using the other to push herself away from an apricot tree, red-dotted with blossom. And each time, under the wooden seat of the swing, a hand's span of lace dipped for an instant over an exquisite leg.

Then she heard us. She slid off the swing. Inclining her small, pale face to one side she gathered up her thin, short morning robe in a protective gesture, which revealed even more. Again you could see her calf in its shiny stocking, and her even brighter shoe. But the strange thing was . . . she did not blush or seem embarrassed. In a childlike, accusing voice which was beautifully modulated and full of meaning she simply said two words, "Good morning"—nothing else. Then without glancing back, she walked slowly, very slowly, into a side path.

We withdrew.

"An experience like a pastel drawing" . . . someone said.

Childlike, I thought, dainty, aesthetic! You understand? No other man had appeared on the scene, no one had called out or said anything, just a murmur : Good morning.

But in the evening, amid the deafening din of the boulevard, I bought this picture. At times I hear the sound of her voice, in the deep silence of the night, often by the sea-shore, in the up-roar of public meetings, through the pounding of wheels and the thudding of ship's engines. At this very moment I can actu-ally smell—you may smile—every scent of that morning, the dampness of the soil, the aroma of the air among the buds, the apricot tree and the warmth above it. You can see how an ex-perience can be etched into you with insane intensity, although at first it was something quite superficial, as easy to wipe away as a trace of breath from a mirror . . . and yet it remains, more powerful and persistent than the colossal impact of the first sight of a new continent, than thwarted ambition or the death of a sister. . . .

I have always cherished thoughts that might save me. That is why I love that picture. There isn't much to it. Simply an old etching, of two old people, very dark, with just a little light around their heads. In my mind I added a few pleasant details. That helped me. I was laid up at the time, sick and dispirited. It was a present from a little girl who used to play the violin in the evenings, somewhere in the suburbs. I can't remember anything about her bearing, nor a single feature of her face. But I do recall how she placed the picture on my blanket, alongside her grey cotton glove—it had a darker patch where it was mended.

This Goya here arrived one morning parcelled up in grey packing paper. Perhaps I was in a bad mood. I ripped it open and tore clean through it, making a great gash in the middle of the scene of the bullfight. Right in the middle, between the horse's belly and the bull drawing in his neck for a toss, and just above the even quicker hilt of the lance.

The Goya was sent to me by a Brazilian with whom I once

travelled through the night from Kowno to the frontier. A bliz-
zard was raging. He talked passionately about his country : the
majestic expanse of the Amazon, the burning nights which the
Brazilians endure by gulping down pots of scalding coffee, and
about flocks of screeching parrots.

The storm hurled itself against the embankment and pressed
with idiot force against the straggling body of the train. We began to feel hot, and together we pulled down the window. It
shattered immediately. The glass peppered our faces. We bled
from countless tiny wounds. The wind burst the other window,
the frames crashed. Snow gagged our mouths when we tried to
speak or call out; we choked, and could hardly breathe. The
Brazilian laughed, "shee". That was all I heard.

Hail slapped against our swollen faces, melted and instantly
froze again into masks of ice. We looked as if we had faces of
glass or red gelatine. We were streaming with blood and
laughing.

In the picture of the bullfight you can make out only the
bottom row of spectators. But a wave of fury and ecstasy seems
to have cascaded down from the top of the amphitheatre and
reared up into these front stalls.

There is a thick pool of blood in the picture.

The engraving is mounted on a piece of old yellow paper
which crackles with passion when the shaft of sunlight stabs it
through the little window.

I remember that night with pleasure.

But even dearer to me is the memory of that summer in which
every day was like that night. (With outstretched arm he pulled
out a large, white-framed etching. Its string stretched taut into the
room. He stood, balancing the picture in the hollow of one hand,
the other thrust into his pocket.) Here you can feel only one
thing : the pale path dominates everything. It winds mysteriously
among the dark hills . . . clumsy, brooding fishermen's huts with
glazed hatches squat alongside by the dunes, and then the phantom telegraph poles accompany it to the cross on the hill . . . it
all seems to create an atmosphere heavy with sorrow and disaster,
and only the feeblest sweet light on the horizon. . . . There's only
one thing that is great, so great that it could do without all the
rest, and that's the long white course of the path. It rises, fades
and slowly with a sinister urge spirals up into the grey skies

above the dunes as if into the monstrous, wicked supernatural beyond.

It is a scene from Bornholm by the young engraver Georgi. I met him on a tanker sailing from Copenhagen to the Faroe Islands. We were the only passengers. And the only foreigners on the Faroes (not counting a little botanist who within three days fell to his death from an impossibly difficult crag). We stayed there from the beginning of July till October when the ice started to drift in from Iceland.

We were each staying in a different fishing village. He spent his time sketching. I was writing—well, not really—I went fishing, hunted birds with a seven-balled bolass, and made love to the hefty girls. A violent gale was blowing most of the time. When it came it felt like something rounded or blue, and you always thought you could grab hold of it somewhere. Many times it seemed to flow from an ever-widening metal funnel, then swelled out over the sea like a sail and flooded the shore leaving behind it waves sculptured in sand.

We would often lie all day on top of a cliff that hurtled vertically to the sea. We buried our heads in our arms because of the raging gale. The sky was very pale, almost white. We could not stand upright. The storm would have swept us over the edge —quite gently perhaps, as if toying with a scrap of cloth, lifting it lightly, whirling it round, swiftly lowering it and then setting it down on the water. Who knows? Now and then, I strained every muscle (he bent his arm as if he were cracking something in the angles of his elbow-joints) to hold up a sketching-pad in front of my friend. He traced lines on it, in breathless haste and as if sheltering behind a barricade. That is how the gale raged.

Once I lay alone on top of the cliff for a whole day in the scorching sun and then through the night, not daring to take a step back until the morning, when the fishermen's girls sailed past below. One of them was wearing a red skirt. She waved at me and called out: "You've climbed up there early in the day . . ." She came from Stora Dimun. And then I did it.

We didn't wear shoes in those days. Bundles of bast were wrapped round our feet. Our island had a little beach. It was surrounded by black rocks rising up several hundred feet. At sea level they formed tiny fjords of excitingly flexible contours in which the waters swirled. The rocks were pitch-black, but at dusk they turned the dark-blue of basalt. At times brighter patches broke away from the rest and became swarms of sea-gulls that blanketed the sky and out-shrieked the sea.

Once a week the steamer from Edinburgh would arrive with tinned food and tobacco. It would dock only when the weather was fine. During the heavy gales it did not come for a whole month. We looked through our field glasses and saw some Americans standing at the rail; they were on their way to Ice-land. It was then that I missed the most important letter of my life. But who cared about letters?

What the hell did I care? I didn't give a damn. . . .

Imagine! That was the time when we had caught a kind of dolphin. Bigger than a man. Folds of velvety white in its gaping jaw. Its eyes deep violet with a faint reddish glow from the sun shining into them. One of the fishermen, with his coloured cap dangling in a long point over his back, thrust a harpoon into its throat and kept on pushing it down, although its eyes were al-ready going out, no longer reflecting the sun, and its body reared up in three convulsive leaps. The sharp-finned tail churned a hole into the sand and, like the frantic piston of a pneumatic hammer, beat a furious tattoo and raised a wind on that still day. A weird thing, that tail : porous, as if spun from jelly, soft steel and something that would surely taste delicious to the tongue, or, in an unusual bowl, enchant the eye—above all, it was of an infinite moist strangeness. I don't think anything more novel had ever happened to me before, nor had I seen anything more bizarre than that fin. Never had I experienced such ecstasy.

What did the most important letter of my life matter to me then?

Not a damn.

There was a difficult cliff between Georgi's village and mine. In the mornings we would fire our guns and make the echoes roll to and fro. That was how we exchanged greetings. In the evening we used to meet on the top of the cliff and gaze down into the interior of the island. It resembled an arena in the centre of which there was a large white rectangle, the building for the only disease that devours these people, dragging them, men and women all jumbled together, from their huts. For a long time the building flashed into the darkness like a shark's belly.

Now this deeply recessed Dutch frame . . .

I should like to think it was painted in the seventeenth century, perhaps even a little earlier, but not a minute later than that. It took me four days searching through twenty-eight antique shops on the Seine before I found it. . . . And while I was doing that I was fated to see a little fair-haired girl run over. Every morning at ten o'clock she would flash me a little smile on the main avenue of the Jardin des Plantes. She was wearing a black silk dress with a lovely yellow ruffle.

I shan't tell you about the picture in this frame, the one with the sailing boats. . . .

On the coldest day I ever spent in Germany I was standing in front of that set of pictures in the corner there. Come to think of it . . . I wasn't standing, I was pacing up and down.

It was so cold. I was walking on a wooden pavement but the cold still burnt into my feet. I walked faster and faster. Three steps towards the picture, three shorter paces alongside to the right, six along its whole length to the left, back to the middle and another three, more slowly backwards . . . over and over again casting ever more hurried glances at it, sinister and silent like the black panther striding behind the bars of his first cage in Frankfurt.

It is Gruenewald's Isenheim Altarpiece. Look at the supernatural power of the ray of light from the top corner, and the body of this leper, already green, putrid and so vegetative that it yearns for the soil and is already half soil. But here it is, captured as the agonised cry of the flesh torn between longing, life and ultimate destiny. All Colmar jingled with cold that day.

I love this picture. It did more than a thousand books ever could : in a surge of intuition it revealed to me, as through a gaping wound, the seething heart of the Middle Ages. . . .

(Raising his arm as if to throw a spear he raked a tiny picture with trembling circles of light from a pocket torch.) Memories of a month in a Scottish country-house. In the evenings silver plate, candlesticks and toasts. At other times, walks along straight paths in the park, lawns, two sisters, Lilith and Jane; rowing with their brothers, who were down from Oxford on vacation, and amid all this liveliness—infinite peace. It gave me an appetite for work for several years to come. As I left I stole this tiny engraving from the hall. It's a scene with monkeys. One of them is dressed as Voltaire. Underneath is written: The Travelling Monkey.

But the tenderest and most painful moments, haphazardly hurled together, are linked with this silhouette here. Germaine cut it out for me, in ultramarine on orange, at our little house by the Tuileries as the fragrance of a summer evening wafted through the curtains. Never, in the relentless flight of time have I loved a woman's body with such devotion as Germaine's. I had her learn every dance that could impart to her limbs new lines, a deeper ardour and more radiant rapture. She was at her most beautiful when, in the evenings, she would lie on a fur by my feet.

She would wear a long white nightgown and dreamily paint her toe nails. Now and then, outside, the dark garden would stir. Occasionally someone would walk past, red sky spread above the curtains and we knew how near the lights of Paris burned across the Seine.

Often Germaine would sit for whole days on her six-legged stool cutting out silhouettes. Then I took her with me to a little place at the sea-side in Brittany. We spent day after day lying in the sand, her body pressed against mine, and when she began to tremble it was dusk. Our bed for the night was a boat, with Germaine's limbs resting on the heavy red blankets like precious stones.

Paul Fort said of her that she was more touching than a butterfly and caused greater heart-ache than a poem of Francis Jammes.

Germaine loved me before she left me, but she had no soul. What she did have were indescribably beautiful knees, incredibly sweet, smaller and more delicate than the breasts of a slim, thirteen-year-old girl from the North of Germany.

I took that Carrière, in the oval frame, from the room of the painter Binetti, after he died of cholera. He had been ill for three days. All through his last day, hour after hour, he kept calling out a curious name. He dictated a letter to me but I didn't understand the address. Binetti kept on crying out and I gave him water. I applied ice-packs. An old woman helped me bathe him. Binetti kept on screaming the name. I could not catch it. In the evening he gesticulated with his arms, time and again making the same weird movement in the air. His stare tried to

force me to understand. Again and again the same gesture, and
a frenzied fear leapt from his eyes. He tried to say it once more
but there was no sound. For a long time his tongue continued to
pierce the air like a dagger, faster and sharper in mounting
agony. But I could not understand.

The letter is filled with desperate anguish. I never found the
address. It was somewhere in Marseilles. The moonlight on the
sea of flat roofs turned them into a flaring chain of mirrors
which blazed into the skies.

From down in the harbour an Arab's insane screams of pain
rang along the street.

Binetti and I had planned to go to Tunis.

I carried the letter in my pocket. Sometimes I repeated his
vague gesture in the air, was astonished and terrified and tried
to force myself to stop doing it. But the gesture had seized me
and outraged my instinct for mimicry, and so I ran along the
quayside, automatically repeating the terrible gestures of the
dying man. And I felt myself starting to call out a name which
slowly rounded itself from an O to a clearer A with strange
palatal sounds behind it. Suddenly I pulled myself together and
ran from the harbour, my head between my clenched fists. Two
sergeants barred my way. I ran into a tree-lined avenue where
a fit of weeping overcame me and thrust me across a bench.

That was the only night I wanted to die.

That Death in wax over your left shoulder there, the colour
of red lead . . . no not this way . . . yes, that's it . . . it was given
to me by the Finnish poet Karelainen, whose real name is
Grönquist. Grönquist is Swedish. Karelainen is Finnish. He calls
himself Karelainen and nothing else. Therein lies his true worth,
for his verses are poor. The gentry and the intelligentsia regard
Swedish as the superior tongue, and use Swedish names. But
against this Karelainen set up a triple opposition—his powerful
chest, fine hands, and especially, the bright wonder of his mezzo-
soprano voice. With these he made propaganda for the Finnish
cause.

But we're not talking about Finland here. We were sitting in
a dirty tavern in a little town on the Lithuanian lake of Ssilkine
where we had been fishing.

"The women of Lithuania are lumps of flesh. Men's love just
washes over them, insensitive creatures that they are, like a wave

over a crab-fisher, or a slap on the thigh. They hardly breathe.
"Lithuanian men have a strange gait. Their blood is thick and
their lust is the lust of oxen.
"But there is no unfaithfulness among them ... never ..."
said Karelainen.
He gave me a searching look. I avoided his glance. Im-
patiently he beckoned a pedlar who was sitting in a corner, with
a miner's lamp strapped to his belly, drinking cheap spirits.
Karelainen bought the red waxen Death off the man and presented it to me.
He knew that I spent every night with the tavern-keeper's
young wife; she was nineteen, had hair that was quite white and
skin as smooth as an eel.
It is not true that Lithuanian women lie in their beds like
lumps of flesh. . . .
Then Karelainen turned his hand, which had been lying flat on
the table, so that it rested on the edge of his slender little finger.
Accompanying himself with frequent faint but sharp raps on the
table he told me that there are only three curses in Finnish. The
first, he said, is "Perkala", the second is "Perrkala" and the third
—a swift, cutting stroke of one of those knives with a handle of
horn and a tip that looks slightly curved, like a pair of seca-
teurs. . . .
It is not true that there are only three curses in Finnish.
There are many intermediate degrees.
For here I am.
Neither is it true that there is no infidelity in Lithuania.
Karelainen was cunning. But his traps were clumsy because he
was too full of jealousy and venom. Anyway, I am not afraid of
men, and in this particular case . . . his voice was mezzo-soprano.
Besides, he was furious with me, because I had caught a trout
a good six inches longer than his biggest. He never forgave me
for that.
The cheap symbolism of his gift, incidentally, makes it immediately obvious that he was a rotten poet.
(Undecided, my friend began to walk hesitantly round a
wood-cut depicting a Japanese torture scene, and he kept turning
his head, now absently looking at me, then staring at the picture.
Suddenly he wheeled round, but before this resolute movement
was complete he seemed to think of a swarm of new things. His

profile, too, had assumed a new sharpness. And then he said "Yes".)

Just, yes.

I, too, said : "Yes".

I didn't know what else to say. Besides, I found the atmosphere hot and oppressive.

He gave me a very distant amazed look. "Yes," I said.

He replied curtly, "Right."

And then :

This also happened in Marseilles. I have been battered by many a city, but I left my best, my brightest blood in that one. When, in my dreams, I find myself aboard a ship and run aground—it is always at the mole of Marseilles. When, in my dreams, they amputate one of my limbs (magnificent Rimbaud!) it is at the yellow hospital in the city's eastern suburb. And when I am crowned with all the insignia my ambition craves, it is in the town hall of Marseilles—and it is from there that I journey into the mockery of my awakening.

And so I hate this town. . . . The plague . . .

In those days I often travelled to Aix. It's not far. An acquaintance of mine was lecturing in bacteriology at the university there. In the evenings, to relax, we used to play Ecarté—four of us : my friend, myself, a Jewish-Russian airman, and my friend's Japanese pupil, who was even smaller than Japanese usually appear to be. There was an attractive lissomness in his movements, and at the back of his eyes : energy. He often came to see me in Marseilles and had mastered the art of making delightful conversation as we played cards—something you can only do at Ecarté. Once I met him with a lady. But he didn't acknowledge me.

At carnival time we all made for one of the large multi-storied cafés, but we soon had to split up. After a while I got involved in an argument with a little colonial officer because I wanted to take over his girl. I recognised her : she was Hessemer's model—the red painter of Lausanne, which isn't very far away; this little sweetheart was got up as a nymph, a band round her loose hair, a short dress and bare legs. I grabbed her round the waist, but she, half drunk, wanted to get back to her lieutenant. She tried to break free. Then Blumenthal, the airman, put his paws round her wrist. Now there was no getting away.

Seething with rage, she hurled herself at my chest and bit deep into my shoulder, right through my dinner-jacket.

Blumenthal saw what happened and let her go; she tore herself away and ran off, with me after her. The lieutenant tackled the airman. I think he wanted to knock the stuffing out of him. But I lost the nymph.

However, on the stairway to the third floor I spotted a young woman in a yellow dress, the most beautiful gown of the evening. I made a grab for her. She laughed, and retreating up the stairs kept pushing her knee against my chest. I laughed too. Suddenly she escaped.

I followed her up a few flights. I wanted to kiss her; so I led her into a niche between two sloping roofs, just beneath a strip of starry sky. Two warm, parted lips, smelling slightly of wine, were placed, with grace and experience, on my mouth; and between each kiss—for I kissed her several times—she interposed in a whisper, "Maman" ... Then she ran off again, and I chased her.

She fled into a powder room. I waited and saw her silhouette framed in the frosted glass of the door. She was putting on rouge. I was spying from behind a pillar. When she came out I stepped forward, and pretending to be terrified she playfully scampered off. We ran across a hall, through pergolas and private rooms and found ourselves in a corridor. I was about to grab her—when I saw, at a high window, a scene that seemed to belong to a puppet play produced with startling suddenness: the little Japanese gesticulating ... faced by a man of markedly Southern, almost Spanish appearance in a vicious posture. Nearby, leaning against the drapery of the window-arch was a lady—pale, almost lifeless, very erect.

I saw the Japanese silently raise his arm, then blood spurting from his opponent's face, and the Japanese jerk the man's arm up across his back. . . .

And now a strange thing happened.

My friend faltered; he was panting. His breath was wheezing from his throat as if someone was scraping a violin bow across broken glass. I jumped up. Stooping a little, he raised his hand in a peremptory gesture. I sat down again.

He hastily rang the bell: "Water ...!"

"Forgive me," he cried, "I was bluffing ... it was too much

for me . . . first I didn't want to tell . . . but then I had to. But it
was a travesty, I altered everything. . . . Not one of the characters
is real, not one is genuine . . . not a single feature. You must
believe me! . . ."

I looked at him coldly.

"This story is quite different," he said, "I thought I could get
it out of my system by telling it, but I couldn't tell it. So I invented the whole thing. But to imagine what might have happened was even worse. . . ."

He stared at the window.

Then he burst into an ugly laugh. His mouth drooped towards
his chin as though dragged down by a pair of fists.

Then he silently turned the wood-cut towards the wall, bowed
and switched off the lamps. His face gradually resuming its
former expression, he asked me to accompany him back to the
other room.

But I stopped in the doorway.

Everything hurled itself upon me with renewed force and
heightened fury.

I could sense it: strange, fantastic happenings corroding the
walls. Human destinies were burning in those frames, straining to
get out. Infinite longings, some fully lived, others merely brushed
against in passing, were swelling the room to bursting point, and
seconds on the tall clock were years racing past.

I saw everything in the room in glittering confusion, as in a
kaleidoscope.

And as I stepped back across the threshold and saw the stoop
in my friend's walk, I was suddenly aware of the tenseness of my
own body and the brutality of my attitude, and I knew then that
I had lived my life well. For it is not a matter of having flashing
experiences and living the searing thrill of adventure (how mean
and trivial that would be); no, it is what we make of our experiences that gives events their form and dignity. . . .

And this collapse brought it home to me:

The right thing is to have no memories. None at all! Ever!
And the one thing we must never do is to create wretched idols
and incarcerate pieces of our life in inanimate objects. We
must not bring a confessional into our home for the day will
come when it forces us on to our knees.

One should cast things aside. Right away. And experiences

should be wiped off one's body, nonchalantly, like lather, in the morning and evening every day, lest sooner or later they humiliate us.

For the relish of adventure is that uncertain and volatile quality: to know that one has done a multitude of things, but not to feel marked or cramped by them. Surging... hectic life ...

That is it.

But in any case this room was a sin against vigour. In some ways its intoxication was a stimulus, in others an opiate, but taken altogether it was constricting. For (as if in mockery) it enshrined the great and the weak, the monstrous and the sweet, the peaks and depths of our experience; they are immeasurably distant and separate from each other and can never be caught in a single grip. They make up and fill our lives, and they resemble these experiences:

The sensation of an express train hurtling at dusk through a little station—and visiting a shop with a glorious spread of silks in the Meisengasse in Strassburg on an all-too-fleeting day of spring.

BIOGRAPHICAL NOTE

Kasimir Edschmid is the pseudonym of Eduard Schmid, born in Darmstadt on 5th October 1890. After studying Romance languages in Munich, Geneva, Giessen, Paris and Strassburg, Edschmid abandoned his projected academic career and became literary editor of the *Frankfurter Zeitung*. With the collections of Novellen, *Die sechs Mündungen* (1915) and *Das rasende Leben* (1916), from the latter of which our story is taken, Edschmid became a leading figure in Expressionism, a movement which he did much to propagate and interpret through his series of pamphlets, *Tribüne der Zeit*. His earlier novels and short stories, e.g. *Timur* (1916), *Die Fürstin* (1918), *Frauen* (1922), *Die achatnen Kugeln* (1920) and *Der Engel mit dem Spleen* (1923), have the bold, visionary conception, the vehemence and the terse dynamic style that are characteristic of the movement. Later on, Edschmid became more of the cosmopolitan journalist and the observer of manners in high society; the novel, *Sport um Gagaly*, 1927, gives an impression of the hectic and frivolous life of the gilded youth of the 1920s that is reminiscent of the works of Aldous Huxley from the same period.

Another genre in which Edschmid has specialised is the fictionalised biography : *Lord Byron* dates back to 1929; *Wenn es Rosen sind, werden sie blühen* (1950) takes as its hero Edschmid's fellow-Darmstädter, the dramatist Georg Büchner; *Der Marschall und die Gnade* (1954) and *Drei Kronen für Rico* (1958) are based on the lives of Simon Bolivar and the Hohenstaufen Emperor Frederick II, respectively. Edschmid is now best known, perhaps, for his numerous travel books, of which the most accomplished is probably *Afrika nackt und angezogen* (1930, 2nd ed. 1951). These books afford Edschmid ample opportunity to indulge his taste for the exotic; they retain an impression of his cultured personality and are well and fluently executed. Edschmid was too cosmopolitan and too flamboyant a character to be acceptable to the Nazis; his work was suppressed and he spent most of the years between 1933 and 1945 in Italy. The collections of essays, *Die doppelköpfige Nymphe* (1920) and *Lebendiger Expressionismus* (1961) are most important contributions to the study of Expressionism.

Franz Kafka

Translated
by
Willa and Edwin Muir

FRANZ KAFKA

A FASTING SHOWMAN

DURING these last decades the interesting professional fasting has markedly diminished. It used to pay very well to stage such great performances under one's own management, but today that is quite impossible. We live in a different world now. At one time the whole town took a lively interest in the fasting showman; from day to day of his fast excitement mounted; everybody wanted to see him at least once a day; there were people who bought season tickets for the last few days and sat from morning till night in front of his small barred cage; even in the night-time there were visiting hours, when the whole effect was heightened by torch-flares; on fine days the cage was set out in the open air, and then it was the children's special treat to see the fasting showman; for their elders he was often just a joke that happened to be in fashion, but the children stood open-mouthed, holding each other's hands for greater security, marvelling at him as he sat there pallid in black tights, with his ribs sticking out so prominently, not even on a seat but down among straw on the ground, sometimes giving a courteous nod, answering questions with a constrained smile, or perhaps stretching an arm through the bars so that one might feel how thin it was, and then again withdrawing deep into himself, paying no attention to anyone or anything, not even to the striking of the clock that was the only piece of furniture in his cage, but merely staring into vacancy with half-shut eyes, now and then taking a sip from a tiny glass of water to moisten his lips.

Besides casual onlookers there were also relays of permanent watchers selected by the public, usually butchers, strangely enough, and it was their task to watch the fasting showman day and night, three of them at a time, in case he should have some secret recourse to nourishment. This was nothing but a formality, instituted to reassure the masses, for the initiates knew well enough that during his fast the artiste would never in any circumstances, not even under forcible compulsion, swallow the smallest morsel of food; the honour of his profession forbade it. Not every watcher, of course, was capable of understanding this, there were often groups of night watchers who were very lax in carrying out their duties and deliberately huddled together in a retired corner to play cards with great absorption, obviously intending to give the fasting showman the chance of a little refreshment, which they supposed he could draw from some private hoard. Nothing annoyed the artiste more than such watchers; they made him miserable; they made his fast seem unendurable; sometimes he mastered his feebleness sufficiently to sing during their watch for as long as he could keep going, to show them how unjust their suspicions were. But that was of little use; they only wondered at his cleverness in being able to fill his mouth even while singing. Much more to his taste were the watchers who sat close up to the bars, who were not content with the dim night lighting of the hall but focused him in the full glare of the electric pocket-torch given them by the impresario. The harsh light did not trouble him at all, in any case he could never sleep properly, and he could always drowse a little, whatever the light, at any hour, even when the hall was thronged with noisy onlookers. He was quite happy at the prospect of spending a sleepless night with such watchers; he was ready to exchange jokes with them, to tell them stories out of his nomadic life, anything at all to keep them awake and demonstrate to them again that he had no eatables in his cage and that he was fasting as not one of them could fast. But his happiest moment was when the morning came and an enormous breakfast was brought them, at his expense, on which they flung themselves with the keen appetites of healthy men after a weary night of wakefulness. Of course there were people who argued that this breakfast was an unfair attempt to bribe the watchers, but that was going rather too far, and when they were invited to take on a night's vigil without a breakfast, merely for the sake of the cause, they made themselves scarce, although they stuck stubbornly to their suspicions.

Such suspicions were, anyhow, a necessary accompaniment to the profession of fasting. No one could possibly watch the fasting showman continuously, day and night, and so no one could produce first hand evidence that the fast had really been rigorous and continuous; only the artiste himself could know that, he was, therefore, bound to be the sole completely satisfied spectator of his own fast. Yet for other reasons he was never satisfied; it was not perhaps mere fasting that had brought him to such skeleton thinness that many people had regretfully to keep away from his exhibitions because the sight of him was too much for them, perhaps it was dissatisfaction with himself that had worn him down. For he alone knew, what no other initiate knew, how easy it was to fast. It was the easiest thing in the world. He made no secret of this, yet people did not believe him, at the best they set him down as modest, most of them however thought he was out for publicity or else was some kind of cheat who found it easy to fast because he had discovered a way of getting round it, and then had the impudence to admit the fact, more or less. He had to put up with all that, and in the course of time had got used to it, but his inner dissatisfaction always rankled, and never yet, after any term of fasting—this must be granted to his credit—had he left the cage of his own free will. The longest time he could fast was fixed by his impresario at forty days, beyond that term he was not allowed to go—not even in great cities, and there was good reason for it, too. Experience had proved that for about forty days the interest of the public could be stimulated by steady pressure of advertisement, but after that the town began to lose interest, sympathetic support began notably to fall off; there were, of course, local variations as between one town and another or one country and another, but as a general rule forty days marked the limit. So on the fortieth day the flower-bedecked cage was opened, enthusiastic spectators filled the hall, a military band played, two doctors entered the cage to measure the results of the fast, which were announced through a megaphone, and finally two young ladies appeared, blissful at having been selected for the honour, to help the fasting showman down the few steps leading to a small table on which was spread a carefully chosen invalid repast. And at this very moment the artiste always turned stubborn. True, he would entrust his bony arms to the outstretched helping hands of the ladies bending over him, but stand up he would not. Why stop fasting at this particular moment, after forty days of it? He had held out for a long time, an illimitably long time; why stop now, when he was in his best fasting form, or rather, not yet quite

in his best fasting form? Why should he be cheated of the fame
he would get for fasting longer, for being not only the record
fasting showman of all time—which presumably he was already
—but for beating his own record by a performance beyond
human imagination, since he felt that there were no limits to his
capacity for fasting. His public pretended to admire him so
much, why should it have so little patience with him; if he could
endure fasting longer, why shouldn't the public endure it? Besides, he was tired, he was comfortable sitting in the straw, and
now he was supposed to lift himself to his full height and go
down to a meal the very thought of which gave him a nausea
that only the presence of the ladies prevented him from betray-
ing, and even that with an effort. And he looked up into the
eyes of the ladies who were apparently so friendly and in reality
so cruel, and shook his head, which felt too heavy on its strength-
less neck. But then there happened yet again what always happened. The impresario came forward, without a word—for the
band made speech impossible—lifted his arms in the air above
the artiste, as if inviting Heaven to look down upon its creature
here in the straw, this suffering martyr, which indeed he was,
although in quite another sense; grasped him round the emaci-
ated waist, with exaggerated caution, so that the frail condition
he was in might be appreciated; and committed him to the care
of the blenching ladies, not without secretly giving him a shaking
so that his legs and body tottered and swayed. The artiste now
submitted completely; his head lolled on his breast as if it had
landed there by chance, his body was hollowed out, his legs in a
spasm of self-preservation clung close to each other at the knees,
yet scraped on the ground as if it were not really solid ground;
and the whole weight of his body, a featherweight after all, re-
lapsed on to one of the ladies, who, looking round for help and
panting a little—this post of honour was not at all what she had
expected it to be—first stretched her neck as far as she could to
keep her face at least free from contact with the artiste, then
finding this impossible, and her more fortunate companion not
coming to her aid but merely holding extended on her own
trembling hand the little bunch of knuckle bones that was the
artiste's, to the great delight of the spectators burst into tears and
had to be replaced by an attendant who had long been stationed
in readiness. Then came the food, a little of which the impresario

managed to get between the artiste's lips, while he sat in a kind
of half-fainting trance, to the accompaniment of cheerful patter
designed to distract the public's attention from the artiste's condition; after that, a toast was drunk to the public, supposedly
prompted by a whisper from the artiste in the impresario's ear;
the band confirmed it with a mighty flourish, the spectators
melted away, and no one had any cause to be dissatisfied with
the proceedings, no one except the fasting showman himself, he
alone, as always.

So he lived for many years, with small regular intervals of
recuperation, in visible glory, honoured by the world, yet in
spite of that troubled in spirit, and all the more troubled because
no one would take his trouble seriously. What comfort could he
possibly need? What more could he possibly wish for? And if
some good-natured person, feeling sorry for him, tried to console
him by pointing out that his melancholy was probably caused
by his fasting, it could happen, especially when he had been
fasting for some time, that he reacted with an outburst of fury
and to the general alarm began to shake the bars of his cage like
a wild animal. Yet the impresario had a way of punishing these
outbreaks which he rather enjoyed putting into operation. He
would apologise publicly for the artiste's behaviour, which was
only to be excused, he admitted, because of the irritability caused
by fasting; a condition hardly to be understood by well-fed
people; then by natural transition he went on to mention the
artiste's equally incomprehensible boast that he could fast for
much longer than he was doing; he praised the high ambition,
the goodwill, the great self-denial undoubtedly implicit in
such a statement; and then quite simply countered it by bringing out photographs, which were also on sale to the public,
showing the artiste on the fortieth day of a fast lying in bed
almost dead from exhaustion. This perversion of the truth,
familiar to the artiste though it was, always unnerved him afresh
and proved too much for him. What was a consequence of the
ending of his fast was here presented as the cause of it! To fight
against this lack of understanding, against a whole world of non-
understanding, was impossible. Time and again in good faith
he stood by the bars listening to the impresario, but as soon as
the photographs appeared he always let go and sank with a

groan back on his straw, and the reassured public could once
more come close and gaze at him.

A few years later when the witnesses of such scenes called them
to mind, they often failed to understand themselves at all. For
in the meantime the aforementioned change in public interest
had set in; it seemed to happen almost overnight; there may
have been profound causes for it, but who was going to bother
about that? At any rate the pampered fasting showman suddenly found himself deserted one fine day by the amusement
seekers, who went streaming past him to other more favoured
attractions. For the last time the impresario hurried him over
half Europe to discover whether the old interest might still sur-
vive here and there; all in vain; everywhere, as if by secret agreement, a positive revulsion from professional fasting was in evidence. Of course it could not really have sprung up so suddenly
as all that, and many premonitory which had not been sufficiently remarked or suppressed during the intoxication of success now came retrospectively to mind, but it was now too late
to take any counter-measures. Fasting would surely come into
fashion again at some future date, yet that was no comfort for
those living in the present. What, then, was the fasting showman
to do? He had been applauded by thousands in his time and
could hardly come down to showing himself in a street booth at
village fairs, and as for adopting another profession, he was not
only too old for that but too fanatically devoted to fasting. So he
took leave of the impresario, his partner in an unparalleled career,
and hired himself to a large circus; in order to spare his own
feelings he avoided reading the conditions of his contract.

A large circus with its enormous traffic in replacing and re-
cruiting men, animals and apparatus, can always find a use for
people at any time, even for a fasting showman, provided, of
course, that he does not ask too much, and in this particular case
anyhow it was not only the artiste who was taken on but his
famous and long-known name as well, indeed, considering the
peculiar nature of his performance, which was not impaired by
advancing age, it could not be objected that here was an artiste
past his prime, no longer at the height of his professional skill,
seeking a refuge in some quiet corner of a circus; on the contrary, the fasting showman averred that he could fast as well as
ever, which was entirely credible, he even alleged that if he

were allowed to fast as he liked, and this was at once promised him without more ado, he could astound the world by establishing a record never yet achieved, a statement which certainly provoked a smile among the other professionals, since it left out of account the change in public opinion, which the fasting showman in his zeal conveniently forgot.

He had not, however, actually lost his sense of the real situation and took it as a matter of course that he and his cage should be stationed, not in the middle of the ring as a main attraction, but outside, near the animal cages, on a site that was after all easily accessible. Large and gaily painted placards made a frame for the cage and announced what was to be seen inside it. When the public came thronging out in the intervals to view the animals, they could hardly avoid passing the fasting showman's cage and stopping there for a moment, perhaps they might even have stayed longer had not those pressing behind them in the narrow gangway, who did not understand why they should be held up on their way towards the excitements of the menagerie, made it impossible for anyone to stand gazing quietly for any length of time. And that was the reason why the fasting showman, who had of course been looking forward to these visiting hours as the main achievement of his life, began instead to shrink from them. At first he could hardly wait for the intervals; it was exhilarating to watch the crowds come streaming his way, until only too soon—not even the most obstinate self-deception, clung to almost consciously, could hold out against the fact— the conviction was borne in upon him that these people, most of them, to judge from their actions, again and again, without exception, were all on their way to the menagerie. And the first sight of them from the distance remained the best. For when they reached his cage he was at once deafened by the storm of shouting and abuse that arose from the two contending factions, which renewed themselves continuously, of those who wanted to stop and stare at him—he soon began to hate them more than the others—not out of real interest but only out of obstinate self-assertiveness, and those who wanted to go straight on to the animals. When the first great rush was past, the stragglers came along, and these, whom nothing could have prevented from stopping to look at him as long as they cared, raced past with long strides, hardly even glancing at him, in their haste to get to the menagerie in time. And all too rarely did it happen that he had a stroke of luck, when some father of a family fetched up before him with his children, pointed a finger at the fasting showman and explained at length what the phenomenon meant, telling stories of earlier years when he himself had watched similar but much more thrilling performances, and the children, still rather incomprehending, since neither inside nor outside school had they been sufficiently prepared for this lesson—fasting was a commonplace for them—yet showed by the brightness of their intent eyes that new and better times might be coming. Perhaps, said the fasting showman to himself many a time, things would be a little better if his cage were set not quite so near the menagerie. That made it too easy for people to make their choice—to say nothing of what he suffered from the stench of the menagerie, the animals' restlessness by night, the carrying past of raw lumps of flesh for the beasts of prey, the roaring at feeding times, which depressed him continually. But he did not dare to present himself to the management; after all, he had the animals to thank for the crowds of people who passed his cage, among whom there might always be one here and there to take an interest in him, and who could tell where they might seclude him if he called attention to his existence and thereby to the fact that, strictly speaking, he was only an impediment on the way to the menagerie?

A small impediment, to be sure, one that grew steadily less. People grew familiar with the strange idea that they could be expected, in times like these, to take an interest in a fasting showman, and with this familiarity the verdict went out against him. He might fast as he could, and he did so; but nothing could save him now, people passed him by. Just try to explain to anyone the art of fasting! Anyone who has no feeling for it cannot be made to understand it. The fine placards grew dirty and illegible, they were torn down; the little notice-board telling the number of fast days achieved, which at first was changed carefully every day, had long stayed at the same figure, for after the first few weeks even this small task seemed pointless to the staff; and so the artiste simply fasted on and on, as he had once dreamed of doing, and it was no trouble to him, just as he had always foretold, but no one counted the days, no one, not even the artiste himself, knew what records he was already breaking, and his heart grew heavy. And when once in a time some leisurely passer-by stopped, made merry over the old figure on the board and spoke of swindling, that was in its way the stupidest lie ever invented by indifference and inborn malice, since it was not the fasting showman who was cheating, he was working honestly, but the world was cheating him of his reward.

More days went by, however, and that too came to an end. An overseer's eye fell on the cage one day and he asked the attendants why this perfectly good cage should be left standing there unused with dirty straw inside it; nobody knew, until one man, helped out by the notice-board, remembered about the fasting showman. They poked into the straw with sticks and found him in it. "Are you still fasting?" asked the overseer. "When on earth do you mean to stop?" "Forgive me, everybody," whispered the fasting showman; only the overseer, who had his ear to the bars, understood him. "Of course," said the overseer and tapped his forehead with a finger to let the attendants know what state the man was in, "we forgive you." "I always wanted you to admire my fasting," said the fasting showman. "We do admire it," said the overseer, affably. "But you shouldn't admire it," said the fasting showman. "Well then we don't admire it," said the overseer, "but why shouldn't we admire it?" "Because I have to fast, I can't do anything else," said the fasting showman. "What a fellow you are," said the overseer, "and why can't you do anything else?" "Because," said the fasting showman, lifting his head a little and speaking with his lips pursed, as if for a kiss, right into the overseer's ear, so that no syllable might be lost, "because I couldn't find any food I liked. If I had found any, believe me, I should have made no bones about it and stuffed myself like you or anyone else." These were his last words, but in his dimming eyes remained the firm though no longer proud persuasion that he was still continuing to fast.

"Well, clear this out now!" said the overseer, and they buried the fasting showman, straw and all. Into the cage they put a young panther. Even the most insensitive felt it refreshing to see this wild creature leaping around the cage that had so long been dreary. The panther was all right. The food he liked was brought him without hesitation by the attendants; he seemed not even to miss his freedom; his noble body, furnished almost

to bursting point with all that it needed, seemed to carry freedom around with it too; somewhere in his jaws it seemed to
lurk; and the joy of life streamed with such ardent passion from
his throat that for the onlookers it was not easy to stand the shock
of it. But they braced themselves, crowded round the cage, and
did not want ever to move away.

BIOGRAPHICAL NOTE

Franz Kafka was born of Jewish parents in Prague on 3rd July
1883. He was educated at German schools in the city and studied
law at the German University. In 1908 he became an official in a
local insurance company and worked in this capacity until forced
by ill-health to retire in 1922. Kafka's life was dominated for years
by his father, who seems to have been an over-weening personality.
From 1912 until 1917 he was emotionally attached—in fact, twice
engaged—to a young woman from Berlin, Felice Bauer, but neither
this relationship nor others which followed it ever led to the marriage and family life which might have rendered his existence rather
happier. Kafka died of tuberculosis in a sanatorium near Vienna on
3rd June 1924. His life and his art were closely bound up with the
German Jewish community in Prague, and the malaise and sense
of isolation that are frequently the theme of his works may well
have been derived from his situation as a member of a minority
within a minority. At the same time, his representation of man as
a being estranged from the world around him, haunted by barely
understood feelings of guilt and governed by an all-powerful and
inscrutable authority seems to have reflected a predicament widely
experienced by modern man. The literary originality and the
impact of his work is largely the result of its apparent cold objectivity and the constricting impression of a single-view narrative,
which holds the reader prisoner as in a nightmare. Basically, his
technique is to turn metaphor back into literal description and narrative. In spite of its morbidity and its terrifying symbolic situations, Kafka's work is by no means devoid of humour. After an
early experimental period in which he barely goes beyond the
idiom of Expressionism, Kafka wrote his first really original and
characteristic work about 1912 : the stories *Das Urteil, Die Ver-
wandlung* and the fragmentary *Der Verschollene* (later published
as *Amerika*). These works appear to be the expression of his
anguished conflict with his own father. In 1914 followed the story
In der Strafkolonie and the novel *Der Prozeß*, works that are fun-

damentally concerned with guilt and punishment, and with religion. Kafka perfected his technique of symbolism in the last years of his life from 1920 to 1924, with stories like *Erstes Leid, Forschungen eines Hundes, Ein Hungerkünstler* and *Josefine, die Sängerin*. Kafka's reputation owes much to the energetic propagation of his work by his friend Max Brod, who edited his literary remains. Brod has published a biography, *Franz Kafka. Eine Biographie*, Frankfurt a. Main, 1954, which is available in an English edition, New York, 1960. M. Dentan, *Humour et création littéraire dans l'Oeuvre de Kafka*, Geneva and Paris, 1961, is a very sound study. An edition of the short stories by J. M. S. Pasley, Oxford University Press, 1963, has a succinct and well-organised introduction and good notes. There is an analysis of *Ein Hungerkünstler* in Benno von Wiese's volume of interpretations, *Die deutsche Novelle von Goethe bis Kafka*, Düsseldorf, 1959, Volume I, pp. 325–42.

Wolfgang Borchert

Translated
by
Richard Thonger

WOLFGANG BORCHERT

THE DANDELION

THE door shut behind me. That often happens, a door being
shut behind you, and one can think of times when it gets locked
as well. Front doors of houses, now, they get locked and then
you're either in or out. Front doors have something special about
them : they have the last word, they close the subject and you're
sold and delivered. And now this particular door is pushed shut
behind me, yes, pushed, as it's so thick that you couldn't slam
it. An ugly door, marked with a number, 432. That's the special
thing about this door : it's got a number, and it's covered with
sheet-iron, which makes it very proud and unapproachable. This
door will entertain no propositions, and passionately uttered
prayers will move it not at all.

And now I've been left alone with a person, not only left alone
but locked up with the one person I'm most afraid of—myself.

Do you know what it's like to be left to yourself, left alone
with yourself, exposed to yourself? It doesn't really need to be
frightening, that I can't say, but still, one of the headiest adven-
tures this world can offer is : meeting oneself. Meeting myself as
I did in cell number 432, naked, helpless, nothing to fix one's
thoughts on but one's own self, no characteristics left, no distractions, nothing left to do at all. That is the worst dishonour,
having genuinely nothing left to do, no bottle to drink from or to
smash, no towel to hang up, no knife to cut one's way out or to
slice through an artery, no pen to write with : having really
nothing—but oneself.

That is damned little in an empty space with four bare walls.
It's less than a spider's got : she can spin a scaffold out of her
backside and risk her life on it—she can take the risk between
falling and being caught. What thread will catch us if we fall?

What thread will catch us? Do we catch ourselves; or does
God catch us? God—is that the force which makes trees grow
and birds fly—is God life? Then he does catch us sometimes—if
we want him to.

When the sun took its finger off the iron bars across the win-

241

dow and night crawled out of the corners, something stepped towards me from the shadows, and I thought it was God. Had someone opened the door? Wasn't I alone any more? I felt there was something there, something that was breathing and growing. The cell was getting too small—I felt that the walls must stand aside before this Thing that was there and which I called God.

You there, number 432, little man, don't drink too much of the night, you're drunk on night! Your fear is with you in your cell, that is all, fear and night. Fear is a monster anyway, and night can play the ghost and terrify us when she has us alone.

Then the moon rolled across the roofs and lit up the walls. You brainless ape, the walls are as narrow as ever, and the cell is as empty as an orange-peel. God, whom they call Good, is not there. And what was there, what was speaking, was in yourself. Perhaps it was a god, made of you—it was you, that's what it was. You must be God too. Spiders and mackerel are God. God is life, that is all. But that is so much that it can't be God any more. And there's nothing else. But this Nothing often overpowers us.

The cell door was as shut as a nut—as if it had never been open, and would never open by itself, it would have to be cracked. The door was as shut as that. And when I was left alone with myself I leaped into bottomless space. But then the spider shouted at me like a sergeant: shouted Weakling! The wind had torn the spider's web and she got busy as an ant and span another and caught my nine-stone-twelve in her breath-fine web. And I thanked her for it, but she took no notice at all.

And so I slowly got used to Me. One can get so light-hearted about being accepted by other people and then hardly be able to bear the thought of oneself. But little by little I found Me really quite entertaining, quite pleasant company, and by day or night I kept discovering the strangest things about myself.

But wait, over this long period I was also losing my grasp on everything, on life, on the world. The days dripped off me rapidly and regularly. I could feel the real world draining out of me and Me filling up with Myself. I was, I felt, moving further and further away from this world which I had only just stepped into.

The walls were so cold and dead that I felt sick with despair and hopelessness. Of course, you can shout your head off for a few days : but you soon get tired of that if no one answers. Or you can beat the walls, and the door, for a few hours : but when they don't open your knuckles soon get sore, and the small area of pain is the only pleasure you have in this desert.

But nothing on earth is really final, nothing, as the imaginary door has opened, and many more like it, and each door is pushing a timid man with a bristly chin out into a long queue and into a courtyard with green grass in the middle and grey walls round the edge.

And then the barking exploded round us and at us—hoarse barking from blue dogs with leather straps round their bellies. They kept us moving and were always on the move themselves, and barked us bow-legged with fear. But when we had enough fear in us and had settled down a bit, we realised they were men, men in washed-out blue uniforms.

We went round in a circle. Once your eyes had got used to the first shattering sight of the sky, you blinked and realised that there were many others besides yourself, seventy or eighty perhaps, trotting along unconnectedly.

And always round in a circle to the wooden-clogged rhythm, clumsy, frightened, and still for half an hour happier than you were at any other time. If the barking dog-faced blue uniforms hadn't been there you could have jogged along for all eternity, no past, no future, just the pleasure of the present, breathing, seeing, walking.

So at first it was like that. Almost a holiday, a little bit of happiness. But in the long run, when you've been letting yourself enjoy it for months, your sense of enjoyment begins to wander. The little bit of happiness isn't enough any more, one is fed up with it, and the world that we've been handed over to dribbles into our glass in muddy drops. And then the day comes when trotting round and round in a circle is torture, and you feel a fool under the high heaven, and the man in front of you and the man behind you are no longer your brothers and comrades in suffering but wandering corpses who are only there to disgust you. You're slatted in between them, you're a slat without a face of its own in an endless slatted fence, and your neighbouring slats can really make you feel sick, they can do that better than anything else. That comes from months of going round in circles between grey walls until you've been barked soft in the head by those washed-out blue uniforms.

The man in front of me had been dead for a long time. Or else he'd escaped from a waxworks show, some demon had grinned as it wound him up and made him behave like a real person. And he'd certainly been dead for quite a while. Oh yes. You see, his bald patch—he has a bald patch wreathed with clusters of dirty grey hair—his bald patch hasn't got the greasy shine of a living bald patch, a shine to play the looking-glass to rain or sun however dull. No, this bald patch has no shine at all, it's as unshiny as a piece of cloth. If this thing, I can't call it a person, this imitation man in front of me didn't move you could take its bald patch for a wig, a dead wig. And not even a wig belonging to a man of letters, or a great drunkard: at best it might belong to a salesman in a stationer's, or a clown in a circus. But it's tough, that wig, out of sheer malice it won't go away— because it knows about me, the man behind, it knows I hate it. Yes, I hate it. Why should the Wig—I'll call the whole man the Wig, it's easier—why should the Wig trot in front of me and be alive, when baby sparrows who don't even know what flying is fall from the gutters and die? And I hate the Wig because it's a coward, what a coward it is. It can feel I hate it while it trots in front of me, the stupid thing, round and round, round and round again between the grey walls, and they can't have any feeling for us either, or else they'd creep secretly away one night and stand round the palace that our Ministers live in.

I've been wondering quite a while now why the Wig is in prison at all. Whatever can it have done, the cowardly thing, it hasn't even the guts to turn round and look at me while I torment it. And I torment it all the time, I keep treading on its heels, intentionally of course, and making sinister noises as if I were coughing my lungs up and spitting four-ounce gobs at its back. When I do that it shudders as though it were hurt, but it just doesn't dare turn round and look at the person who's hurting it, no, it couldn't do that, it hasn't got the guts. It just gives a stiff-necked fraction of a turn towards me, but never dares to make it 180 degrees so that our four eyes meet.

Whatever did it do? Did it embezzle something, or even steal it? Or try a bit of the dirty old man stuff? Yes, I suppose it might have. Just for once some hump-backed Cupid jerked it out of its timidity into straight idiotic randiness, and now there it is trotting in front of me, smug with pleasure and still startled that it had ever dared to do anything.

But do you know, I believe it trembles secretly now, because it knows I'm behind it, and I'm going to kill it. Oh yes, I could easily kill it and I could think of ways of doing it that wouldn't show at all. I'd only have to stick my leg out : the Wig's legs are much too spindly, it would go head over heels and probably knock its head in, and the breath would escape from it with a puff-noise like a bicycle puncture. Its head would split open in the middle like white-and-yellow wax, and the few drops of red ink that came out would look absurdly artificial, like raspberry-juice on the blue silk shirt of an actor who's been stabbed to death.

That was how I hated the Wig, someone whose face I'd never seen, whose voice I'd never heard, whom I only knew by his stuffy moth-ball smell. The Wig must have had a gentle, tired voice without a shred of feeling in it, as feeble as its milky-white fingers. And it must have had bulging eyes like a calf and a thick flabby lower lip always ready to eat chocolates, a proper lecher's face, no personality at all, and about as much guts as a stationery salesman with soft midwife hands that often do nothing all day but sell an exercise book and stroke the coppers off the counter.

No, not another word about the Wig! I hate it to such a degree that I might easily clamber into a fit of rage and expose myself unduly. Stop. Enough. I'll never mention it again, never!

But when you want to shut up about a thing and there it goes, shambling along on its knock knees in front of you, on and on to a tune like a barrel-organ tragedy, you can't get rid of it. It's like a tickle on your back that you can't reach, it keeps urging you to think about it and feel it and hate it.

I do feel I must kill the Wig. But I feel afraid that it would play me up after it was dead. It would suddenly let out a vulgar laugh to remind me that it used to be a clown in a circus and then wallow up out of its own blood and stand there, looking a bit embarrassed perhaps, as though it hadn't been able to hold its blood. Like other people who can't hold their urine. And it would blunder head first through the prison circus, treating the warders like jumping jackasses and driving them demented, and then in a flurry of artificial fright leaping on to the wall and sticking out its floorcloth tongue at us and then vanishing for ever.

It is quite unthinkable to imagine all the things that might happen if each of us suddenly realised what he is.

Don't imagine that my hatred for the Wig, for the man in front, is empty and unmotivated. It is perfectly possible to get into situations where you're so running over with hate, bursting your banks and flooded away by it, that you can hardly find your way back to yourself afterwards. Hatred has turned you into a desert.

I know it is hard to listen to me and to feel as I feel. But you shouldn't just listen as you might if someone was reading Gottfried Keller or Dickens to you. You should walk with me in that narrow circle between those relentless walls. And you shouldn't imagine it and walk beside me, you should do it properly and walk behind me. You should be the Man Behind. And then you'd see how quickly you would learn to hate me, because when you shamble round with us (I say "us", we've all got this one thing in common) in our knock-kneed circle, the love drains out of you and you get so empty that the hatred foams up in you like champagne. And you let it foam, just to stop that terrible empty feeling. And your empty heart and empty belly won't move you to any great deeds of brotherly love, believe me!

And so you'll have all the goodness emptied out of you and you'll trundle along behind me and for months you'll be stuck with me and only me and my narrow shoulders and the flabby back of my neck and my baggy trousers which ought, according to the rules of anatomy, to have more stuffing in them. But chiefly you'll have to look at my legs. All Men Behind look at the legs of the Man In Front and have to submit to the way he walks and copy it, strange and uncomfortable as it is. Oh yes, and the hate will tear your hair like a jealous woman when you notice that I can't walk. No, I can't, it isn't walking at all. There really are people who can't walk, they move in a jumble of styles which never amount to a rhythm. I'm one of those. And that is why you'll hate me with the same senseless and deeply motivated hatred that I feel for the Wig because I am the man behind It. When you've just got used to my wobbling, careless walk you'll get a jolt: suddenly I'll begin to march in a firm decisive manner, and you'll hardly have time to take in my new style of walking before I relapse a few paces further on into a gutless untidy shamble. Oh no, you'll get no joy or friendship out of the sight of me. You'll just have to hate me. All Men Behind hate their Man In Front.

Things might get very different if the Men In Front would only look round from time to time and make contact with their Men Behind. But all the Men Behind are like that, they only look at their Man In Front and hate him. And they disown their Man Behind, so he feels he is a Man In Front. That is the way it is in our circle between the grey walls, and it may be much the same in other places. Perhaps everywhere.

I really ought to have killed the Wig. Once it really got my blood to boiling point. That was the time I made my discovery. Nothing very much. Just something quite small that I discovered.

Have I already said that every morning we spent half an hour going round a grubby little green patch of grass? In the middle of the ring in our strange circus there was a pale gathering of blades of grass, and each blade was pale and had no face. They were like us, running round in an unbearable slatted fence. And as I looked for something living, something with colour in it, I ran my eye casually and accidentally, not very hopefully, over the few small blades of grass. When they noticed me looking they couldn't help shrinking together and nodding their heads at me. And there among them my wandering eye fell on a barely perceptible yellow dot standing like a tiny geisha in a great green meadow. It was such a shock to make this discovery that I thought everyone must have seen it, and my eyes became glued to this yellow thing, whatever it was, until I wrenched them away and stared with great attention at the Man In Front's wooden clogs. But it was the same as when you're talking to someone and you just have to keep staring at the pimple on his nose and making him feel awkward : my eyes kept longing for that little yellow dot. I got a bit closer to it as I went past and walked as casually as I could, and saw what it was. It was a flower and it was yellow, a dandelion, a little yellow dandelion.

It was growing about half a yard to the left of our path, that circular track where we did homage every morning to the fresh air. Fear took me by the throat as I imagined that one of the blue jobs was slanting his goggle eyeballs towards the object of my eyes' caress, but conditioned as our watch-dogs were to react with furious barking to individual movement by any slat in the fence, not one of them had shared my discovery. The small dandelion was still my property, all mine.

It was all my joy, that flower, but only for a few days, until the certainty came to me that it ought to be mine, and mine alone. Each day at the end of our circular trundle I had to jerk myself away, and I'd have given my day's bread ration, and that meant something, to have the flower in my possession. I was so filled with desire to have some living thing in my cell that that flower, that shy small dandelion, soon became worth as much as a person, a secret mistress, someone I could no longer live without, up there between the four dead walls.

And then the business with the Wig happened. I began very craftily. Every time I passed my flower I walked nice and casually a foot's breadth off the path on to the grass. We've all got a good dose of herd instinct in us, and this is what I'd counted on. And I hadn't been mistaken. My Man Behind, and his Man Behind, and his, and his, all shambled faithfully after me, and in four days I had the footpath so close to my dandelion that I could have put my hand on it. If I'd bent down. My operation did in fact cause a score or so of the pale blades of grass to die a dusty death beneath the soles of our wooden clogs, but what are a few squashed blades of grass when you're out to pick a flower?

I was getting near to the fulfilment of my desire. I rehearsed a few times, making my left-hand sock slip down and stooping with a cross face and evident absence of guilty intent to hitch it up again. No one thought anything of it. Right. Tomorrow.

You don't need to laugh at this. Next day when I walked into the courtyard my heart was banging away and my hands were moist and twitching. It seemed such an incredible thing after months of solitary deprivation to have the chance of a mistress walking unannounced into one's cell.

We had nearly finished our daily stint of monotonous wooden-soled clip-clop. The last round but one was coming, and then I would go into action. But suddenly the Wig did it, the dirtiest, most treacherous thing you could imagine.

We'd just turned into the last round but one. The blue jobs held their giant key-rings and rattled them importantly, and I was getting near to the scene of my intended crime, from which my flower was watching me with anxious eyes. I may well have never been so excited before or since. Twenty paces to go. Fifteen paces to go, ten, five . . .

Then it happened, the monstrous thing happened. Suddenly the Wig jerked its skinny arms into the air as though it were striking up a tarantella, gracefully hoisted its right leg as high as its navel and did a backwards half turn on its left foot. I'll never understand where it got the courage. It flashed its gloating face at me as though it knew everything, rolled its silly eyes until the whites began to glitter: then it collapsed, like a dropped marionette. So it was a fact after all—it must have been a clown in a circus, since everyone burst out laughing.

But the blue uniforms barked out and the laughter was wiped clean away as though it had never been there. And one of the blue jobs stepped up to the thing lying on the ground and spoke as ordinarily as if he'd said, it's raining, and said, he's dead.

To be honest with myself there's something more I have to admit. As soon as I was face to face with the man I called the Wig and felt that he'd been defeated, not by me but by life itself, instantly the hatred ran off me, like a wave running off a beach, and there was nothing left but a feeling of emptiness. A slat had broken out of the fence, death had come whistling by and missed me by a hair. When things are like that you suddenly get busy being kind to people. And looking back, I still concede the Wig his victory over me: I suppose it was a victory after all.

Next morning I had a new Man In Front who drove the Wig straight out of my mind. He had a hypocritical look about him, like a theological student, but I'd think he'd been given a leave-pass from Hell just to put a spoke in my flower-picking operation.

He had a horrible cheeky way of making himself obvious. Everybody laughed at him, even the washed-out blue dog-faces couldn't suppress a human grin, and that was something very strange to see. Every inch a government official, these screws were, but the rough-hewn dignified look on their professional military faces was all bent and twisted. They didn't want to laugh, by God they didn't, but they had to. You know that condescending feeling you get when you're angry with some-

one and both your faces are masks of unforgiving hatred, and
then something funny happens that forces you both to laugh,
you don't want to laugh, by God you don't, but your faces have
to give in at last and stretch sideways as though you were eating
a sour apple. And that's what happened to the blue jobs, and
it was the only human thing we ever saw them do. Oh yes, he
was a one, that theological student. He was smart enough to be
weak in the head, but his head was never weak enough to spoil
his smartness.

There were seventy-seven of us in that circus ring, and we
had a pack of twelve creatures in uniform with revolvers to
bark at us. Some of them may have been on the job barking
away for twenty years or more, as their mouths had been pro-
cessing many thousands of patients in the course of years and
had become very dog-like. Still, getting nearer to the animal
kingdom had subtracted nothing from their opinion of themselves. You could have taken any one of them just as he was
and used him as a model for a statue called "L'Etat c'est moi".

The theology student—later I heard he was really a fitter by
trade and had a fatal accident working on a church, God took
care of his own kind—was either mad, or smart enough to show
a deep respect for the blue dog-faces. And deep respect is hardly
the word. He took the blue jobs' dignity and puffed it up into
a super-sized balloon that they themselves hadn't a notion of,
and grin as they might at his idiotic behaviour, they still swelled
with secret pride, and strained their leather belly-bands.

Every time the theology type went past one of the watch-dogs
straddling their power over us and baring their teeth to snarl
whenever they got a chance, every time, he'd do a proper polite-
looking bow and say in a sweet sincere voice "Merry Christmas,
Sergeant" so nicely that even a God couldn't have been angry
with him, let alone the stuck-up windbags in their uniforms. Do
you know, he bowed so humbly every time that he looked as if
he was dodging a clip over the ear-hole.

And now the Devil had put this comic theologian into the
ring as my Man In Front, and his craziness shone out of him so
brightly and took up so much of my time that I almost forgot
my new little love, my dandelion. I hardly had the time to spare
her a tender glance as I was taken up with a terrible battle,
nerve against nerve, and dripping cold sweat out of every pore.

Every time the Theologian made his little bow and dripped his Merry Christmas Sergeant off his tongue like honey, I had to brace all my muscles not to copy what he was doing. I felt so dreadfully tempted that several times I had already smiled a welcome at the blue pillars of the State and only managed at the very last moment to keep myself from bowing and to hold my tongue.

Every day we went round and round that courtyard for roughly half an hour, that was twenty times round per day, with twelve uniforms standing outside our moving circle. So the Theologian bowed at least two hundred and forty times a day, and therefore, two hundred and forty times a day I had to concentrate to bursting point to stop myself going round the bend. When I'd done it for three days I knew I'd be sure to get extenuating circumstances. This chap was more than I could cope with.

I was all in when I got back to my cell, and all night long I dreamed I was walking along an endless rank of blue uniforms, and they all looked like Bismarck. All night long I bowed low to millions of washed-out blue Bismarcks and gave each of them a Merry Christmas Sergeant.

Next day I worked out how to make the others overtake me and give me a new Man In Front. I lost a clog, made a hash of getting it on again and shambled back between the slats. God be thanked, at last the sun had risen. Or rather, it had gone behind a cloud : my new Man In Front was such a hell of a height that my five-foot-eleven melted into his shadow. So there is such a thing as Providence after all, you've just got to help it along with your wooden clog. The new chap's great limbs thrashed about aimlessly and the strange thing was that he moved forward at all in spite of certainly not knowing what his arms and legs were doing. But I came to love the beggar, yes, I actually prayed that he wouldn't up and fall down dead like the Wig or go dotty and start bowing to people. I prayed him a long life and excellent mental health. I felt so safe in his shadow that I let my glances linger longer than usual on my little dandelion and never feared I'd be betrayed. This was a Man In Front straight from Heaven, and I even forgave him his horrible nasal voice, I actually held back from calling him names like the Oboe or the Cuttlefish or the Praying Mantis.

Now I only had eyes for my flower, I didn't mind the Man In Front any more, he could be as long or as dumb as he liked.

That day was just like any other except that the prisoner from cell number 432 used the half-hour to acquire a galloping pulse, and his eyes filled with artificial innocence and badly-concealed anxiety.

We turned into the last round but one, and once again the great key-rings came to life and the slatted fence dozed along through the thin rays of sunshine, it might have been behind an endless railing.

But what's this? One of the slats wasn't dozing at all. It was wide awake and so excited that it changed step every few yards. Didn't anyone notice? Not a soul, and suddenly slat number 432 was bending double and fumbling with his slipped-down sock and flashed a hand sideways at a small frightened flower and grabbed her and picked her: and along went the old routine as seventy-seven slats clattered into the last round.

Funny, isn't it? Sophisticated young citizen of gramophone-record and space age stands deeply contrite below high-up window in cell number 432 and with his lonely hands displays a small yellow flower to the narrow shaft of light. A common dandelion, very common. And then this chap, who used to have gunpowder and perfume and petrol and gin and lipstick to smell, and hasn't had a thing to sniff at for months except his plank bed and dust and the sweat of fear, then he lifts this dandelion to his famished nostrils and breathes the soul from her tiny yellow body into himself so hungrily that all he is is just a nose.

And something opens inside him and pours out like light into the cramped space, something he had never known before, an incomparable tenderness and warmth and submissiveness towards the flower seeps through him and fills his whole being.

He couldn't bear the cell any more and shut his eyes and thought in wonder: You smell of earth, you smell of the sun and the sea and honey, you darling scrap of life. And he felt the flower's chaste coolness, like his father's voice, which he'd never paid much attention to and which was a comfort now, all the comfort you get from a quiet man. And he felt it like a dark-haired woman's pale shoulder.

Tenderly he bore the little creature in his arms like a mistress, took her to his tin mug, cooled her tired body in the water. It took him minutes, sitting down very, very slowly, face to face with his darling flower.

He felt so free and happy that all his worries slipped from him like old clothes, all his worries, the prison, the loneliness, the longing for love, the helpless pain of his twenty-two years, all this and present and future too, and the world, and Christianity —even that fell away and left him.

He was a brown man from Bali, a savage of a savage race who feared the sea and the lightning and trees, and worshipped them, and treated coconuts and codfish and humming-birds with respect and wonder, and ate them, and didn't understand them. He'd never felt so free or so ready to accept goodness as when he whispered to his flower . . . want to be like you . . .

All night long his fortunate hands clasped the trusty tin of his drinking-mug and as he slept he could feel Her piling earth on him, dark rich earth, and he took to the earth and became like Her, and flowers grew out of him, anemones, columbines, dandelions : tiny scraps, but glowing suns.

BIOGRAPHICAL NOTE

Born at Hamburg on 20th May 1921, Wolfgang Borchert developed into an emotional and irreverent youth interested neither in the Third Reich nor in a proper career. He wrote derivative verse and effusive letters; his admiration for Rilke caused the Gestapo to suspect him of effeminacy. The outbreak of war found him working in a book-shop while he took lessons in acting, and he achieved three months with a touring company before being called up in 1941. At the Russian front his health began to fail, but his emotional disregard of authority exposed him to even greater danger. He spent six weeks in prison and narrowly escaped the death penalty on a charge of self-inflicted wounding, and in 1943, due to be discharged as medically unfit and to become an actor in troop shows, he spoilt his chance by parodying Goebbels in a barrack-room, and spent nine months in solitary confinement in prison awaiting trial. Late in 1944 the authorities put him back into the army, and early in 1945 his unit surrendered to the French, but he escaped from the convoy and walked over 350 miles back to his parents in Hamburg.

Borchert returned to the theatre and to cabaret, but his health broke down again, and in his sick-bed he really began to write. *The Dandelion (Die Hundeblume)*, written in early 1946, brought him recognition and self-confidence, and his first big success arrived with

Draussen vor der Tür, the radio play first broadcast in February 1947 in a particularly cold winter. This vivid, bitter fantasy brings Unteroffizier Beckmann back from Russia to the ruins of Hamburg —Beckmann to whom all doors seem closed, whom the Elbe refuses to accept as a suicide, who limps along laden with war's guilt and horror and can only reiterate his own unanswered questions. The play inspired enthusiasm as well as many interpretations (some linking Beckmann with defeated Germany) in the cold post-war ruins, but it truly derives from Borchert's own inner struggle for relief from guilt and escape into nothingness.

Borchert died at Basle, already famous, on 20th November 1947, the day before his play was staged at the Hamburger Kammerspiele. His prose pieces, full of colour and sharply observed detail, carry his most substantial achievement, and his personal, bitter-sweet moods in stories of people, evocations of Hamburg, vignettes of the Russian front, or denunciations of war, outclass his occasional humour (as in *Schischyphusch*) or emotional optimism.

The original radio version of *Draussen vor der Tür* is preserved on an LP recording in the *Cottas Hörspielbühne* series (Artur Müller, 1959); the stage version and the bulk of Borchert's other work appears in the *Gesamtwerk* (1949), and a posthumous selection in *Die Traurigen Geranien* (1962, both published by Rowohlt). Borchert's life and works are covered by Peter Rühmkorf in No. 58 of Rowohlt's *Monographien* (1961), and by Dr. Hans Popper on pp. 269–303 of *German Men of Letters*, Series III (Oswald Wolff, 1964). Dr. P. B. Salmon has written an introduction and full notes for Harrap's edition of *Draussen vor der Tür* (1963), and the play has been translated by David Porter for *The Man Outside* (Hutchinson International Authors Ltd., 1962), which contains all Borchert's published work except the verse and for which Stephen Spender wrote an introduction.

ACKNOWLEDGEMENTS

Acknowledgements are due for permission to print these stories in their English versions to the authors and to the following publishers :

Nymphenburger Verlagshandlung, München, for *The White Slave Trader* by Georg Britting ©1959;

R. Piper & Co. Verlag, München, for *The Girl from India* by Ludwig Thoma © 1948;

Aufbau-Verlag, Berlin W.8, for *Abdication* by Heinrich Mann;

Suhrkamp Verlag, Frankfurt am Main, for *The Treasure* by Ernst Penzoldt (from "Süsse Bitternis" © 1951);

S. Fischer Verlag, Frankfurt am Main, for *Love Story* by Carl Zuckmayer (© 1934 by S. Fischer Verlag AG, Berlin);

Verlag der Arche, Zürich, for *Experience on an Island* by Werner Bergengruen © 1952;

Rowohlt Verlag GmbH, Hamburg, for *The Dandelion* by Wolfgang Borchert (from "Das Gesamtwerk" © 1949);

Three of the stories have been published before in English, and acknowledgement is made to the publishers due to their version :

To Messrs. Routledge & Kegan Paul Ltd., London, for the story taken from *Selected Prose* by Hugo von Hofmannstahl;

To the Henry Regnery Company, Chicago, for the story taken from *The Judgement of the Sea* by Gertrud von le Fort;

To Messrs. Martin Secker & Warburg Ltd., London, for the story taken from *In the Penal Settlement* by Franz Kafka.